MICHAEL BLATHERWICK

PHOTOGRAPH AND THE DAUGHTERS OF INVENTION

BOOK TWO
OF THE
PHOTOGRAPH
CHRONICLES

Also by Michael Blatherwick

Photograph Chronicles Series

Photograph and the Atomic Juggernaut (Book One)

Photograph and the Daughters of Invention

Book Two of the Photograph Chronicles

Michael Blatherwick

Paperback: ISBN 979-8-9867772-3-8
eBook: ISBN 979-8-9867772-4-5

Library of Congress Control Number: 2023941604
First paperback edition: July 2023

Development Editor/Copy Editor: Amy Reeve
Additional Editing and Proofreading: Cleo Miele
Cover by MiblArt

Jackowick Publishing
Bordentown, NJ 08620
michaelblatherwick.com

The characters and events in this book are fictitious. Any similarity to real persons, living or dead, is coincidental and not of any intention or inference by the author.

If you or someone you know is challenged by PTSD or its symptoms, please reach out for help. Please visit https://www.ptsd.va.gov/

For Dad

Chapter 1

Higher Place – Journey

The New Mexico winds spoke lightly, passing gentle words of mystery and peace across the highway. The two lanes sat empty in both directions, the only occupant a lone red pickup truck with new registration plates. The sun rested low and dusted the sparse vegetation on the slight hills set back from the road, creating faint shadows. The winds exhaled a final sigh as the grains of sand settled on the red hood of the Ford Ranger pickup and the cooling asphalt of the spring evening.

Dana Jefferson stepped out of the cab and stood in the middle of the road to survey the barren landscape. In the distance ahead, a lone dust devil died on its final journey to the shoulder to the delight of a prairie dog who emerged from one hole to cross the road into another. Dana smiled at the sinking sun, unpacking her cargo from the back of the truck. *It's been a while . . . too long*, she reminded herself.

She dropped her canvas bag to the ground, then lifted out each shiny gunmetal shin guard. The repairs were noticeable but clean, the new strands of fiber and metal connecting the guards to the boxy roller skates. The boots were marked with scorch marks and scrapes—medals of honor from their prior adventures with Dana, their pilot and caretaker. Dana smiled at the word "LEFT" painted in white on the skate she called Laverne, a recent addition after some confusion during the repairs. Shirley, her right skate, bore more wear than Laverne from their last skirmish but looked fresher after its rehab. Dana stepped into each skate and felt the new magnetic clasps click, forming a second skin, her toes perfectly aligned to the complex pedal mechanisms that responded to her instinctual reactions and guided the motors. She shuffled in place, letting the rollers glide back and forth on the blacktop, crushing the tiny sand pellets into a fine powder under her weight.

She clicked on her Bluetooth earpiece and donned her goggles, single blade shooter's glasses, lightly tinted and shatterproof. As she shook out her loose ebony curls, the breeze picked up again. Anticipating a drop in temperature, she zipped her cropped black leather jacket and smoothed the tuxedo-style tails that fluttered around her hips. Her pre-ride rituals complete, Dana drew in a slow breath, then exhaled as her toes pressed into the accelerators. The motors attached to each ankle hummed with the torrent of electrons now unleashed as the servos came to life. Setting one foot back, she crouched into the stance of a sprinter at a starting block.

With a grunt, Dana pushed off on her front foot and began to move, unleashing the sound of metallic clanging as the steel-coiled wheels vibrated like the notes of a guitar melting into a distorted power chord. Every surge forward increased her speed as the wheels sparked, showering the pavement behind her in a soft shimmering glow.

The desolate highway was exactly what Dana needed. She was in recovery. The past year had left her questioning her life, and she had finally began to confront the unyielding sadness from her parents' passing in her early years. She accelerated faster on the highway, burning any stray dead brush that had the misfortune of getting in her way. She knew burning—she understood burning. She had burned down all her relationships in the past—until she met Nick Andrews, who had helped her recover her heart and soul before it could petrify. His unselfish friendship had shown her how to accept her place in the universe. Now she was here, ready to start a new life in the place where she was born.

"Photograph"—the nickname Nick and his father, Mitch, had given her back in New Jersey because that was the only way to catch a girl like her—now felt like her identity. Her peanut-hued cheeks rose into a smile as she thought of Nick, who had arrived in her life just as she was searching for clues about the legacy of her father and grandfather. The image of the Atomic Juggernaut, the terrifying military robot her father and grandfather had helped create, burned in her mind's eye with each push against the pavement.

Laverne and Shirley had been crippled during her final confrontation with the machine and the ominous organization One Hundred Roads, a government contractor hoping to sell the Atomic Juggernaut to the highest bidder, no matter their allegiances or intentions. But Dana was sure the skates would hold now with Nick's enhancements. Her father's blueprints had guided Nick's hands as he repaired their delicate and ingenious circuits and motors. Nick understood that it was not enough for the skates to be fast; they had to respond to her movements, delicate or aggressive, as she pushed her toes against the controls.

Dana soared over the crest in the road. She leapt, and the sparks arced behind her and marked her ascent with a glistening comet trail. She began to spin, one arm raised above her head, as a burst of fireworks sprang from her heels. She felt alive, steeped in the kind of joy and madness that only Laverne and Shirley—and sometimes Nick—brought to her world. She raced down the highway, keeping one eye on the setting sun as she lifted her back trailing leg and held a graceful Arabesque pose, an artifact of her youthful skating lessons before she had become a brawling roller derby player. She missed her former derby team back in New Jersey, not just for the friendships but the sisterhood of the sport itself, and wondered what her former teammate and lover, Angela, was doing to keep herself busy.

Angela was still a loyal friend, having come to Dana's side after their breakup to help rescue her from One Hundred Roads in the middle of the Pine Barrens. Images of the statuesque, beautiful blonde flashed into Dana's mind—as did the memory of a knife going into Angela's side when she was stabbed by Olsen, the enforcer of One Hundred Roads. Dana had rarely felt so helpless.

A small stone slipped under Laverne and popped under the weight and force of her acceleration, sounding like a gunshot.

A gunshot.

Alone at night, Dana was haunted by the gunshot that had almost killed Nick—the moment she had felt the world drop, and the trigger that had led her to break Olsen's back in a vengeful moment of rage. That gunshot still resonated, not just in her memory but in her ears now. The ringing rose underneath the churning of her skates and the shallow breaths in her chest.

The whirring of the skates melted into a flat tone as her heart raced. She felt the wind recede on her face as the wheels began to sputter. Her breaths grew quicker, her intake shallower, choking her slowly as the horizon swallowed the sun. Her left leg gave out before her right; her strides stuttered before she fell. Her body rolled across the empty highway, each rotation announced with a clunk as the skates smashed against the pavement. Dana settled on her back as her lungs released their grip and granted her full breaths.

Air.

She stared at the sky above, a freckling of clouds against the purple, a single star announcing the night was here. She had missed this sky. The same one that she and her mother had watched while camping just north of Roswell, playfully guessing which stars were alien worlds with little green men planning to visit a little girl and take her away from her parents to a utopian planet.

Star.

Her parents had sometimes called her that, rather than *princess* or *angel* or any of the other common nicknames used by mothers and fathers for their daughters. A tear rolled down her cheek. She had long ago accepted that there were no aliens coming to get her, but her parents had still been seized from her life far too early for any girl to endure.

But my mom may still be alive, somewhere out here, *today.*

She tapped the button on her Bluetooth.

"Nick, can you come pick me up? Look for your truck and then you'll see a pile of meat a few miles north." She propped herself on her elbows and waved at a prairie dog a few yards away, frozen in an upright stance. "Take your time. And grab me a burrito and a ginger ale."

Chapter 2

Thunder Island – Jay Ferguson

The wind swatted at Nick's short tuft of blond hair through the cracked driver's side window of his red Ford Ranger pickup. His Honda CRF 450R dirt bike, strapped upright in the back of the truck bed, rattled against the unsecured milk crate containing Dana's skates. He threw the shifter into park as he pulled into the driveway, jolting to a stop. Dana hopped out and retrieved the crate, then stared across the expanse surrounding the small mesa, beyond the wooden pillared fence along the side of the yard.

This house had been chosen by her father, Samuel David Jefferson Jr., because of its remote location in the New Mexican desert—on the very far outskirts of the "big" city Alamogordo—and its proximity to the Mescalero Apache reservation. Her grandfather, Colonel Samuel David Jefferson Sr., had worked a few assignments at the military facility at White Sands to the west before moving to New Jersey, but Dana preferred to explore to the east, past the reservation, on the rolling hills of tan and orange soil.

Nick took the crate from her as they walked up to the front of the dirty white rancher, now legally hers. The automatic lights, installed by Nick in a single afternoon, popped on, illuminating the porch and front foyer visible through the double doors. The back spotlight flashed momentarily as a rabbit dashed too close to the side porch. It charged into the gray shadows farther out in the yard, disappearing into the brush just as its human companions disappeared into the house.

"Did you have a good day at school, roomie?" she inquired as she kicked the dust off her chukka boots. This was still new to her—real, true companionship. It was comforting to have Nick's calm, reasoning aura around the house. He was enrolled at the local university but took advantage of online courses whenever possible to stay close to her—"just in case," as he put it.

"Yes, *roomie*," he admitted with a half smile. Nick stared at the tidy pyramid of toolboxes and packages near the garage door. "This is all going to have to go with me to the reservation tomorrow." He kicked the largest box on the bottom. "The junction boxes for the solar panels are going to be a pain to install, but at least I'm getting paid."

"Ah, yes," she said, poking him between the shoulder blades, "in cash *and* in eggs and firewood. You're like a garage sale Marco Polo. Or maybe Lewis and Clark—I like that one better. You're Clark."

"You know, I still don't understand your jokes sometimes."

"And I don't understand your need for obsessive compulsive organization around the house."

As per the terms of their move out west—and after clearing Dana of any property damages accrued by her encounters with One Hundred Roads—the government had paid for Nick's tuition as well as covered the fees for Dana's assumption of the title for the house. All that had been helpful, of course, but liquid cash evaporated quickly without additional income. Nick had found a welcome compromise by performing electrical contracting jobs for the Mescalero reservation's unofficial public works team, for which he was often paid with a mix of cash and goods. Without a valid electrician's license and insurance, he was happy to work "off the books" until he could find an insured contractor to work for while he finished his degree. Despite a handful of experiences with New Jersey's Native American history, he was ignorant of much of their modern-day challenges. Dana assisted him in his dealings with the tribe, using what she knew of them from her abbreviated youth in New Mexico.

Dana hoisted herself onto the kitchen island and watched Nick continue his evening routine. He hung up his coat, checked the doors and windows, and flicked the manual switch off and on for the outside floodlights. He motioned for her to scooch across the island, then reached into a drawer for a pack of batteries.

"I should probably keep an extra set of these downstairs in the workshop," he concluded. The house had come with a few surprises, the biggest one being the basement and all the devices and treasures left there by Dana's father.

Nick opened the basement door and propped open the handcrafted self-closing two-way hinge next to the heavy crossbar to barricade the cellar from imaginary cyclones or intruders—a door fit for a CIA agent's safehouse panic room, not a scientist's hobby lab. A steel-lined stairwell led down to the finished room, almost the size of the entire house. Nick flipped the switch and the lights began to hum along the ceiling, bathing the subterranean room and its tiled floor with antiseptic white light. He slowly descended the steps, wanting to allow time for any critters or crawlers, usually scorpions or desert mice, to scurry into hiding first.

The far wall of the basement housed the computer bank full of mostly obsolete curiosities, including magnetic data reel-to-reel, various-sized floppy disk drives, and several hard drives surrounding a series of monochrome monitors. The large metal workbench was now clear after hours of Nick and Dana cataloging and storing the variety of parts, alloys, and blueprints that had lain dormant for years until their arrival.

Dana listened to the short echoes of Nick's footsteps fading down the stairs as she sauntered through their house. *Her* house. She felt a surge of warmth as she studied the painting of the ocean that hung over the fireplace. It bore her mother's signature, "Simone J.", along the bottom in white paint. Her mother had spent many afternoons teaching her how to draw before she became sick—allegedly became sick, that is—and disappeared into the ether. Dana peered into the painted waves and dune grasses in the foreground, searching for some clue in it her mother may have left. She extended her pinky and traced the looping letter *J* on the canvas.

Just because I love you, her mom had signed her birthday cards. Dana had lost them all during a dorm move one year at boarding school, but she had read them over and over before then and could still hear her mother's voice in her mind. Being in this house again, Dana felt like Simone could one day just walk through the door and throw her arms around her. *Maybe.*

She crept down the stairs and sat on the bottom step in silence, observing Nick. She watched as he moved slowly to the middle table, which held a diorama of an industrial park surrounding a central geodesic dome. As he leaned over the model, his short sandy-blond hair glowed under the lighting, creating an angelic halo that Dana found quite charming. The model was a design of her father's perpetual power station, an energy plant that he had hoped to develop as a side project while working on the Atomic Juggernaut program. Nick quietly lifted various diorama pieces and placed them back in their positions, his eyes wide as he touched the top of the dome.

"That's the big one, right there," Dana said, interrupting Nick's introspection. "He hid the key part of the design for that in my skate blueprints, right?"

He nodded. "Your father was a clever guy. I mean, he was ridiculously brilliant. And yes, hiding the missing circuitry routes for this building in your skate design was a nice middle finger to more than a few people." Nick ran his thumb through a dusty drift on the end of the diorama. "I still don't know if it would work. It *should* work, but I'm not confident I'm smart enough to *make* it work."

"You think you *could* build it?"

"Oh, no, no, no. I can enter this into the modeling programs at school and simulate it, but to build this, we'd need a lot more space—and a lot more money." He looked over at Dana, her hands resting under her chin, and noticed a sliver of a tear sliding down her cheek.

"He was an amazing man, my dad. And you are, too, Jersey boy genius. You're very talented. College is suiting you well." She wiped her eyes. "*Your* dad is going to be very proud when you tell him all this stuff."

They walked up the stairs together, Nick shutting off the light and closing the door behind him. They lay down on the large sectional couch that faced the glass patio doors, their "go bags" sitting next to the door just in case One Hundred Roads or some other nefarious individuals came looking for them—a reminder of the dread of pursuit. Dana unpacked her sleep roll and set it next to the coffee table.

"I'm going to sleep out here again tonight," she whispered. She knew that sleeping out in the main room made Nick uncomfortable, but her recent night terror spells had receded when she slept in the large open room with starlight shining through from many directions. Any night without dreams of gunshots and stabbings was a victory, and victories were hard to come by as of late.

"You do have a rather nice bedroom with a new, comfy bed, but whatever you want. It's your house."

"I know. *My* house, but *our* home. You have a bigger room here than you did in New Jersey." She fanned a linen sheet over the sleeping bag.

"Smells better, too."

Dana stared out into the stars that had rapidly bloomed in the deep blue sky and framed the cloudless nighttime desert. The low hills slept in the dark, refusing to wake even as a lone coyote bayed far away. A low throbbing noise announced the presence of a helicopter flying along the southern border, slinking away over the hills.

Dana sunk into her bed for the night and looked up at Nick. He was still sitting on the couch, watching the dragonflies drift through the darkness outside.

"Hey, you're allowed to sleep," she said. "You don't have to stay up to keep watch over me."

"I know," he whispered, settling deeper into the couch.

Chapter 3

The Ghost of Tom Joad – Rage Against the Machine

Aaron Olsen lifted his right leg with both hands and swung it out of the Hummer with a restrained grunt. He pivoted his hips and lowered his left leg to the dry concrete, then mounted his arm crutches—the finest money could buy, layered in carbon fiber and spring-loaded for optional shock absorption. The cuffs of his tailored pants were dusty, a souvenir of the desert that he shook out in a fit as best his numbed limbs could muster. His driver walked around and placed her gloved hand gingerly on his shoulder.

"Major, shall I?"

"I'm fine," he barked. He looked up at her high cheeks and steel-blue eyes, crosscut by her pageboy haircut whipping in the light breeze. "I am sorry, Nina," he apologized, his Australian accent softening his tone. "Some days are worse than others, but every day is worse than I used to be. Because of *her*."

"That roller-skating bitch, Dana Jefferson," she snarked. Her angular features tightened into a scowl as she slowly shook her short blond tresses.

"Dana Jefferson." He held up his hand, trembling lightly from nerve damage. He repeated her name at a lower volume. "Dana Jefferson."

The partners crossed the pavement toward the permanently mounted trailer adorned with a large blue-and-yellow sign stating the rules of the reservation. They walked up to the door marked with a simple placard reading OFFICE and Olsen rapped with his crutch to announce their presence. A tall barrel-chested man with a fine black buzz cut opened the door. The whine of a low-flying crop duster's engine drowned out his initial salutation.

"Come in! Major Olsen? Nice to meet you in person. I'm Frank Irons. And I assume you are Nina Rhodes? You're a yellow rose in the desert, ma'am." Frank extended a hand to her. She met his hand with her own gloved grip.

They stepped into his office and Frank closed the door behind them, extending his hand to indicate they should sit. Olsen wasted no more time on the meeting's formalities.

"Mr. Irons, I know you've read my proposal, and I know your financial situation, so let's cut to the chase. Are we in agreement?" Olsen kept a closed-mouth smile under his arching brows, still knotted from squinting into the high noon sun on the drive to the Mescalero reservation.

"In short, and with due respect, no. We're not there yet. I'm not kicking you out, but this isn't the first time someone has asked to mine the hills." Frank leaned back in his desk chair and clicked the window air conditioner up one fan speed. He placed two fingers on top of a glass dome on the desk blotter, drawing Nina's gaze to the dull silvery rock trapped inside.

"May I?" She gestured toward the glass trinket. Before he could respond, she carefully removed the glass and held the metallic form in her hands. She rubbed a black leathery thumb across the ragged edges and frowned.

"Such a shame," she sighed. "The geological studies we've run from the air suggest a small but easily mineable cache close to the surface. Several tons, but not more than ten. We can be in and out in fifteen months with a little luck."

"Well," Frank countered, "for us, it's not just about letting someone pay to pull that—"

"Palladium," interrupted Nina.

"Yes, palladium. It's not the price, it's the impact. We have a pretty fragile ecology in this part of the state, so fragile that I'm terrified of a hole in the ground significantly altering the rain runoff. And obviously, we have to consider the industrial pollution. I wish there was another way."

"Double," snapped Olsen. "Double your price. For half the output. We mine out four tons and leave the rest to you. You'll be getting at least another four, maybe even six or eight tons."

Frank rubbed the back of his neck and looked over the partners seated under the window. Olsen felt more comfortable than Nina in the trailer's stagnant heat; he had spent much more time in the desert, the jungle, and other weather extremes than Nina, who specialized in pacing up and down three-story atriums in the headquarters of financial corporations. She pulled up her outer sleeve to check her smartwatch, strapped over, not under, her performance spandex, and winked at Olsen.

"We're not going to harass you to make this happen," Nina responded. "But we are going to be much more favorable to deal with than the government once they know you have a palladium source. I don't want to sound culturally insensitive, but you know how they are when it comes to wanting something on tribal lands."

"If that's a threat, it's pretty weak." Frank stood up and grabbed a yellow folder from his inbox. "Do you know what this is?" He flapped it at their faces. "This is *not* another hotel complex and conference center. Not a casino for the *white man*. This is a campus for the University of New Mexico agriculture and veterinary sciences programs. *This* is productivity.

Opportunity. You're offering me a short-term paycheck. *This*"—he waved the folder again—"is *wealth*." His eyes widened to match his smile. "More than a few alumni will pay handsomely to repave a road around here and name it after them."

Olsen raised both hands into the air and mimed a surrender pose.

"Okay, mate, I get it. Kudos to you on that. You have a sense of perspective and strategy, and that puts us in the same canoe." Nina groaned under her breath. "But mate, here's the last bit I'd like to ask. If the cache is underneath, say, your property line—your *own* property—would it be fair to offer compensation for a one-and-done extraction? Not with the tribe, but with you, the property owner."

"From what I could tell from the survey you provided, that ore starts under the grazing area at the foot of the hills. It's not my land. *It's the tribe's*."

Nina placed a hand on Olsen's forearm and squeezed, strangling his tendons.

"Major, I think we should thank Mr. Irons for his time. I think we're at an impasse. But I would like to revisit this once you have more details on the campus. We are interested in investing in this area in one way or another."

After a brief and rather insincere parting, Nina assisted Olsen to the Hummer. He preferred to drive, even with the pain in his leg, but she felt it best to keep up the appearance of his executive status during their departure. Now all he wanted was to go home and sulk. He glanced across the reservation, noting the power lines crisscrossing the sky, the two-story houses and run-down ranchers, sheds and horse stables dotting the landscape. A few houses displayed new solar panels that liberated them from the power lines, and there were more satellite dishes than Olsen had expected to see based on his preconceived notions of reservation poverty. As Nina helped him into the car, he noticed Frank leave the trailer and walk down to a covered paddock featuring picnic tables and paper lantern lights that rattled in the smallest breeze.

"Nina."

"Yes?"

"If we can't obtain the palladium for our collaborators, we're going to need an alternate plan." He closed the truck door and placed his crutches across his lap.

"You don't want to go with a spontaneous wildfire to burn them into negotiating?"

"No, I don't want to burn this place to the ground. When they have nothing, negotiations are a futile exercise." He stared out at the far clouds. "Do you know what tribal genocide is, Nina? It's when you massacre everyone, even children, so that the military-industrial complex can dig holes. I won't be party to that again. There has to be a better way."

"We're still working out the details of the train transfer."

"Still?" He rubbed his chin and glanced at her profile, her gaze fixed on the road. Her striking features betrayed the darkness in her heart. The trauma and rage inside her manifested into ruthlessness and cunning, the perfect combination for their cause. "Just keep me in the loop. Our window is open again."

Nina pushed the gas pedal to the floor, and the Hummer barreled down the main road toward the edge of the reservation. Olsen watched the cars passing in the opposite direction with minimal interest. A commuter van full of children. Two compact cars in various states of disrepair. A late-model SUV with plastic drainpipes strapped to the roof rack. A weathered red pickup truck . . .

Olsen stared at the driver as they passed by. He studied the neat and tidy blond hair, the canvas work jacket, and the motor bike mounted in the back bed.

"I'll be damned. Nina, I think Providence has made her presence known.

Head back to the compound. I'm going to make a few calls."

"Are you calling Silver?"

Olsen recoiled at the thought. His list of resources came with price tags, some of which he could not afford to pay.

"Do not contact Silver. Don't even mention that name."

"Fine."

"I mean it—no one hears that name." He touched his shirt and felt the scar underneath the fine weave of the material. "Get me Nails."

Chapter 4

Dark Skies – CJ Burnett

Frank Irons, a trucker hat high on his head, watched from the trailer porch as Nick unloaded the boxes of electrical cable and components. "Bad news, Nick. The panels didn't make the delivery truck, so you're not going to be able to put those up today."

Nick wiped his brow with his forearm and stared at his motorbike strapped in the Ford's bed. He might have some free time for once to do a little riding. "Any chance I can get an advance on the eggs and milk?"

"No problem. Don't want them to go to waste."

A small wave of relief unknotted the muscles in Nick's back. The drive to the reservation was easy, but it was a solid hour in each direction. It would at least be worth the effort for some free groceries.

Nick looked past the trailer, where there was a dirt path leading to the remains of a failed garden.

The mountains blurred in the distance in the desert heat. "Hey, Frank, what are those things out there?" Nick asked, pointing to a set of poles lined up at the base of the mountains.

"That, Nick, is a railroad line. The train only runs once every couple of months, but it's an offshoot of the commercial lines through Albuquerque and Taos."

"Where's it heading?"

"Well, see, just past the mountains, on the other side, is an annex. Once the reservation was established, the government stayed out of our business—that is, until the United States Army Air Corps was reconstituted as the Air Force and Washington D.C. decided we should be neighbors. On the plus side, there are economic benefits to them using our land. And, might I add, the complex brought along with it civilian jobs. But in reality, this land has become a tactical buffer zone.

"Anyhow, the train brings cargo to the base while on its way to the high-security prisons out here and up in Colorado. The rumor—heck, every rumor out here—is that the base has something to do with UFOs." He pushed the brim of his hat up with his finger. "Sorry to disappoint, but there are no aliens. The train just brings a resupply of toilet paper and food and fuel for the bases. Our reservation is their driveway."

"Does anyone else try to get use of your land?"

"Plenty. There were a couple people here just today. They offered the big bucks immediately—that's always a red flag. The tribe, we have a lot of pride in preserving this area, and that's not just a heritage point. This is *undisturbed*." He spread his hands out wide. "*Sacred* as an act of nature. Despite the tense relationship between our nation and yours, I like to believe there's more good than bad out there, and if we help the good folks over the mountains at the base, then that's okay, but I don't like the idea of opening it up to just anyone."

"Fair enough."

"Let me grab you those egg cartons. You don't need to waste more time on tribal history." Frank waved him along and headed into the trailer with the shuffle of an athletic but worn-down middle-aged man. Nick saw a glimmer of his dad in Frank's cadence and smiled to himself.

He turned to face the mountains once more just before heading inside. Despite the glare of the midday sun, a faint flash beyond the rail line caught his attention. It was longer in duration than a camera flash but blinked off after a second or two. It reappeared again a bit farther away, then flashed off. It repeated the pattern without adhering to a set cadence, a series of flickers moving at a high speed along the foot of the mountain. As a cloud rolled over the far landscape, he could make out the tiny silhouette of a person just ahead of each flare. Nick chuckled at the lone skater charging across the desert road.

"Dana, just take a day off," he murmured with a smirk before stepping into the trailer and letting the cool breeze from the air conditioner blow over his forearms, producing goosebumps. "Those visitors you were just talking about," he asked Frank, "did they come in that Hummer I saw leaving when I came in?"

"Yep. I always laugh when they come to negotiate in an ostentatious vehicle with a high price tag. Not a good look. A few 'landlubbers' trying to charter a ship for desert treasure." He tapped the glass containing the palladium sample on the desk.

"Is that silver?" Nick reached out to touch it, then thought twice. Frank nodded his permission, so Nick carefully lifted the small container to examine the rock.

"Palladium, Nick. One of the weirder metals. Used in—"

"Electronics. Catalytic converters. It's used as a diffuser, absorbs gases, and holds a lower boiling point than the rest of the platinum family," Nick explained with aplomb. Frank's lower lip jutted out and his eyebrows raised at the tiny dissertation.

"I guess they still teach stuff at college, eh? Yep, all that is correct, from what I'm told. My son's graduating from high school this year. His senior project was on palladium, given our exposure to it. He said the Americas' deposits are inferior to those in Russia and Africa, so we're possibly sitting on a strategic supply, right here on the reservation." He tapped the glass encapsulating the sample. "Possibly."

Nick saw the use of palladium factored across many of Dana's father's blueprints, as well as a potential tool in maintaining and upgrading her skates.

"Frank, the guys in the Hummer. Did they seem a little . . . aggressive?"

"That's an interesting choice of words. Not totally. The guy was serious, but not exactly threatening—had a couple of those canes you strap to your wrists. The girl? I wasn't sure what to make of her, besides that she was very well put together. Quite the looker, but she's no Dana." He winked at Nick, who responded with a blush.

"You know she's not my girlfriend, right? We're just roommates." Nick cleared his throat.

"Whatever you say, buddy, but I get the feeling you got a little crush on her. You can't cohabitate for too long before things . . . you know." Frank exhaled with a blast and unfurled his hand in a mock explosion. "Sparks."

"We're both fresh off of our respective breakups." Nick lowered the register of his voice. "And her last relationship was with a *girl*friend. I don't where her head is, so I'm not going to poke her to get back on the horse."

"Are you saying you might *be* the horse?" Frank grinned.

"You're worse than my dad," Nick groaned, wanting to get back to what was really bothering him. "But seriously, I don't have a good feeling about those two visitors of yours. Can I see what they left with you?"

"Sure. It's a mining proposal." He handed a folder over to Nick. "I don't see the harm in you looking at this. It's not like I plan on agreeing to it."

Nick scanned the papers inside the folio. His jaw clenched as he read the names. *Olsen. Rhodes.* The sudden dampness on his palms transferred to the edge of the pages.

"The guy. Short buzz cut? Australian?"

"You got it. No accent for the woman, but she's got a heck of a handshake."

That might be Rhodes's daughter, Nick thought.

"These people who visited you, Frank, they're bad news. How tight are you with local law enforcement here?"

"How tight? My brother is a local deputy."

"Good to know."

Chapter 5

As Cool as I Am – Dar Williams

The box labeled KITCHEN sat open and alone in the center of the island, balled-up packing tape beside it. Inside was a perfect alignment of spatulas, bread knives, ladles, and miscellaneous cooking implements layered between sheets of newspaper and paper towels that Nick had used as makeshift packaging. Dana sat on the wooden stool, chin planted on the counter, gaze unfocused as she peered beyond the box and through the window.

"Tomorrow. You guys have a stay of execution," she sighed as she tossed the ball of tape into the garbage.

The aura of permanence attached to a home was unfamiliar to her. But now, as they had spent many late nights cleaning and dusting, she and Nick had rapidly begun to dream about the future of the house as their own. Buying decorative pillows, painting floor trim, someday replacing the open truss beams of the vaulted ceiling—all these things were added to their imaginary to-do list. Even now, the thought of unpacking a box of kitchenware was insurmountable without Nick's help to review what to keep and what to throw away from their combined collection. She closed the flaps of the box with a sigh and placed it in the cabinet under the island.

Dana heard Nick's truck roll into the driveway and threw herself onto the couch, swinging one leg over the armrest, hoping to give off the vibe of a distressed heiress on the French Riviera from a stuffy art film. As he walked in, she threw her hand against her forehead in feigned despair.

"*Darling,*" she declared with absolutely ostentatious pronunciation, "why did we lay off the staff when we have so much to do in the chalet?"

Nick dropped his toolbox. "How did you get home so fast?" he said with a raised eyebrow.

"I beg your pardon? I've been here lounging all day without any maids or butlers." She shed her faux accent. "I've had to check the job listings online without anyone to click my mouse for me." She giggled. Nick remained by the door, decidedly not laughing and instead looking rather serious.

"I saw you lighting it up by the railroad on the reservation. I thought you were going to take a day off from skating. Did you hoof it back here at top speed?"

She sat up. Her eyes widened as the merriment drained from her face.

"I've been here all day. What are you talking about?"

"You weren't out skating?"

"No."

"You didn't go out to the reservation?"

"*No.*"

"So, I saw a *different* woman on what appeared to be *your* skates?"

The words punched her in the gut as her lungs began to squeeze in her chest.

"What did you see? Nick, I swear, I've been here all day."

He sat down on the couch next to her. She clutched the forearm of his coat, still permeated with desert dust and spots of stubborn New Jersey pine sap that refused to wash out.

"Dana, when I was at Frank's, I saw someone out past the rail line. A woman, definitely a woman. She was flying along, sparks shooting from her heels, just cruising. I know it wasn't an optical illusion. I *saw* her."

Dana firmed her grip on his forearm and struggled to process the feeling creeping into her throat. Horror, fear, excitement, and confusion scrambled into her vocal cords all at once, fighting for dominance.

"Did anyone else see?"

"No, it was just me. Frank had gone back into the trailer when I saw it. So, who the hell was she?"

"I don't know, but we definitely can skip unpacking the final box of kitchen stuff while we try to find out, that's for sure."

Nick walked to the patio doors and leaned on the glass. Dana came to his side and stared at his profile, noting the increasingly worried look on his face. "Nick, what else is wrong?"

"There's something else I didn't tell you yet. I'm still wrapping my head around it." He took a deep breath and turned to face her directly.

"Which is?"

"Someone came to the reservation before me. Two people. Dana . . ." Nick paused to take a deep breath. "It was our friend Agent Ninety-Nine— Olsen—and a woman named *Rhodes*."

Dana's knees buckled at the mere mention of those names. Nick clutched her to hold her upright. She wheezed and gasped, her eyes darting with the frenzy of a pinball machine turned upside down. Instinct drove her muscle memory as her thighs tightened and she pushed her toes down in her socks, reaching for the imaginary controls in the pads of her roller skates.

"Okay, you probably should have *led* with that," she deadpanned once she regained some composure. "Olsen is . . . walking around? I thought all this time I'd turned his spine into saltine crackers. And the woman named

Rhodes, she must be related to Colin Rhodes. Is she young? Old?"

"I'm not sure. I didn't see her myself, but Frank seemed to think she was around your age."

This makes no sense. Nothing is making any sense. Dana balled up her fists and held them tight against her sides.

"Okay. Let's work this out. They show up at the same time as some mystery woman with skates like mine." Dana paced back to the kitchen and marched around the island counter with her hands folded behind her head. "So maybe they think this other person on skates is me, and they're sniffing around. That's a possible scenario." She paced faster and faster.

"Focus," Nick said calmly. "The two events may be related, or maybe they're unrelated. We need to keep both paths open until we get more information to rule one out."

Dana stopped circling the counter and surveyed the house. Other than the painting by her mother that had been here when they arrived, the rooms were full of pieces from each of their lives, merging into this new joint life— one that now seemed to be suddenly teetering on the brink of destruction. What Nick told her signaled a coming storm of unknown magnitude. She stared at his toolbox, their backpacks by the door, her favorite flannel blanket draped over the back of his couch, the milk crate with her old Asbury Angels roller derby uniform and skates. The shock of the news churned in her stomach, kicking her adrenaline into high gear and refocusing her brain.

"Nick, you work on the reservation angle. Someone else *has* to have seen them or interacted with them. You poke around. They would stand out like a sore thumb."

"What about you?"

"If someone else really is out there on *my* skates, I think I know where I might find them." She grinned as she held up her old jersey, sky-blue sleeves attached to a faded black torso, to her chest. "I'm going to join the local derby team." She pirouetted and pumped one arm. "I'm back, baby!"

"Dana, that's one hell of a swing of emotions you just went through. It's, uh . . . a bit worrying. Are you sure you're alright?"

"I'm fine, Nick," she said, seemingly trying to convince herself as much as him. "Once I get my skates back on, I'm good. And there's no better place to work out my issues than at the roller derby track. There's a *wooft-da* team right in town."

"Woof-what?"

"Women's Flat Track Derby Association. W-F-T-D-A."

"Wooft-da. Right," he replied. "I'll go to the reservation, and you go and . . . join a roller derby team. Makes perfect sense."

Chapter 6

Rock Candy – Montrose

Nina grabbed the handle for the two-hundred-pound hangar door and leaned her shoulder into the frame. The rusty wheels creaked and stuttered as they yielded to her brute force. Olsen's assembled team gawked as the door rolled and slowly revealed her muscular body contracting and rippling under her neoprene bodysuit. She brushed her gloved hands against each other and stared back at the assembled men, frozen at their task stations next to a fleet of box trucks.

"Nina, you know there's a motor," Agent Seventy-Four said in his quiet manner that belied his massive bulk. He pointed his scarred and calloused hand to a set of red and green buttons.

"I've been sitting all day," she sighed, "and I needed to get out some pent-up energy."

Olsen lumbered behind her on his canes. Each step required a focused effort, a sharp contrast to Nina's elegant and precise cadence, but he refused to let the men—many of whom he had served with abroad and ran unspeakable missions of violence with across the globe—see him in a wheelchair. Retaining an image of strength and resilience was critical.

He glared at the men as they openly gaped at Nina as she walked by, none of them hiding their interest. Whenever she walked into the room, they seemed to forget that she was the daughter of the man who had given them their jobs and now sat in a federal prison sentenced to a lengthy list of fraud and racketeering charges, as well as attempted theft of government property. She was now deemed Agent Ninety-Nine with Olsen out of commission and, most importantly, she was a medical marvel and technological wonder—the apex of biomechanical advancement, a survivor of medical maladies now weaponized and lethal, serving the greater good of their cause. Olsen knew that she held their attention for those reasons, but she also knew how to use their base desires to manipulate each and every one for whatever task or goal she pursued. Olsen might still be the boss—now Agent One Hundred to her Agent Ninety-Nine—but *she* was in charge. He stopped and whistled a sweeping shrill note to refocus the men.

"Thirty-Six and Thirty-Seven, where are the long crates?" he barked. A set of identical twins emerged from the back of the farthest truck, their long scraggly beards wet with perspiration and spit. "Do I need to come up there myself?"

The closest brother, Agent Thirty-Six, came to the lip of the cargo hold, his visible limp the only thing to set him apart from his brother. Agent Thirty-Seven waved a crowbar and flipped it to his sibling. "This would go a lot smoother if we had a forklift or bobcat," he said, a hint of insubordination in his tone. The brothers leaned into the closest wooden crate and cracked the lid with the crowbar in a joint effort. Thirty-Six held up a gun, a Colt M4 carbine equipped with a scope and laser sight. "We've got a half dozen of these in here. Ammo is in the next crate behind it," he noted, smoothing out his beard and running his hand through an imaginary hairline. "Agent Ninety-Nine, can you please give us a hand?"

The twins pushed each long box to the edge of the truck. Nina grabbed the first box and hoisted it over her head to the floor with a loud thud.

"Careful, those cost us a lot of money," Olsen interjected, wincing at her roughness. He was painfully aware of the money spent on the operation so far between the cash deals for the arms, the heavy payout to the airstrip owner to "close" the airport, and food and gas. Nina just nodded and continued to move the crates from the truck to the floor until it was empty. Olsen inspected the crates before taking a seat in a folding chair at a makeshift sawhorse desk topped with his laptop and a stack of papers.

"How has it come to this?" Olsen asked of no one in particular, a look of disdain on his face. "I feel like a goddamn goldfish flopping around barking orders to barracudas." He lowered his voice. "I can't possibly be the leader your father was . . . like this." He looked with disgust at his canes.

Nina placed a cold gloved hand on his shoulder. "Olsen, we are following my father's instructions, and I'm confident we'll get this done. When we get paid, and we will get paid *royally*, we'll give you the best body money can buy. My father wouldn't have it any other way as a reward for your service."

"Let me be clear: I'm not going to buy a new body from Silver." In the world of mercenaries, debt was a burden and a ghost. Silver was the most prolific inventor alive in the field of biomechanical advancements. He had made Nina the amazing machine she was—for a significant price—and could do the same for him, but Olsen would rather have been crippled than owe a steep debt to a ghastly mad scientist who held significant leverage over the most ruthless mercenaries and dictators in the world. He wanted nothing to do with the man. *I just want my final paycheck for one final job, and then I can disappear.*

"Your call," she replied flippantly.

Olsen watched her saunter over to group of men assembling steel shelving units. She patted one of them on the rear as she walked by, her lack of decorum and need to be the center of attention silently roiling Olsen. *If they only knew what was under her skin, they'd run for the hills, and I don't mean her artificial limbs.* Any initial attraction to her had waned almost instantly once he became aware of her blind loyalty to her father. She threw out all logic and common sense in favor of "father knows best."

Olsen ran his eyes over the papers strewn across the plywood desktop: maps of railroad lines, topographical mining surveys, blueprints for assorted weapons, both handheld and vehicle-mounted. He slid a sheet of handwritten train schedules to the top of the pile, but he couldn't bring himself to care about it. Paperwork, planning, logistics—it wasn't what he did best, wasn't what he wanted to be doing.

He stared beyond the open hangar doors and watched the watercolor sky bleed into new hues. He had gained a new appreciation for every moment of daylight after he was arraigned with Rhodes back in New Jersey and spent a bit of time in custody before being freed on a technicality. His freedom felt outside of his control, a feeling that did not sit well with him. He turned back to the papers, but focus would not come. A new line item manifested on his mental list of priorities.

"Dana Jefferson. Where are you at, girl?"

Chapter 7

Raise Your Hands – Bon Jovi

Dana leaned forward and rested her wrist braces on her kneepads, their baby-blue paint chipped and scraped away in most places—a memory of countless roller derby battles back in New Jersey. She coasted onto the track, feeling right at home in her old derby skates—the left named Lenny; the right, Squiggy—as a flush of excitement covered her cheeks and neck. She placed two fingers between her lips and blasted a shrill, note-bending whistle to get the attention of the team manager.

"Photograph, ready for launch."

Dana set the toe of her skate on the painter's tape that indicated the starting line on the floor of the Walt Whitman Community Center's expansive rec room. She pulled the strap on her wrist guards one more time before raising her arms to a charging posture. Nine other women assumed their positions along the line, wearing a mishmash of vintage sweatshirts, concert tees, and torn roller derby jerseys from defunct teams. Only Dana and the woman next to her wore spandex white caps stretched over their helmets to indicate their role as jammers, the point scorers for their respective teams. Dana relished the position; she was already beaming with anticipation for being responsible for scoring points for the supporting blockers on her squad. In truth, she was a pivot, a player designated to switch from blocker to jammer—a quarterback of sorts for the overall game—but she knew that as a "rookie" trying out here, she would take any role designated by the team's senior members.

The team manager had introduced herself at the beginning of tryouts as Janice Oketra—pronouncing her name with punched annunciation—and now stood before them with her arms folded intimidatingly. She glared at Dana and shook her head, swatting her thin shoulders with her long brown ponytail.

"Just run the jam, old woman," she shouted. "And don't hurt anyone."

Janice set her whistle at her lips and fired an explosive echoing bleat. Dana drove her lead foot into the wooden floor and launched past the first blockers before they could gain any momentum. Another blocker, a muscular woman with a long black French braid, attempted to intercept Dana but only clutched an armful of empty space, falling into the path of the oncoming skaters.

"Middle, middle!" Dana yelled, receiving no reaction from the assembled rookies. *Doesn't anyone here know directions?* "Out!" she snarled. "OUT!"

Dana pivoted with a brief stutter step toward the outside of the track and dodged a hip-check from the final blocker before breaking away from the pack. Janice blew the whistle and threw her clipboard down on the floor.

"Photograph! Get over here!"

As the pack slowed to take a casual lap around the makeshift track, Dana slid over to Janice in a heel-toe pose and skid into a T-stop, feet perpendicular to each other. Janice avoided eye contact as she scanned the gang of girls on skates, shaking her head with a fervor that rattled her hoop earrings against her cheeks.

"Dammit . . . you weren't bragging," she said with a scowl, but Dana noticed the corners of her lips twitching, fighting a smile. "You *are* the best girl here. By a long shot. You know we suck, right? We're barely able to field a team, and I'm struggling to keep us registered with WFTDA. Hell, I considered letting a high school girl on the team last week just so we'd have a body for our next event."

Dana panted as she removed her helmet, slightly out of breath from the sprints. Lenny and Squiggy required much more effort to maneuver than Laverne and Shirley, but muscle memory and instinct had taken her through tryouts with ease. She had outperformed all the moves, ran through an orange traffic-cone slalom in what felt like record time based on the other girls' slacked-jaw reactions, and landed a graceful Axel jump after warmups to ensure she caught Janice's attention early. The rush of competition and the reckless fun on the track had successfully made Dana forget about the constant lurking fear that had engulfed her since the move to New Mexico. She had to remind herself that her goal was to find out exactly who Nick saw skating.

"Just happy to be given a shot," Dana replied with a mock salute. "My life is a little up and down right now. This is good for me."

At the top of the bleachers, a thick woman in a denim vest decorated with handsewn patches folded up a tripod and packed it into her camera bag. She pointed at Dana aggressively as she descended the stairs.

"Hey! I know who you are," the woman bellowed, her heavy footsteps on the metal bleachers echoing in the open room. "You played for Asbury. I read in a few of the group chats that you bailed on them last season." She walked over to Dana and leaned into her face, close enough that Dana could smell the sweat and barbecue scent on her breath. "We're waiting on three girls—*three*—to come back from medical. We don't need a quitter taking up space for someone who *wants* to be here."

Dana's pulse increased. She felt warmth creep up her neck and face as her eardrums popped. This level of conflict was uncharacteristic on most teams, and across the derby leagues in general. An invisible fist constricted in her chest. She pushed the rising rage down as she struggled to form words, any words, to try and deescalate things.

"Well, my ex-girlfriend was on the team and got stabbed. So, yeah, I didn't finish the season. And neither did she, thanks for your concern."

The woman gave an unsympathetic nod, then turned and walked toward the hallway. Janice stood silent until the doors closed behind the woman.

"What's her deal?" Dana asked.

"That's Kendra. She's got some . . . anger issues. She's the most senior member of the group—she's pretty protective of the team. She helped us a lot with fundraisers when we started out. Worked out a deal for us to skate here at a reduced rate." Janice squished her face, her smooth features wrinkling tightly. "She had a back injury, started to get crotchety, and hasn't been the same since."

"Maybe she's not thrilled you held a tryout scrimmage this close to a first match."

"Not any choice, really." The two women both watched the ragtag group of recruits either freeskating or taking off their gear. "We used to do a recruitment night and teach some basic skills, but we can't afford as many nights renting out this place, even with Kendra's help, and the skate population is a bit thin. So, we cut right to the chase and held a rookie scrimmage." She picked up her clipboard. "Thank God you're not fresh meat, Photograph."

"Off the track, just call me Dana."

"Ok, *Dana*. You get your handle on your jersey when you say yes to the team. And I hope you do." Janice tilted her head and smirked. "You okay, girl? You look a little pale."

"I'm fine. Just knocking the rust out." Dana finished removing her pads and stuffed them into her gym bag. She packed up her skates and headed toward the exit.

"I'll call you about practice!" Janice yelled after her, mimicking holding a phone to her ear.

Dana didn't look back, picking up speed until she was through the exit doors and in the parking lot. Her forehead felt hot, her knees wobbly. She collapsed next to a light pole. Her hands trembled—numbness ran through her fingertips up to her elbows. She closed her eyes.

The slideshow started again in her head.

The knife slicing into Angela's side.

A spray of blood erupting from Nick's shoulder.

Nick falling onto the tarmac.

She felt the asphalt on the back of her head. Behind her eyelids, a blinding rainbow pulsed. White noise rose in her ears. The warmth of the afternoon sun pressed on her cheeks.

"Are you going to be sick?" asked a female voice, piercing the swelling din inside her head.

Dana opened her eyes and saw a black French braid dangling over her face. The woman attached to it smiled gently, her long eyelashes fluttering lavishly with each blink, framing large dark-brown eyes. She extended her hand, still strapped in a pink wrist guard, and pulled Dana to a sitting position.

"I'm Lilly. You're a really good skater. Like, so good. So good, I just want to quit."

"Um, thank you. You were pretty good, too." Dana kept her hand locked on Lilly's wrist guard. "I just need a second . . . I'm Dana."

"Sure. Dana Jefferson, Asbury Angels, right? I followed you. Online. Er, your team—I followed your team online. I've never been to the East Coast."

Lilly held out a water bottle that Dana accepted and poured over her head.

"I guess I got a little overheated . . . it's a recent thing. It's been a weird transition, coming back to New Mexico." Dana pointed to the silver barrette shaped like a wolf that Lilly had pinned close to her forehead. "So, what tribe are you from?"

"Me? I'm not Native American. I'm *Indian*. Lilly Patel."

Dana smacked herself in the head. "I'm sorry. The hair, your features . . . boy, did I make a really bad assumption right there. I'm an idiot and obviously culturally ignorant. I went to boarding school with lots of rich white folk . . . okay, I'll shut up now."

Lilly giggled. Dana accepted the gesture as forgiveness, even as she simmered in the juices of her own embarrassment.

"It's totally fine. I get a lot of looks out here. Everywhere I go, I seem to get second-class treatment. That's partly why I wanted to join the derby team—a good way to meet people and look tough at the same time. You know, forced friendship."

Dana laughed as she put her head between her knees to draw one more deep breath before standing up. "Yeah, making friends is tough as a grown-up. So, new friend, want to walk me to my truck?"

"Are you sure you can drive? I had to be an Uber for some girl last week. She was barely sixteen. Don't know how she got here, but she begged me to drop her off at the bus stop afterward. It's too bad we have a minimum age, because she skated almost as well as you." Lilly sheepishly grinned. "Maybe even better."

"Really?!" Dana hoped she didn't seem overly excited, but she had just wandered into an informational jackpot thanks to this serendipitous meeting. "Tell you what, give me your number. We'll go get some fries together, and I'll give you some skating tips as an elder statesman of the sport." She grabbed an unpaid parking ticket from the visor and a pen from the dashboard so Lilly could write it down. "So, what bus stop did you drop her off at?" she asked as nonchalantly as possible. "I mean, I'm just curious where the closest bus stop is."

"The corner at Horizon Boulevard, two blocks up. Next to Ram Gas."

"Great, thanks. So, I'll call you soon for fries and a beer!"

Dana jumped in the truck and turned the ignition, immediately blasting the air conditioner, her heart and lungs battling for the cold breeze. She glanced at the footwell in the passenger seat where Laverne and Shirley sat tucked safely in their bag.

"We've got something. There's no way this is coincidence."

Chapter 8

I Gotta Try – Michael McDonald

Nick poked his head out from the basement doorway. "Why is our living room floor covered in bus schedules? I think there are some board games in the closet if you're looking for something to do. They're right next to the cleaning supplies and vacuum, in case you haven't seen those."

Dana ignored him and continued shuffling through maps and pamphlets. She gingerly refolded one of the maps to lay over another one and drew a line with a pink highlighter across both papers.

"Dee? Hello?"

"I got an idea, my dear Watson. I think my doppelgänger may be somewhere in this area." She poked a finger through a fresh hole in the map and grimaced. "If you get on this bus, take this transfer, you'd get close to the highways by the reservation." Proud of her deductions, she turned to Nick with an ostentatious openmouthed smile. "Ya dig?"

Nick arched his eyebrows and crossed his arms. His sleeves rolled up over his biceps, revealing a dark tan line. "How do you where she's coming from?"

Dana ignored his question. "Got a little sun there," she noted.

"Yeah, well, working outside, on a roof, in *this* climate to put up solar panels for eggs and cash isn't fun, but it's what we have to do. Or at least what *I* have to do, since the bills are all in my name."

"It's not my fault I don't have a credit score above two digits. And besides, we're trying to keep my profile on the down-low, remember?" She crumpled a bus schedule and lobbed it at his head. He scowled as he unsuccessfully dodged the paper projectile, which bounced off his forehead.

"I know, but it seems we were right to be paranoid since the remnants of One Hundred Roads are afoot." He nodded toward the basement. "Want to see what I've been doing?"

Dana walked slowly down the stairs behind Nick into the fluorescent lights of the basement. She usually avoided the cellar, not only because of her fear of insects and tiny beasts that liked to live in the cool and uncommon feature of their home, but because the specter of her father loomed heavily, pricking her happy memories with spikes of sadness. All his work— unfinished, unlauded, unwanted—remained here, his genius hidden from the world.

She quickly saw what Nick had been up to. The laboratory space was now clean, save for the pile of scraps around the shop vac in the corner of the room. The old computers sparkled and shined with renewed luster. Nick had connected the working CPUs to a set of color tube TVs he had acquired in a barter with Frank Irons. A keyboard ran through a series of adapters into a channel switch box that spread into a trellis of cables.

"Welcome to our new secret headquarters! Now we can run each of the old computers to check the files your dad left behind, and we can copy and save them here." He slid Dana's laptop across the table and held up a lone cable.

"Wow," she breathed, genuinely impressed. She held the cable up to her nose and smelled it. "Still a little musky. Any idea what's on them yet? Text-based video games? Maybe a Sears catalog from 1986?"

"I'm not sure, but a few of the files have similar names, each with a different two-digit number at the end. I think the files are meant to be used together. Maybe for that?" He pointed to the power plant diorama at the far end of the basement. "If I can pull it off—building that, I mean—I say we give it to the reservation. Assuming it works."

"Well, before you go into a technical dissertation of just how you'll do that, I want to tell you what I found out about the skater today."

"Shoot."

"See, I had another episode at the tryouts—not while I was skating, but after practice—and this girl was helping me—"

"Hold up, you had another one? Dana, you should have told me right away."

"I'm trying to tell you now! Anyhow, this old-timer derby troll got in my face about not being reliable. I told her about Angela getting stabbed. And then, boom, panic." She held up her hands and mimicked fireworks.

"Hey," he said gently, "it's a big deal what you went through. All the layers can add up. Do you think, and I'm not by any means a psychologist—"

"Are you taking a class in that, too?"

"Funny. I'm just wondering if maybe you have some PTSD. Flashbacks, panic attacks, zoning out . . . those are all symptoms." He fiddled with a small screwdriver and avoided eye contact as he said it.

"I wouldn't be surprised." She took a punctuated deep breath. "I just wish it would stop happening when I'm around skating. It's the one thing I love. It's not fair." She crossed her arms and shrugged.

"You're right, Dana. It's *not* fair. One of the guys back when I was with the electric company in Jersey had it, PTSD. His partner fell out of a bucket from a cherry picker truck and hit a line. The guy died, and he watched it. He had to quit, filed for disability. Last I heard, he had a breakdown . . ." He trailed off as he saw Dana's eyes widen. "Not that you will. Everyone is different, from what I know."

Dana stood in front of the bank of monitors and rubbed her eyes. "It's just hard."

"Maybe we should find someone for you to talk to. Like a counselor, or a group. I know they host things like that at the community center on the reservation. I can look at the schedule. Plus"—he splayed his hands and shrugged—"it's free."

She smiled at that. "Okay, fine, if it's a free mental health check, I can try. But I need to find out more about the girl on the skates first. The girl that helped me after my 'incident,' she told me about a teenager who tried out for the team the week before. She said she was good—as good as me."

Nick leaned back on the table and shook his head. "I'm voting against finding her for now and voting for you getting some help first."

"Maybe this isn't a thing you get a vote on," she countered as she stepped toward him and playfully poked his chest with two fingers. "But I will go talk to someone. I promise."

Nick patted her on the shoulder as he walked past her to the stairs and headed up. Dana slowly wandered over to the table of the power plant diorama and ran her fingers along the sides of a tiny tower closest to her. She admired her father's work, cleaned up by Nick, arrayed in a pattern of circles and squares. There was still so little she knew of his actual plans, yet here she was off chasing phantom skaters while Nick was the one immersed in her dad's world. *I need to do more,* she told herself. She was tired of being a bystander here in New Mexico. She didn't want to feel broken and useless. Especially not with Nick.

"I'll do better," she whispered—partly to herself, maybe partly to her dad—before turning back to the stairs.

Chapter 9

Nothin' for Nothin' – Cinderella

Flight A301's passengers exited the gate at Roswell International Air Center in a muddled mob, darting and pushing to find the big board listing the connecting flights. The plane had landed an hour late due to the weather over Oklahoma, and the business travelers shoved and nudged each other in a chaotic stampede. A stocky young man in a black sport coat stopped short, frantically slapping his hips for his wallet. Another man, a septuagenarian with short sleeves and a wide striped tie, performed a similar ritual in front of an information desk. All over the arrival hub, people hurriedly emptied their pockets and carry-on bags, dumped out their laptop totes, and turned their jackets inside out searching for their IDs, phones, or car keys, disorganized and disheveled.

All the while, Brian "Nails" Nelson strode confidently through the chaos as he entered the terminal from the gate. His aviator sunglasses shone above his wide toothy smile and pencil-thin moustache. He made his way to the airport map, then confidently turned toward the escalator that descended to the pickup area. His black button-down shirt and crisp jeans flattered his muscled athletic frame, forged by years in active combat zones around the world, and he relished the attention he attracted from the flight attendants he walked past, close enough to smell their discount-store herbal shampoos. He lifted his sunglasses to wink at one as he strode into the parking lot and adjusted his small but heavy backpack.

"Well, well, well, it's my paycheck!" he announced in a loud voice that echoed against the concrete, rising above the engine whine of shuttle buses and idling taxis.

Olsen balanced on his canes, wincing from standing so long but refusing to lean against his black SUV. "I'm pretty sure you're the one who owes me."

Brian dropped his bag and hugged him, placing a hand on the back of Olsen's neck and smashing their foreheads together.

"I got you a gift." Brian emptied his pockets and fanned some stolen wallets and passports from Flight A301 before him like a deck of cards. "Let's go run up a few bar tabs for old times' sake." He had not seen his brother-in-arms in a few years, but the bond from battle was still strong between them.

"I guess you had a good flight, then." Olsen smirked and steadied himself. "Things have . . . changed since we last worked together."

"It pains me to see you like this, buddy," Brian whispered, lifting his sunglasses to the top of his head.

The driver's side door of the SUV swung open, and a blond woman stepped out in a long black duster over a bodysuit. She walked coolly up to Brian and stood inches from his face. Her eyes carefully took him in while her hair whipped across her open lips as a large bus barreled down the lane just behind them.

"Well, hello there," she purred. "Nina Rhodes. I'm your new boss. Nice to finally meet you, *Brian*."

"Bonjour, my little sugar cookie. Have you killed anyone today with those looks?" He snickered.

Olsen rolled his eyes but smiled. "Get in."

The SUV roared down the highway, the airport shrinking in the sideview mirror. Olsen was glad Brian was here. *He's a good fit*, he thought. Their prior missions, especially the ones that had gone sideways, had shown Olsen just how reliable Brian could be in crisis mode, his ability to stick to the mission no matter the cost. When a situation called for extreme force, Brian never hesitated to be the first to do whatever was necessary.

"So, Brian, the contact on the plane. How did you get the laptop from him?"

"Oh, our government idiot? Boy, he was a talker. Very unhappily married. Kept him talking all the way to the restroom once we got off the plane. Then I incapacitated him"—he pantomimed squeezing a syringe—"got his computer, dug his password book out of his bag—these guys always have one of those." He rapped his knuckles on the laptop bag on the seat next to him. "So, *Aaron Olsen*, what other fun do I get to have on this little trip? Duping that guy can't be the only reason you called me."

Olsen looked down at his canes. If he weren't injured, he and Brian could have run this whole op, just the two of them. Their connection and unspoken communication made them a formidable team, whether in dangerous missions or a pick-up soccer game.

"Now I need you for your *other* expertise. I need surveillance, a world-class tracker like yourself." He turned to look Brian directly in the eyes.

"Ah, with those canes, I'm guessing the only place you could infiltrate would be a nursing home." He laughed at his own joke. "Please tell me I get to go after whoever did that to you."

Olsen's chin jutted out as his nose flared. One thing he had never liked about Brian was his caustic sense of humor. But he hadn't brought him here for laughs—rather, for his sociopathic dedication to the hunt. They had met on a special operations security detail in India when they played a crime lord and a terrorist organization against each other and emerged from the ensuing shootout as the only survivors. Their partnership had been cemented then and there. When One Hundred Roads came calling, Olsen was handpicked by Mr. Rhodes, but Brian was deemed too unstable for such top-secret work. But now, Olsen needed a rook to sweep the chessboard.

"You'll hear more when we get to our location. But yes, it has something to do with the woman who did this to me. She has something we need, and I also need to make sure she doesn't get in the way of our current deal." Olsen stared back at Brian through the side mirror. "But let me be clear, *I* make the decisions on this op. If you jump the gun and off her before we exhaust her usefulness, I will, indeed, not only fire you—I just may kill you."

"Look at you! You can barely walk, but you're throwing down. I love you, man!" Brian slapped his chest and laughed. "You don't have to worry about it, buddy. I won't let you down. I'm sure I'll get my fix elsewhere. Hey, speaking of fixes, any chance we can stop at . . ."—he paused as he checked his phone—"the parking lot of the Lore Suites off Route 70? I'm supposed to meet a guy there." He winked at Olsen in the mirror.

"Sounds like fun," Nina replied, putting on the turn signal and navigating the SUV toward downtown Roswell. "By the way, why do they call you 'Nails,' my new friend?"

Brian pulled his collar flat and smoothed the buttons on his shirt.

"One, because I seal coffins." He licked his fingers and smoothed his eyebrows. "You play your cards right, and you'll find out the other reason why."

Olsen shook his head. "Brian, rule number one: never mess with the boss. Rule number two: never forget the first rule."

Nina smiled to herself and kept driving.

Chapter 10

September Gurls – Big Star

Dana stood in front of the glass doors to the community center. She unzipped her leather jacket, adjusted her backpack straps, and drew another swig from her water bottle. The door handles were well worn, sandblasted from years in the desert, revealing the brass under the brown utilitarian paint. Beyond the entrance she could see double doors propped open, revealing a small conference room with a circle of folding chairs—some occupied—and a table with a coffee pot and plates of snack foods. She placed her hand on the handle but could not bring herself to pull the door open.

"Excuse me, miss."

A middle-aged woman with stringy brown hair and graying temples politely opened the door and nodded for Dana to enter.

"Thanks. It's my first time here," Dana said with a forced smile.

"Everyone has a first time," the woman replied. "I'm Christina."

"Dana. Dana Jefferson," she answered, and then scowled immediately. "Sorry, no last names, right?"

Christina nodded as they walked inside together. The attendance for the evening tallied twelve people, a full blend of ages, gender identities, and ethnicities. Dana chose the seat next to Christina and slid her backpack containing Laverne and Shirley under her chair. *I don't know why I brought them,* she thought to herself. Before she could finish assessing the crowd and the well-kept but dated room, a tan woman with jet-black hair stood to conduct the session.

"Welcome, all. My name is Tara. This is the depression and anxiety weekly group. For our new members, this group is for those who are challenged and looking for support. All are welcome to speak or remain silent. Please respect the time of others, and do not interrupt. We are all working through our depression or anxiety, or both, and for some of us, this will always be something we deal with and aim to control. There are no permanent fixes; there is no judgement. We are all roadrunners."

Dana snorted before she could stop herself.

Tara looked kindly at her. "Is there something you want to share?"

"No, just the roadrunner image . . . was just . . . funny. I'm sorry . . ."

"Well, the roadrunner is our mascot. See, a roadrunner's wings don't work very well, but the roadrunner adapted and evolved in this world—it learned to run instead. We, too, can adapt and evolve, can run if our wings don't work. We can still move forward."

Dana nodded and leaned back in her chair.

"Would you like to start first? Introduce yourself?" Tara asked her, extending an open hand and a gracious smile under her worn cheeks.

"Um, sure. My name is Dana, and I'm trying to figure out some things. I'm a bit of a talker when I get on a roll, so throw a flag or blow a whistle if you have to. Anyway, I'm a boarding school kid. My parents died when I was young, and my grandfather, who was my caretaker, also died."

Christina placed her hand on Dana's arm while Tara gently responded, "The death of a parent is challenging, let alone multiple guardians."

Dana cleared her throat and opened her mouth to talk but, despite her own warning of talking too much, nothing came out. She certainly couldn't share the details of her lineage creating a walking golem of destruction, her ex-girlfriend being stabbed, and her best friend getting shot right before she crippled a man by breaking his back. "Roller-skating," she said abruptly. "I mean, I love to roller skate—roller derby. My mom and I would roller skate around the house sometimes when my dad was away for work. And now I have trouble doing it. It, like, triggers some bad things, like I can't breathe, I get dizzy, I . . . I'll stop there." The faces around her smiled kindly and nodded. Dana waved her hands to indicate she was done.

A young man with a dark military crew cut across the circle raised his hand. Tara pointed.

"Darren, go ahead."

"I'm Darren. Welcome, Dana. I was a pilot, and my crew, well, we had a training accident with a helicopter. I loved flying. I was going to go commercial after I got out of the military. But now, I can't leave the ground. I acknowledge now that the idea of being responsible for people's lives became a big conflict in my head. I couldn't go back to flying. I couldn't do what I love." He paused and smiled warmly at Dana. "But I *can* teach, help people get their license. And I can be on the ground, in the control tower. It brings me some joy, but it still feels . . . it's just not fair." He looked down at his hands in his lap.

Dana felt warm appreciation for Darren's disclosure and nodded at him in empathy. *This place is alright.* She removed her jacket and folded it on her lap.

"Looks like you're going to stick around?" Christina whispered before Tara gestured to her to see if she wanted to talk next.

"My name is Christina. I'm in recovery from addiction, like many people in here are. I acknowledge that I cannot cure my addiction, but I confront and face it every day, especially since it's still widespread in our community."

Around the circle, people continued to speak. A man in his early twenties admitted his relapse with drugs. Another man, arms covered in faded tattoos, discussed turning to alcohol after the death of his wife and daughter at the hands of a drunk driver. One woman close to Dana's age discussed being the target of a hate crime when she had moved into a mostly white neighborhood. A middle-aged man—who stared at Dana a little too much for her comfort—discussed how his wife had committed suicide and left him with three kids to raise on his own. Dana soaked in these strangers' stories, their challenges and failures as well as their successes. Each time they spoke, Tara skillfully led them into acknowledgements of their problems but also their value and worth, and their ability to move forward.

At the end of the meeting, after a group affirmation, Dana placed her folding chair against the wall with the others and lingered by the cookie plate until Tara ended a small conversation with Darren. She then turned to Dana with a broad smile.

"Thank you for coming, Dana. I hope we see you again. We meet weekly, but many people come on an irregular basis. So, whenever you need strength, just come."

"Thank you for having me. It's a bit surreal, sitting down and talking things out with strangers." She blushed. "I don't know how to talk to people about feelings and stuff. Anything you said in boarding school was used against you by the pretty girls who ran the asylum, if you catch my drift." She opened and closed her fists. "I don't know what to do with my hands sometimes. Kind of a nervous thing."

"You know," Tara said as she stacked unused disposable coffee cups, "it sounds like you grew up with a lot of instability. If I may, it seems to me that you have two choices. You can be a roadrunner who tries to *outrun* the pain and predators, or you can be a roadrunner who *adapts* and *evolves*. Maybe change the reason that you run."

Dana's eyes widened as she leaned back. "That's some crazy mojo."

"I got it from a book for addicts. I'm a recovering addict, like most people in the group."

"Is addiction a big problem here?" Dana pulled on her coat and strapped on her backpack. "I'm sorry, that's like *way* too probing."

"No, that's alright. It was for a while, a big uptick in substance abuse, then it slowed down. But it's always going to be a challenge." Tara leaned in closer, so near that Dana caught a whiff of coffee and lavender soap. "In fact, I was talking to Mr. Irons about it, and it sounds like there's a new source in the community—a courier bringing stuff in."

"A courier?" Dana noticed that only she and Tara remained in the room as the doors shut behind the last group member.

"I keep an ear to the ground, which goes far in a small community. One person said it was a girl on skates bringing in prescriptions scripts."

Dana slid an arm behind her back, suddenly protective of the skates in her pack.

Tara continued, "You mentioned loving skating. Wonder if you've heard anything in your roller derby circle?"

Dana shook her head vigorously back and forth. "No, not exactly. See, I'm actually *looking* for a girl on skates myself. Not because I think she's running opioids or, gosh, even aspirin. Although, I do think this girl could be dangerous, or maybe she's *in* danger? Maybe both? I guess we could be looking for the same person."

Tara didn't respond. She seemed to be considering Dana in a new light. Dana couldn't stand wondering what she might be thinking, opting to break the silence. "Listen, I don't want you to get the wrong idea. I've done some things, not bad things—well, at least not for good reason—but this girl might know some things I need to know. I just . . . need to find her."

"Well, let me know if you do." Tara turned back to the table and slid some leftover cookies into a resealable bag. "And come back to the group, even if you don't find her, for your own good. My mojo radar isn't what it used to be, but I think you're on the side of the light, not the darkness."

"I like to think I'm one of the good guys."

Tara pressed the bag of cookies into Dana's hand. "I have a gift for seeing people's true colors, and I do think you are a good one, *roadrunner*."

Chapter 11

Waterfalls – TLC

Nick slid his thumbnail across the flower's stem, gently cutting it to liberate it from the main stalk. The name, he didn't know; the flora of New Mexico differed from New Jersey, where he had known the names of every flower he planted with his mom on warm spring weekends. He held up a multi-petaled ornamental white bloom and decided to name it "Mrs. Andrews."

His father had loved to call her Mrs. Andrews when he was feeling affectionate, and his mother had always preferred to receive flowers over gifts. Nick placed the freshly cut flower next to the others, completing a small but beautiful rainbow bouquet of desert blooms. Dana's shadow passed over him from behind before he heard her footsteps in the sand.

"It's so pretty out here," she said wistfully, sighing as she sat down next to him. "I just can't get over it." She rested her head on his shoulder. Her dark locks danced in the breeze, a stray piece tickling his cheek for a moment. She dug her heels into the dry soil.

"So, how'd it go?" Nick asked, slowly tilting his head away from the tendrils of her hair.

"Good. I got another lead."

"I meant the meeting." His hand covertly moved the tiny bunch of flowers under his leg, out of her line of sight.

"It was . . . helpful, I think. I'll go back. I have a lot on my mind, Nicky." She shuffled her feet back and forth, creating shallow footprint trenches in the sandy soil. "Did you talk to your dad?"

"I did. He's good. Stories about the cardiologist, stories about the raccoons in the trash. Ten minutes on the amazing turkey sandwich he got at the deli last week."

Nick looked out over the plain and focused on the low mountains on the horizon. The range melted from orange to purple as the sun dripped its rays lower and lower, the sunset imminent. He did not overlook when Dana had called him Nicky; she used it when she no longer wanted to discuss a tenuous topic or decision.

Nick learned this during the move out to New Mexico every time he had pivoted the subject to a critical personal revelation, resulting in an awkward and silent three-hour ride across Texas after he had asked her if she thought her mother might still be alive out here.

The mountains offered no wisdom on how to deal with other people despite their millennia of experiences.

"What's on your mind, Detective Andrews?" She reached forward and picked a yellow wildflower from a dark green plant at her feet.

"It's just . . . if One Hundred Roads is here, and they're looking for you, or this other skater is working for them, we're screwed. We don't have anything—well, except your 'leads,' but they haven't gotten you very far yet."

Dana snapped to attention and sat upright. "Joshua!"

She fumbled in her pants pocket for her wallet. Once liberated from the tight fabric, she dumped the contents onto the sandy ground and poked two fingers inside a ripped seam. Her eyes lit up as she gently pulled a tiny envelope, no bigger than a credit card, from the hidden pocket. Nick cocked his head and squinted as she retrieved a black unmarked credit card, a business card with several numbers printed in raised black ink, and a photo of man in a Hawaiian shirt sitting with a woman in an orange dress and an infant boy on her lap.

"Joshua Green!" she exclaimed again. "The guy from the government? The one who gave me the deed to my dad's house that we're living in?"

"Yes, I remember the guy who tracked all the evidence to make sure Rhodes was locked up for good."

Nick had met Joshua during his recovery in the hospital. After discussing video games and their favorite New Jersey sports team—the state only had one, technically; the hockey team, the Devils—Nick listened to the government agent's account of the Atomic Juggernaut project and the attempts by One Hundred Roads to steal the monstrosity.

Joshua also took the lead to get the government to help with their relocation to New Mexico. Dana was right to guess he may be able to help figure out if there was another plot in motion. Nick gently pulled the card from Dana's fingers.

"So, Dana, if we call Joshua, what are we going to ask him to do? Ask him if he knows why One Hundred Roads would be looking to buy precious metal mines from Apache businessmen? Maybe something more *obtuse*?"

She winked and nodded with an openmouthed smile. "Didn't you say Frank Irons was offered a bunch of money by our eerily familiar businessmen? We can at least ask him to look into it." She stood up and dusted her knees. "If I was going to buy a mine from a bunch of Native Americans, I'd probably keep the money hidden until I was ready to write the check. It's just like we did with the electric bill last month, right? I didn't hand you the money until I finished rolling the quarters and changing my singles into twenties." She smiled sheepishly. Nick shook his head slowly. "Otherwise, I'd have marched down to the reservation and bought that cute baby-blue flannel shirt I saw last month at the store." She winked at him. "That's a birthday hint you can stash away for a few months."

"Wait, we're at the stage where we exchange birthday gifts now?"

"Think of the tips I can get if I'm wearing that shirt! Assuming I get a new bartending gig." She poked a finger into one of her dimples and batted her eyelashes. "Am I making you uncomfortable?"

"Maybe a little." *Maybe a lot.*

"Okay, so you call Joshua. And I'll head to the reservation to get some additional details. Maybe there's another bread crumb to pick up." As he stood up, he gently placed the tiny wildflower bouquet in his back pocket. They walked back toward the house together, her arm locked in his. He swallowed hard and cleared his throat of the residual desert dust.

"What was that credit card, by the way?"

"That," she said, hesitating slightly, "was something he gave me in case of emergency." She released her grip on Nick's arm. "I haven't used it. It expires a month after a purchase activates it. The government set it up to, like, self-destruct."

"Wow, I'm surprised you didn't tell me." Dana looked slightly worried until the corners of his mouth turned up. "Does a new truck count as an emergency? That old Ford is sentimental, but boy, I would love a new one." He held his hands up with his thumbs and fingers touching in a photographer's viewfinder pose. "Extended cab. Lift package. Maybe a roll bar with an excessive amount of fog lights. Just the type of extravagant ride I need to pick up burritos and blend in out here. Or back in South Jersey."

"You just said the *B* word. I think you picked dinner tonight." Dana opened the back door and held it open for Nick.

"So, you're definitely going to go back to a meeting? Say yes or I'm not getting the *pico de gallo* with your order."

"Yes, I think I shall, my good man. And don't ever bribe me again with pico."

He stopped and looked back at the mountains. "A motorcycle. I'd love to get a real motorcycle, too." He shook his head before entering the house. "Keep that credit card away from me, Dee."

Chapter 12

King of Wishful Thinking – Go West

The brakes on the bus hissed as the aging diesel engine rumbled to a stop at the front gate at the Mescalero reservation. Fresh graffiti adorned the covered bench at the bus stop. A handful of tired men in soiled work clothes stepped off together, laughing wearily as they exchanged jovial arm punches and discussed beer and dinner options. As the group embarked on the walk down the road into the Apache Nation territory, Dana hoisted her backpack off the grimy bench and boarded the bus.

The early evening passenger manifest skewed heavily toward the working-class middle-aged men of the area, but Dana immediately noted the demographic outliers as she selected a seat toward the back. Behind the driver sat a couple in their sixties, dressed for a night out. A few seats behind them a trio of teenage girls tapped on their phones, each taking turns urgently sharing their screens with the others. Two rows ahead of Dana, an athletic man with perfectly combed dark hair wearing a black tailored dress shirt crossed his denim-adorned legs as he flipped the pages of a sports betting magazine. He smoothed his thin moustache and licked his fingers between page turns. *He seems like a total tool*, Dana noted.

The bus rambled down the highway toward the next town, Carrizozo, where Dana hoped to find another clue to the identity of the mystery skater. For the past two weeks, she had taken the bus from Mescalero through a radius of locations during the afternoon and evening routes, traveling hours sometimes to stalk random teenage girls who might have been the one she was hunting. The trio of girls on today's route were familiar; she had seen them before, but it was the one next to the window, wearing a fitted vest and always carrying a hiking backpack, who was the most frequent traveler. Her face looked young, although she seemed to be in her late teens, and was framed by chin-length light-brown hair with large swaths of blond sections. Her tanned skin was a shade lighter than Dana's own, but still a color tone akin to a peanut. She said very little, even when the other girls asked her opinions on such pressing matters as which boy was the cutest or what bar was letting the underage girls drink without IDs. Most promising, though, was that her backpack made a metallic clanking noise whenever the bus strayed onto the rumble strips at the edges of the highway or hit a pothole.

As the bus slowed to the stop at the corner of the La Rosa Steakhouse, Dana watched the next wave of passengers leave. The row of girls emptied, except for her target. As casually as possible, Dana switched to the seat diagonal from the girl before the last incoming passenger walked down the aisle. She wanted to be ready to get off quickly to follow the girl at the next stop where she always got off and seemed to disappear immediately.

After a short acceleration and deceleration, the transit bus stopped at a covered bench in Alamorosa plastered with legal ads. The teen girl stood, heaved her bag on to her shoulders, and used quick, light steps to walk off the bus. Dana grabbed her own backpack and sprinted to the front just as the driver reached for the handle to close the doors.

"Hold up, that's me, thank you, you're a peach," Dana stammered as she forced herself through the closing bifold panels. She twisted her head left and right, but the girl was nowhere in sight. A small bird rested on top of a street sign for La Luz Gate Road, silhouetted by the setting sun. The taillights of the public bus faded as the diesel exhaust cloud dissipated into the evening air. Dana walked to the corner of the intersection, her mouth agape as she scoured the surroundings.

No girl.

"Dammit."

She hit the Call button on her phone and slipped in her earpiece. "Nick, she just vanished on me . . . again. Stepped off the bus, and she's gone."

"Are you sure? Maybe she went inside somewhere?" he proposed as Dana pressed the earpiece into her ear, the volume competing against the roar of a passing truck.

"Not that fast. There's only one store here, the convenience store or whatever mart." The store on the corner was lit up only by the aging mercury bulbs in its parking lot and the yellow-and-white sign on the corner post. "And I think I would have noticed if she went in. The door is on the front, so unless she hopped into the dumpster—"

Dana stopped talking, speechless and dumbfounded as the girl emerged, indeed, from behind the dumpster, the poor light in the space making it hard to see her well. The girl appeared to be gliding forward, as if the parking lot was covered in ice. She then pulled a white motocross helmet from her now flaccid backpack. As she slipped the helmet over her head, a single spark erupted from her left foot.

"Nicky, Nicky, Nicky! I got her! Gotta go!"

"Wait, how do you know—"

"Gotta go!" Dana pushed the button on her earpiece to hang up before he could finish his question. The girl glanced over both shoulders and, clearly not noticing Dana squatting behind one of the few parked cars, pumped her legs to rev her wheels. Dana heard the whine and grind of their metallic rollers ascend into a major chord as the girl shot off down the road in a blast of sizzling fireworks.

"Oh my God," Dana whispered. There was no denying that *this* was the girl—and that her skates were *just* like Dana's.

Dana tossed her backpack onto the shoulder of the road and clawed inside to get to Laverne and Shirley.

"Laverne, it's go time! Wake up Shirley!" She jammed the skates onto her feet, tripping as she pulled the shin guards into their magnetic latches, splaying herself on the sandy shoulder of the road. She tossed her shoes into the backpack as she scooped it onto her shoulder and set off, her wheels singing their dissonant jangling song. The magnets for the latches clicked into place as she moved, the skate boots tightened on her feet, and the rollers roared as her toes pushed into the control pads.

Behind her, a cascade of sparks fell to the road. Ahead, the far and faint flickers of the mystery girl's skates left her a sparkling trail to follow.

Inside the convenience store, Brian Nelson watched first the teenage girl and then Dana soar off into the night. He folded his sports betting magazine under his arm and lit a cigarette. The cashier, a scrawny kid wearing a green vest with the store logo and a name tag that spelled Thom, sheepishly approached him from behind.

"Uh, sir, you can't smoke inside," he said in a soft voice, fighting a stutter.

Brian turned and lifted the hem of his shirt to reveal the concealed holster strapped across his prominently defined abs. "How about you mind your business, *Thom*," Brian declared with a flick of the cashier's name tag, "and let me smoke my cigarette. I'm celebrating here, Thom, celebrating! I just found *Dana Jefferson!*"

"I don't want any trouble, sir," Thom mumbled, slowly backing away.

"Thom, buddy, is this your first night on the job at a convenience store? You better toughen up if this is how you react to threats after dark."

Brian clutched Thom's cheek and pinched it between his thumb and finger. "I'm going to take a six pack from the third aisle." He removed a hundred-dollar bill from his pocket and placed it on the counter. "This will cover that, and the rest is yours, as a thank-you for erasing the security camera tape and not telling anyone I was here."

His menacing smile flattened to a single line. He pinched the lit end of his cigarette with two heavily calloused fingers and slowly blew a billowing smoke cloud out of his nostrils. "Or I *will* come back, and I *don't* think you want that." With a wink, he left the boy alone, a small wet spot spreading down Thom's leg.

Chapter 13

Dancin' – The Tubes and Olivia Newton-John

I see you, you little brat!"

In the silence between convoys of big wheelers, Dana watched the teenage girl in the white motocross helmet glide silently down the highway's double yellow line, her skates lit up from the tiny sparks coming from the motors and wheels in their tattered housings. The sign for Roswell glowed in the ambient light of the streetlamps. The highway was dusted with a fine layer of sand, blasted off occasionally by a gust of wind or a truck hauling gasoline or building materials that barreled through the evening darkness.

The mercury and sun dropped, and a chill rose with the moon and stars. Dana zippered her jacket and pulled her collar under her chin. She was within striking distance now. A car approached from behind, illuminating both skaters and pushing long shadows ahead of each one. The rogue skater seemed surprised to see a second shadow paralleling hers and turned her head just in time to meet Dana's gaze as she pulled alongside.

"What's up? I'm Photograph." Dana matched the girl's speed and coasted next to her, both pairs of skates sparking in unison. The girl glanced at her, blinking slowly behind her clear visor.

"Nice to meet you. I'm Phoenix. Now go away. Bye!"

"Wait!" Dana yelled as Phoenix charged ahead, scattering ashes of road debris underfoot with each quick stride. Dana immediately pushed her toes into the foot panels and surged forward. Finally seeing her up close, Dana noted that the girl was in her mid-teens, a hand or two shorter than Dana at full height. Her backpack flapped and fluttered behind her as she continued to accelerate away from Dana.

"Hey, Phoenix! We're phonics buddies! Phoenix, Photograph. Get it?" Dana pushed through her thighs and closed the elastic gap between the two again. Ahead, a lone streetlight stood sentry to the town limits of Roswell. The glowing dome of the businesses and traffic lights, houses and diners, and the infamous downtown honkytonk tourist district broke the blackness as they approached the tiny metropolis. Dana added the downtown to her list of places to see, someday, when she felt settled in. *Right now, I need to catch this dumb kid.*

Shooting through the first ring of the city's outskirts, Phoenix straddled the double yellow lines as they roared past the first traffic light. The four lanes of the main road, two in each direction, steadily grew denser with cars and pickup trucks. In the oncoming lanes, two mammoth diesel trucks pulling long cargo trailer boxes blared their horns. The trucks drove side by side and accelerated, yielding barely a few inches of pavement. Phoenix glanced over her shoulder to confirm Dana's position before darting into the closest oncoming lane.

"Hey! PHOENIX!" Dana yelled, screaming above the roar of traffic, but she was gone, disappearing down the dotted white line directly between the trucks. *This kid is nuts,* Dana thought just before zipping behind her trail. The slipstream as the trucks enveloped her tore through Dana's hair. She felt road chum splatter onto her face and exhaust fumes fill her nostrils as she maintained her speed and emerged from between the trailers.

Phoenix slowed down and shook her head. "Get lost!" she growled at Dana. "I don't have any business with you!"

"Oh, come on, we're roller buddies! Speaking of," Dana yelled, pumping her legs with the rhythm of the skate motors, "I'll tell you where I got mine if you tell me where you got yours!"

Phoenix extended a middle finger and dropped her right shoulder suddenly. She crossed her skates one over another as she flew into a turn at the next intersection, losing little of her speed. Dana tipped her skates back and rocked forward, leaping over the corner curb to close the distance. She struck her shoulder into Phoenix's arm upon landing next to her.

"Hey, girl, we can do this the easy way, or I can put some *Jersey* into my next hit."

Phoenix threw an elbow into Dana's chest. "That one had a little *Albuquerque* in it, Jersey girl!" The traffic light ahead flickered from yellow to a menacing red, the cars in front of them slowing to a stop.

"Oh, you gotta be kidding me," Dana said out loud, grimacing in anticipation. She extended her leg in a hurdler's stride as she leapt over the hood of a stopped car. Phoenix dropped to one knee and spun around another's rear bumper. Both women erupted into the intersection, prompting honks from the drivers witnessing the chaos. Dana powered over to Phoenix and grabbed her elbow in the blinding stream of headlights and skate sparks.

"I just want to talk!" Dana coasted and pulled back on Phoenix's arm, gaining the advantage as Phoenix squirmed in an unsuccessful attempt to accelerate.

"Let go!" She slapped at Dana's grip. "I'm warning you, I *know* people!"

"That's what I'm hoping!"

A whooping siren blared behind the entangled girls. Two police cars swung into their lane, flashing high beams behind the skating rivals. The intercom crackled.

"Ladies, pull over and put your hands behind your heads. NOW."

Phoenix's eyes locked with Dana's. Dana nodded and shoved the younger skater to the left as she dove right. Each girl dropped into a crouch on opposite sides of the cruisers, and the cruisers continued right past them. The scent of scorched rubber and sound of skidding engulfed the roadway. The patrol car in the right lane cut the wheel and spun into the opposite lane, smacking into a pickup truck's rear. The hood erupted with a shower of hissing steam while the other police car skidded to a stop, only to find himself fenced in by two cars that sideswiped each other and blocked the road.

The girls turned on their heels and sped back toward the outskirts of town, the traffic thinning as they headed into the open desert. Phoenix smiled at Dana, which Dana happily returned.

"Heads up," she yelled as she kicked out the teen's leg, sending Phoenix tumbling into a ditch along the side of the road. Dana tackled her in the dirt, forcing her full body weight onto the smaller girl's torso.

"Can we talk now, baby doll?"

Phoenix snapped her head back, then forward, cracking Dana's forehead with her helmet.

"*Shasta!* Ow! You brat!" Dana squealed as she reeled backward. "Alcatraz! Shit, shit, shit!" Dana pressed her fingers into her head, stars filling her eyes. Phoenix skittered toward Dana and unlatched the metallic snaps on Shirley with a flick. Dana attempted to stand up and tripped out of the boot as her momentum sent her teetering face-first into the dirt. Phoenix leapt onto the pavement and blasted a cascade of cinders onto Dana's back. The din of the wheels receded quickly, the elder skater realizing she was now alone on the side of the road with a mouthful of sand.

"Now *that,*" Dana gasped, "had some Jersey in it."

She groaned as she maneuvered her arm out from under her body to reach the Bluetooth receiver in her ear. Spitting a gritty wad of saliva onto the sandy earth, she pressed the Call button while she rubbed her temples and waited for Nick to pick up. His voice came through calm and collected, as she had come to expect.

"Dana, hey, what's up? How'd it go?"

"I'm outside of Roswell. I got my ass handed to me by a teenager. I need a toothbrush . . . and an ice pack."

Chapter 14

Einstein on the Beach – Counting Crows

Nick smiled at the waitress as she approached the vinyl-padded booth. Dana smiled as she pointed to a cut on her chin. "Does this look infected?"

"Stop it. Here she comes."

The waitress pulled a black pen out from the nest of silver and brown hair twisted on top of her head. One eyelid twitched, much like the blinking neon OPEN sign sputtering outside the long glass panels of the front window. Dana looked down and noticed the waitress's dirty Keds were patched with duct tape.

"My name is Miranda. Welcome to the Roswell Silver Saucer Diner, home of New Mexico's best Philly Cheesesteak," she droned.

Dana mouthed the words "New Mexico's best Philly Cheesesteak" and received a shrug from Nick.

"Are you ready to order, or do you need another minute?" Miranda announced before bridging the gap between herself and the table.

"Burger, well done, fries, and two glasses of ice water," Dana chimed in. "And get my manservant here an iced tea and a grilled cheese if he has sufficient funds, *Miranda*."

"Will that be all?" Miranda asked as she tapped her pen on her notepad.

"Yes," Nick quickly replied. "We're good. Take your time." Dana shot him a smirk as he watched Miranda head back to the kitchen.

Nick clawed his forehead as his cheeks flushed. "Must you do that every single time we eat out?" He grinned back at her despite himself. "It was a heck of a drive here to pick you up. I'm still in my sleep pants."

"I appreciate it, pumpkin. There was no way I was going to make it back on my own two legs after that girl gave me a healthy headbutt." Dana waved a hand across her field of vision. "What colors do you see with a concussion? I'm seeing flashes of red and blue." Nick tapped the window and pointed up at the neon sign. Dana pursed her lips and looked down at her placemat. "Shame . . . I have so much shame."

"So, let's talk about the girl while you have the details fresh inside your dented head. Skates? Age, height, hair color?"

"Ok, so. This girl. She's mid-teens, like, *definitely* would get carded if she tried to buy alcohol. She had hair down to like, here," she said, gesticulating toward her collar, "and I think it was light brown. No—blond dye job, done either really poorly or stylized. Eyes, same color as me from what I could tell. She was wearing a motocross helmet. White, I think?"

"She's a white girl?"

"No, the helmet was white. I mean, maybe she was white, or biracial like me. Her skin tone was close to mine." Dana exhaled and knotted her eyebrows. "And I'm not positive because there were only streetlights, but she had light-brown eyes like me. I think. Wait, did I say that already?" The evening was melting into fondue in her brain, as though everything was covered in a thick sauce. She knocked on the tabletop in a staccato rhythm, trying to recall details about the skates. Miranda stomped over to the table and produced the beverages.

"A little busy, miss. You don't have to knock. I didn't forget you."

"Oh, no, not you. I'm trying to think of something. I'm from New Jersey—we're a little abrupt. I mean, I'm from out here originally, but once you drink the water in Jersey, you get a little, you know." Dana turned up her nose and made a menacing face. "Nice girls get meaner. Oh, and do you know what the signs are for a concussion?"

Miranda backed away from the table slowly, never unlocking her eyes from Dana's until she receded into the kitchen.

"You know," Nick said as he waved a butter knife along with his words, "she's going to spit in our food."

"Sigh. I'm sorry. It's just so crazy . . . this girl had my skates. They were almost the same, except no shin guards. They looked like a high-top sneaker style. And the wheels! They spat out the same sparks. Same glow." Dana frittered her fingers to illustrate in the air. "It was like I had a mini-me that turned to the dark side."

"Or a clone. Or a little sister." Nick laughed and slid down in his seat.

Dana felt a hot hole burning in her head. *No, that's not possible. Is it?*

Miranda returned with their food, gently laying each plate down on the paper placemat. She slid a folded towel toward Dana.

"There's a disposable ice pack in here, *Jersey*. Even if you're not concussed, you're going to want to take care of that bruise." She smiled and lifted her chin, showing off a long and jagged scar across her lower jawline. "Pretty faces fade when no one takes care of them." She slid back to the kitchen again. Nick's jaw fell slack as he waited for the kitchen door to swing shut.

"What a really odd thing to say."

"I think she likes you, pretty boy. She figured out the vibe here," she said, pointing back and forth between herself and Nick, "and knows you're an eligible bachelor." Dana winked, then winced as the cut on her chin reopened. "But I'm eligible too if she's, you know, 'on my team.'"

"You *are* really loopy, girl. Did anyone else see you two?"

"Just the cops."

Nick splayed his arms and folded his fingers on top of his matted hair.

"*Just* the cops? Oh, perfect! That's sure to help us stay low-key while we're trying to figure out what One Hundred Roads, or at least their remnants, are doing in our backyard!" He stared up at the ceiling, his fingers still interlocked on the back of his head. "Dana, promise me that we're going to have at least one day in the near future that doesn't involve unwinding some crime caper? But for now, what do we do next?"

Dana funneled her French fries into her maw and chewed deliberately. She leaned over her plate and placed a greasy hand on his forearm.

"Nicky," she sputtered, a glob of masticated fry landing on the table, "you are my hero. Every day. Let's just finish our food and head home. We can think about this all tomorrow. I just want to lay down on the couch, take off my road clothes, and let you give me a foot massage. Let's cross that boundary as friends. Foot massages."

Miranda suddenly emerged from behind the booth to take their plates.

"Honey," she said as she leaned over Nick, "if you come back tomorrow and give me a foot massage, you can eat for free."

"Ma'am, if I come back here tomorrow night, it probably means something has gone terribly, terribly wrong."

Dana leaned on her hands and fluttered her lashes at Miranda. "I'll give you a foot massage right now for a cheesecake to go?"

Chapter 15

Whatcha Gonna Do? – Pablo Cruise

What are you doing, Nails?"

Olsen moved slowly on his arm crutches across the hangar, his left foot dragging prominently as he tensed his back and straightened his spine as best as he could through the discomfort. He stopped short of Brian, who rustled through a wooden crate stuffed with stale-smelling hay and sawdust. Brian glanced over his shoulder with a tooth-filled grin.

"I was looking for something, and I just found it." Brian revealed a short carbine rifle with an ammo clip already loaded into the stock. He examined the sides of the SA80, a delightful rifle Olsen and Brian had plenty of experience using, a standard-issue arm used by the British Armed Forces. Brian blew the dust off the laser scope mechanism strapped to the barrel and presented it to Olsen, who declined the invitation with a wave.

"Not for me, mate. My sharpshooting days are done."

"You can't be serious," countered Brian, spinning the gun back to his shoulder and aiming it at an imaginary target in the rafters. "I saw you take out a rearview mirror on a taxi from a half mile."

"Not anymore."

Olsen grasped the rifle and turned on the targeting beam. The red dot danced across the floor as he raised the stock to his shoulder and stared down the barrel sight. The dot settled on the back of Agent Thirty-Six, head down and counting ammunition clips on a folding table in the middle of the room. The target spot danced and fluttered in a small circle on the unknowing agent's body. Olsen firmed his grip, but the red dot continued its prancing pattern.

"There's too much nerve damage," Olsen muttered. He squinted and grunted as his hands trembled slightly on the gun's grip. "I can get my brute strength back, according to the hopeful doctors, but the finer motor skills are still lost. I may get it back in time." He chewed his lip. "Right now, I'm as useful as a bouncer at a roadhouse. Good for bashing drunks, not counting the cash register."

"That's a shame," sighed Brian, "but also explains why you asked me to hop on this op." He snatched the rifle from Olsen and spun to his left, leveling the barrel at the zipper running down the front of Nina's bodysuit as she nonchalantly strolled toward them.

"Brian. *Nails*," she cooed, pressing her sternum against the barrel. "Daddy would be upset if you killed me." He ran his gaze up and down her bodysuit.

"*Daddy* is in a high-security military prison."

Olsen lumbered into the huddle with an ostentatious clack of his canes.

"If you please, you two can finish this later." He nodded at Nina and Brian to follow him to the makeshift desk. "Accounting isn't my forte, but it's where I'm currently focusing my efforts. There're still a few alternatives to obtaining the mining rights to that palladium from the little nation." He handed a topographical map to Brian.

"So, am I on the team with the shovels to dig this out? Or do you have an extra piggy bank with the additional millions we need to run a strip mine and delivery system?"

"That's not what we do. Instead, we *sell* the rights to a shell corporation from one of the factions in the bidding pool. That way, we not only profit from the sale but, given the ore's proximity to a certain military installation"—he traced his finger across the map to the White Sands military testing area—"we also give them a shadow op to set up right next to the dragon's teeth." He ran his fingers across the paper, his fingertips fluttering on each highway line and city dot. "Then we run the table and short the palladium on the market, loading our coffers from the eventual rout when we also sell to the United States government."

Brian scratched the black stubble on his chin before licking a fingertip and smearing his moustache into place.

"I don't get it."

"We're trying to buy low, then sell high to the bad guys. Enemies of the state, terror cells, whoever wants to cough up for the minerals and strategic position." Olsen felt the specter of doubt in his decision to recruit Brian creep up but continued. "Then we offer up the bad guys for a bounty and certain legal conditions. During the whole affair, we're running the financial market on our goods." He slid a few random sheets of paper around, attempting to look organized. "We're setting a financial and strategic snare to flush out our enemies and walk them right into an enormous trap."

"Like insider trading? You know this is way too complicated, right?" Olsen ignored Brian's terse counterargument and opened his laptop. "Olsen, why would we set this all up just to hope the Big Ol' United States of Big Ol' America will pay us instead of seizing the information we offer? One Hundred Roads is *disavowed*. Done. No longer legit."

The laptop on the table glowed with a green iridescence while Olsen punched the keys and opened a folder of schematic files. He pivoted the screen to face Brian.

"Because we'll have this, too."

The diagrams on the screen formed the shape of two cylinders, each the size of a soda can, one ribbed horizontally and the other vertically. Olsen tapped a button on the screen and initialized a graphic of the two diagrams merging into a single elongated cylinder. He had become more comfortable with technology now that he was useless as a fighter in their ragtag operation. Even so, every day was a fight between his growing education and looming ignorance in how to run a covert subversive organization, and the schematics seemed to mock his shallow understanding of their workings. He tried to recall the phrases used by one of their tech contacts when they had decrypted the files.

"These were obtained from the remnants of the files we were able to scavenge from the Atomic Juggernaut lab. The first, the vertically lined canister is a power inverter. The other, the horizontally lined one, is the micro centrifuge where energy is born." His eyes darted between Brian and Nina. They both nodded, although it wasn't clear if they were actually following. "Together, they could power a network of autonomous drones or missiles," he noted, tapping the screen. Nina peered into the display and slacked her jaw.

"That would be a missile that's much smaller and doesn't need a fuel tank or combustion afterburner to leave a heat signature," he announced. "It would be invisible to the naked eye at a low height, under the radar. And then it would just, you know, hover. Circle the target, menace, for however long it needed to be airborne. Hours, *days,* even. And it would create its own location neural network, like airborne Wi-Fi. They can't be scrambled or tracked via satellite because they are their own web, talking to each other with artificial intelligence, which, I might add, would also need a lot of continuous power that these batteries can provide."

Nina nodded, her eyes displaying admiration. "So, a weapon you never have to fire?"

"Nina wins the prize. Yes, you just let it go like a pack of super-intelligent junkyard dogs and let them bark on the other side of your enemy's fence." Olsen closed the laptop. "But to reiterate, palladium is essential for the casing, the targeting system, and the power cell."

Nina pulled herself up onto the tabletop and crossed her legs. Her shins clinked and her knees whirred as she swung her feet back and forth.

"Then we'll get it. The prototypes for the components are on their way. Some of the secrets of our dearly departed benefactor, Samuel Jefferson Jr., were still in the hands of the science boys in the DOD. And some of Jefferson's little side projects were outside of my father's jurisdiction, which is why we need to finish your little tracking assignment and find Dana, the wheeled wonder."

"Right. Even with both these parts"—he tapped the screen again—"we don't have the connection. You can slap these together, but they won't work. They might even explode. And my best guess is Dana has the plans, or knows where they are, that tell us how these connect." Olsen raised his hand to form a trembling pinching gesture. "She stumbled across the Atomic Juggernaut, which her grandfather was clever enough to lock up using her biosignature. I have a hunch she is the key to this, too, and probably doesn't even know it. We're in the neighborhood."

"I told you that I have her travel pattern," Brian sighed, "but I still haven't located her home base yet."

"We need it." Olsen stood up on his crutches with effort. "The power supply's missing links must be at Samuel Jefferson's home, wherever that is. New Mexico is where he developed this perpetual power supply theory. And according to his service records, this was where he had a few addresses while he worked in New Jersey on the juggernaut. Why else would Dana be out here if she wasn't having a little homecoming and revisiting her past?"

Nina shook her head slowly, pulling her gloves tightly over her gaunt digits. "I really don't see how this all works out, the endgame. There's something we're *missing* here, Olsen. But anyway, let me get a look at those schedules Brian obtained from his friend on the flight when you're done."

Brian lowered the SA80 from his shoulder to his hip. "So, while I'm chasing some bimbo on roller skates, what is *she* doing, exactly?" He pointed the rifle at Nina's chest.

"I have the easy job," Nina sneered. "I get to rob a train."

Chapter 16

Die Young — Kesha

Dana collapsed into the folding chair next to Lilly, their breathing synced as they inhaled and exhaled, recovering from the barrage of blows. The opposing team, the Santa Fe Femme Fatales, had coasted to a lopsided victory over the newly monikered Roswell Roses, the winning name suggested by Lilly for the team's rebranding. Dana removed her helmet and shook out her hair, flailing sweat onto her teammate.

"Oh, Lil, I'm sorry," she apologized. "You totally should be on the jam next time, or at least a pivot. You block well, but you just don't have the right leverage." She gripped her teammate's bicep and squeezed. "You need to eat a couple dozen chicken legs and hit the heavy weights. Those girls kept knocking you out."

"Yeah, I was there," Lilly replied, still gasping and winded. "You're our best skater. You're our best shot at points. You're our best *everything*." She lifted a tangle of sticky, sweaty hair from Dana's eyebrow with a delicate finger. "That's better."

Dana leaned back and admired the friendly scrum as the teams shook hands and traded hugs in the center of the rink, the camaraderie after a match serving as the antithesis to the brutal chaos during. Memories of the team back in Asbury filled her heart with a calming warmth, yet it made it ache, too. Before today's match, the creeping dread had continuously whispered in her ears. *Angela. Nick.* The traumas they had all endured because of her actions. But now, after facing her fears and even in the agony of defeat, Dana embraced the joy and endorphins of skating again. One of the girls on the opposing team, a long-legged blonde, flexed her arms in victory before punching the air—a move she saw Angela do back in Jersey on many nights, ones that ended with too many drinks and either a shared bed or another lover's argument between them. *She was a pain in the ass, but she always had my back,* Dana mused. She felt Lilly smack her arm, bringing her back to the present.

"We should hang out soon."

"That sounds like fun," Dana replied. "Clean our skates, braid each other's hair, tickle fights, that kind of thing. Right now, I'm going to go talk to Kendra and Janice." She stood and spun a full rotation. "Oh, and do yourself a favor: go out there and congratulate someone on the other team. Make some friends. That's what derby is all about."

Dana coasted over to the senior team members and skidded on her toe to announce her arrival.

"Janice, how about we put Lilly on the jam and set me into more blocking next weekend?"

Janice looked up from her tablet and opened her mouth to speak. Kendra elbowed her and planted herself between the two women.

"Dana. *Photograph,*" Kendra intoned with intentional mockery, "just let us do our job, and maybe next time you'll be able to do yours. *We* make sure everyone is in their best position, not you."

"Hey, I'm just making a suggestion," Dana scoffed, taken aback by the abrupt command. There was no room for this type of barking in the unwritten rules of derby. "We're all here to have fun, and if we win, that's the cherry on top. But Lilly deserves a shot. She's *really* good, and I think a confidence boost will push her along." Dana attempted to fold her arms, felt the coating of sweat, and defaulted to her hands digging into her hips.

"Listen, just go have a beer or something with the girls. I got business to figure out." Kendra stomped away from Janice, who looked up from her tablet with a wincing grin.

"I don't know what's gotten into Kendra lately," she confided to Dana as the rink slowly emptied. Janice scanned the small pack of spectators that remained and noticed a blond man waving in their direction. "Is that *your* Nick?"

Dana smiled down at the floor. "Sigh. Yes. My roommate, chauffer, meal ticket when I have a bad week of tips, if I even work at all." *Best friend.*

Nick attempted to leap over the row in front of him but tripped. He recovered, glancing over his shoulder for witnesses, and walked toward Dana and Janice. "Hi, I'm Nick."

"I'm Janice."

"Nice to meet you. Um, Dana, can I borrow you a minute?" His hand slipped off her forearm as he attempted to grab and pull her along.

"Sweaty. Really sweaty, Nick."

"Just—will you check this out?" Nick locked his elbow around her elbow pad and dragged her on her skates toward the exit at the far end of the community center. Despite the perpetually running air conditioning, the back door sat propped open to allow the arid air from outside to move the stale humid air inside. Dana peeked out the door into the parking lot.

"What am I looking for, Columbo?"

"That woman who was yelling at you. I saw her meet a young girl at the door here during the match." He leaned out to inspect the parking lot.

"And then?"

"Dana, I think the girl was selling her drugs or something. I'm not really in that world and don't have any experience outside of a bunch of movies, but there was *definitely* a handoff and money exchanged. She gave that woman a paper bag."

"*And?*"

"The girl was wearing skates."

Dana's cheeks retreated into a Cheshire cat smile. *Oh, you big, loveable idiot.*

"Nicky, most of the girls here are wearing skates."

"No." He pulled his cheeks back in imitation of her sarcastic expression. "*The* skates. *Your* skates."

The words had barely floated into Dana's ear canal when a female voice interjected from behind them.

"So, what's the conspiracy?" Janice stood with her tablet against her chest.

"Janice!" Dana said loudly, startled by her appearance. "Is Kendra, like, into drugs?"

"Subtle," Nick admonished, his voice tapering to a mumble.

"Kendra? She got methed up after one of her injuries, but she's clean now from what I can tell." Janice tilted her head with a thoughtful gaze up to the red EXIT sign over the door. "Although she is acting a lot like a tweaker recently."

"You mean the frequent chewing off of my head, and so on?"

"Yeah." Janice glanced back at the remaining skaters as they packed their bags and shouted names of local bars at each other for the after-party. "We had to let go of a few girls last year after we found out they were dealing and scoring at the meets. That's why we're a little strapped on the roster this year. WFTDA helped me figure out the best plan so the good girls wouldn't get punished by having the team shut down." She opened the tablet and presented a photo of the team from last year. "Two in rehab, one clean after she broke her hip during a frenzy in practice, and this one down here, she was arrested for dealing." She traced a circle around one face next to Kendra's in the picture. "I thought we had this all flushed out."

Dana scanned the photos with a knotted brow. None of these girls looked familiar. Nick ostentatiously cleared his throat. *I know that noise,* Dana thought. *His big brain is burning.*

"Janice, when someone tries out, don't they have to fill out a form for liability? Next of kin stuff? Address or contact number?"

Dana winked at Nick as she picked up where he was going with this. "Specifically, Jan, do you have anything on that teenager that tried out a few weeks before me?"

Janice flipped back through the screens on her tablet to land on the email app, followed by a few flicks. She smiled and presented the screen back to Dana.

"Here you go. 'Ashley Phoenix' was the name she wrote down. I think her address was phony, though. She put down a Taos address, which is north and across the state. I was bored one day and looked it up. It was for an *art gallery.* She punked us good, but she also screwed up by using what I'm guessing is her real birth date, not realizing we can't take players under eighteen."

"Ashley Phoenix," Nick repeated. "If she's really from Taos, that's like five hours of driving."

"Or skating," Dana interjected.

"Should I ask why you want to know?" Janice asked.

"Better if you don't. Thanks, Janice, and good night."

Dana and Nick headed out, watching the last skaters from both teams pile into the remaining cars. A station wagon covered in stickers squealed and fishtailed out the driveway into traffic. Dana reached into her bag and handed Nick a bottle of water.

"Wanna follow that party wagon and hit the post-game party?"

"I've got work tomorrow," Nick said flatly as he twisted the cap. "You know, Dana, if you had a full-time job, you could enjoy all the spoils of employment just like me."

"I have a full-time job," she retorted as she stepped into the cab of Nick's truck, now alone in the parking lot. "I'm the superhero. You're the sidekick." She slammed the door and put her feet on the dashboard.

Chapter 17

Answering Machine – Rupert Holmes

Nick grunted as he held the breaker box in place on the wall. The weight of it was a challenge when combined with the awkward angle created by a series of shelves, a doorframe, and an upright washer-dryer combo unit.

"Mr. Irons, a little help, if you please." Frank rummaged through the bottom of his toolbox, the clanging and clinking of metal handles and drill bits mixing with his muttered curses. His fingers wrapped around a plastic handle under the entanglement, and he heaved out the narrow drywall saw with a triumphant yell.

"Nick! Right here!"

"Just cut that last part," Nick grunted through his teeth, "and we're in!"

Frank ran the jagged blade against the opening, and the box fell into place. The two men high-fived and immediately reached for their respective open bottles of lukewarm beer on the floor.

"Nick, thanks so much for doing this. I can't pay you the balance for the final work until we have everything inspected, but at least this will save us a few hours of union labor rates." Frank clinked his bottle against Nick's. He forced a smile. He and Dana needed money ASAP. Dana's job hunt, or lack thereof, was frustrating, but at least she was spending some of her free time going to the support group now instead of just flipping through the cable channels.

"No problem. It was a way to pass the time while Dana's at her meeting." Nick peered through the storm door into the darkness beyond the porch light and observed a small group of people outside the community center. "Looks like they're done now. Anyway, now that the washer and dryer are on their own circuit, the farmhands can just wash and go home at the end of the day. It'll be a nice quality of life enhancement."

Frank reached into his back pocket and produced a thick envelope. He slapped it across his hand for a moment and stared out the door.

"You know, I trust you, Nick. Consider this an advance on your payment." He held out his outstretched hand. Nick opened the envelope and unfolded a few bills wrapped around a copy of the mining contract proposal from Olsen.

"Thank you, Frank. In return, we might have a lead on your drug dealer problem."

His eyes lit up with interest. "Go on."

"There's a girl, a teenager, and we think she's the dealer. She has some sort of connection to the local roller derby team. At least, that's Dana's best theory right now."

Frank's cheeks lifted into a broad smile. "Oh, you mean Ashley? Oh, wait, what does she call herself? The Phoenix! Oh, yeah, we know all about her. We can thank the dumb kids and their social media posts for that."

Nick's jaw dropped. "You *know*?"

"Oh yeah," Frank chortled. "Sorry, Sherlock Holmes." Nick's bewilderment amused him. "Nick, Nick, Nick, we know who she is; it's just that we can't catch her. She just disappears without a trace. I don't know how she does it—no cars or bikes pulling up or dropping her off. I mean, there's always a new dealer. They rotate in, get busted, rotate out. But this one, she's been such a pain in my side for the past couple of months. It's almost comical how much we've failed to trip her up at this point."

The crowd outside the community center had mostly dissolved. Nick watched as Dana skipped away from the group and toward the trailer.

"What if I told you Dana can catch her?"

Frank pointed his bottle at Nick. "What are you going to do, stage a sting? You think we haven't tried that with my brother working in law enforcement? The moment things go sideways, she's gone."

Dana bounded into the doorway and gestured toward the remaining beer in the six-pack holder.

"Hook a girl up. Nick, did you share the big news on Ashley?"

Nick rolled his head through a full rotation over his shoulders. "Yeah . . . not such big news after all."

"Did you tell him about our plan, though? She has these super rocket skates she uses to whip around town, and, fun fact, I have the same ones! *They're from a secret government thing*," she whispered conspiratorially.

"Dana! Cease the info dumping," Nick admonished as he tossed a beer bottle in her direction.

"Sorry, I thought he was cool."

Frank swallowed a long sip from his bottle and wiped his wet stubble on his forearm. "You kids are crazy, you know that? This reads like a science fiction story. I'm basically just the ranch manager and you two, a pair of supersleuths."

Dana and Nick shared a smile across the room.

"So, tell me, now that we're all on the same page, what exactly is going on?"

Nick wiped a line of sweat droplets off his forehead and sighed. The complications churned in his mind as he sorted his thoughts into some sort of orderly explanation.

"Well, we got into a bad situation back in New Jersey with the people who are trying to buy your land, and they're bad news—*real* bad. *National security threat* bad."

"What's that got to do with Ashley?"

"The skates that Dana has and it seems Ashley also has? They're high-tech roller skates from a government project those guys were involved with. It can't be a coincidence that your drug mule—Ashley, the Phoenix, whatever she calls herself—has the same skates, which means . . . something." His voiced evaporated. "I don't know what, but if *she's* around here and *they're* around here, there's a good chance something's going down—that someone could get hurt."

"So, what you're saying is, if I see her around here, let you know?" Frank's eyes locked on Dana's. "Can you get her to stop dealing to the tribe?"

Dana vigorously nodded her head. "I can try."

Frank stood up and placed one hand on her shoulder, the other on Nick's bicep. "Stop this girl. *Please.* I was making light of it before, Nick, because honestly, it's just a part of life now, but people have been hurt, and worse, by the addiction situation out here. If you can, you know, *take care* of things without law enforcement, that's fine by me." He drew a deep breath. "I am very close to landing some amazing development projects that are going to truly change people's lives here. I don't need a drug dealing operation muddying the waters. Keep it out of the press, out of the public record. We *need* this for the next generation."

With their makeshift plan solidified, Nick and Dana said good night. As they rolled down the road toward the highway, the sun's glow over the horizon dissipated, and the night's blue haze rose up behind the mountains.

Nick caught Dana peering over at him, alternating her attention between him and the dusty edges of the asphalt where the nocturnal animals lay in wait.

"What?"

"You're upset. I'm the one in group therapy—I can tell something's wrong. Talk."

Nick opened his mouth to talk but reconsidered and closed it. Dana swiveled in her seatbelt as best as she could to face him.

"Nicky, what is it?"

"I can't put my finger on it. We're missing something. We need to start thinking and acting like OHR. We need to sort out all the pieces we have."

Suddenly, Nick veered into the shoulder and slammed the truck into park. Dana fell forward into the dashboard, scowling her disapproval of the abrupt pit stop.

"Dana! One Hundred Roads doesn't know where we are. Otherwise, they'd already have come for us."

"Okay, that's true. So, if they don't know where we are, they can't follow us to Taos."

"Taos?"

"You just said we should sort out the pieces of things we know. So, let's start with the gallery in Taos, where Ashley 'lives.' It's the only clue we haven't followed yet, right?" She drummed on the dashboard. "It'll be fun! Let's pretend we're old people on a trip and going to visit an art gallery. You'll have to wear some better pants."

"What's wrong with my jeans?"

"Really? Oh, Nick, you're adorable." She poked a finger through a hole in his knee and blew him a kiss. "You are the most clueless yet smartest boy in the world sometimes. Come on, lend me ten bucks. I'm buying you a coffee."

Chapter 18

Lido Shuffle – Boz Scaggs

W ake up, we're here."

Dana heard the words first, then felt a finger poking her shoulder repeatedly. She wiped a string of drool off her chin. The right side of her face felt numb, having been pressed against the truck window for much of the past five hours on the way to Taos. The morning sun stung her eyes.

She stretched languidly and wiped her face. "Breakfast? Coffee, at a minimum?"

Nick had exited the truck and was already standing on the sidewalk, slowly turning in a circle. Dana stepped out of the cabin and marveled at the congruence in the architecture of the downtown art district. Storefronts lined a walking path, each with a building-length white balcony that hung over the muddy orange pueblo facade. Dana hitched her arm through Nick's and pointed to the plank benches in front of a small café.

"Coffee in there. You grab, I'll look for the address."

As Nick walked away, Dana unfolded a piece of paper with the street and number she had obtained from Ashley's roller derby waiver. She peered at the wood-and-brass signs hanging over the tourist-friendly establishments and noticed a handful of galleries occupying the upper floors, reached via long white public staircases. Dana found a tiny number on an external mailbox and from there counted the storefronts, pointing at each door and mouthing the digits. Nick soon reappeared at her side with two coffees and a bag that emitted a thick buttery aroma.

Dana pointed to a door under a staircase landing. "That's the one. Just like Janice said, it's an art gallery. The sign says 'Dune Bloom.' A bit tacky."

"Seems par for the course. 'Cactus Folk Art,' 'Taos and Out Consignment,' and a gratuitous 'Desert Treasures' over there." He sipped his coffee. "Ok, we go inside. Maybe she's sleeping on the floor or a cot." He bounced toward the shop with a light step after another swig from his paper cup.

Upon opening, the door rattled with the muted clanking of metallic discs hanging on a wreath of desert brush branches. Dana scanned the interior and identified the four quadrants of the well-organized store: a series of shelves stocked with small hand-painted ceramics and books from obscure local authors; a corner lined with tables of sweaters, scarves, and shirts; a cash register station staffed by a young woman in a woven poncho possibly sleeping; and an area of paintings resting on tripods and hanging on the walls. Dana approached the dark wooden countertop and caught herself smiling at a small taxidermy jackalope on the counter.

"Hi, hello?"

The cashier bolted upright in an explosion of dirty-blond dreadlocks.

"Oh, hey. Welcome to Dune Bloom. I'm Nell. You want that jackalope?" She smoothed the front of her poncho and smiled under a pair of nose rings decorated in turquoise stones.

"No, thank you, not yet, anyway. Hey, is there someone who works here named Ashley?"

Nell placed a pair of thick-framed black glasses on the end of her nose and drew a sour face. "She's supposed to, but she barely works her hours. She couldn't get fired if she tried."

"Huh."

Nick stared at the largest painting on the wall, a horizontal orientation depicting the Rio Grande Gorge Bridge outside of town. Dana had been asleep when they had crossed over the real-life version earlier that morning.

"That bridge scared the dickens out of me," he admitted. Dana adored the way he refused to use curses and sometimes spoke like an old man. She stepped behind him and leaned over his shoulder.

"And I missed the whole thing. Do we go back over it when we leave?" Dana reached out, moving her finger along the road in the painting.

"Hopefully not."

"Nell? Who's the artist?" Dana shouted. The cashier circled around the counter and stopped next to the duo. She coughed as she gently pushed Dana's hand away from the canvas.

"Jessica is the artist. She's, like, a genius and stuff with paint."

Dana's eyes widened, and her eyebrows clawed up her forehead. She clutched Nick's arm furiously. "Nick, what does that look like?" she asked with shortening breaths. She reached out again, this time toward the artist's signature: a looping cursive *J* followed by a *W* and a scrawl of flowing penmanship.

"It looks like a *J* for Jessica and her last name."

"Nick!" She whispered. "*Look* at it."

Nell leaned between their heads, her matted dreads too close for comfort. "Guys, what are we looking at?" she whispered in reply.

"It's the same as the painting in our living room!" Dana blurted the words in a shrill squeal.

"Did you buy one here? Because honestly, I've done

some . . . things . . . and my memory only goes back a few months."

"*Nell*, would you excuse us?" He grasped Dana's leather jacket sleeve and gently led Dana to the far corner of the room. "What are you blathering about?" he asked in a shrill whisper.

"Nick, think! The painting in our living room! The one my mom painted like a billion years ago! The signature is the same! My mom signed hers *S. Jefferson*, but I'm telling you, it's the same signature. The *J* is the same!"

The paper coffee cup started to slide out from Nick's relaxed grip, but he caught it just in time.

"Nell?" Dana jogged the tiny distance between herself and the counter. "The artist, what's her full name?"

"Jessica Walker."

"Walker. Does she live around here?"

"No, she only stops in when there's a new series she's debuting so she can personally take the payments from the high-end buyers. Lots of rich folks swing out here. It's like wine country but with more trucks."

"Right, whatever. So, when's the next time she'll be in?"

"Beats me. She doesn't even drop off her small paintings between events. Her daughter runs them between her place and the shop."

"Her daughter? Can I meet her daughter?" Dana took a gulp of coffee and wiped a smear of froth from her upper lip.

"She's not in today, but whenever Ashley does come in, I'll tell her you were looking for her."

This time, the paper coffee cup slid completely out of Nick's hand and splattered on the concrete floor.

"I'll clean that up," Nick noted.

"Ashley is Jessica's daughter?" she asked Nell before turning to Nick, excited, and shouting, "*Ashley is Jessica's daughter!*"

Nick kneeled on the floor, attempting to tend to the puddle of coffee with a tiny stack of napkins from the bag of pastries in his hand, but Dana pulled him back up by the collar of his work jacket.

"Nick, did you hear what I said?!"

"Yeah, Ashley is Jessica's daughter." He froze. "Wait. *What?*"

Dana clutched his arms. Suddenly, her broad smile changed. Her eyes clouded over. "Nick, I'm going to need a minute."

She bolted out the door and collapsed onto a wooden bench. Nick watched through the window as she put her face in her hands and her body convulsed. He looked back at the painting, trying to burn the flowing letters of the artist's signature into his retinas. Yes, he saw it too; there was no denying it was the same signature as on the painting at home. Nell stood behind the counter with a notepad and an oversized pen adorned with images of generic coyotes and Native American teepees.

"So, you want me to leave Ashley a message or something?"

"Um, yeah, I do, and write this down exactly. Tell *Phoenix* that *Photograph* needs to talk to her." He crossed his arms and puffed his chest. Nell shrugged and wrote the words on the paper as her glasses slowly slid off the tip of her nose.

"*Okay* . . . that makes no sense, but I'll get it to her."

Nick flung the door open and approached Dana slowly. He kneeled in front of where she sat on the street bench, rubbing her eyes. Nick placed his hand on her cheek gently and ran his thumb across her jaw. She was so brave, yet so fragile when caught off guard. But more and more often, when she had a meltdown, she let him pick up the pieces—as much as she would allow him to touch.

"Hey. Hey, Dana. It's okay. You just took a direct hit." Her gasps grew shallow. "Slow breaths, Dana. Slow."

She clutched the bag out of his hand and dumped the pastries into her lap. She slammed the bag over her mouth and nose and took deep long breaths in and out, in and out. A violent cough erupted from her chest and tore the bag.

"Crumbs . . . I inhaled crumbs."

"Just slow down your breathing. Big things. Little steps. Small breaths."

Dana locked her eyes with his, the bag back over her mouth. She rested her hand in his, syncing her breathing to his own, in and out, in and out.

She thought about camping with her mom under the desert sky when her father took his trips back to New Jersey and the lab.

She thought about roller-skating on the hardwood floors with her mother. Her mom carefully buffed the scuffs out from Dana's skates so that her grandfather would remain oblivious to their shenanigans.

She thought about her mom painting on the patio and encouraging her to finger paint on her own tiny canvas made of paper plates.

She thought about her mom.

Simone Florence Jefferson.

Or Jessica Walker?

"Dana, come back. Dana, just breathe."

Dana fell off the bench, collapsing into Nick's arms.

"Nick, oh God, she's alive, and she's out here. I know it now—*I feel it*."

"I know, I know."

Nick lifted her gently from his chest and rolled into a seated position on the ground next to her. Dana looked down at his hand, wrapped around hers. The world as she had known it just a handful of minutes earlier was gone, replaced by a new unknown. Except for Nick. He was her constant—he was her friend. She squeezed his palm.

"Things just got a heck of a lot more interesting, Nick."

"I know, Dee. Just breathe. We'll make a new plan."

"We'll make a new plan. Yes."

Chapter 19

She Is Beautiful – Andrew W.K.

The late afternoon heat had subsided in Taos. Couples linked arm in arm and laughing families shuffled along, blindly following the walkway of shops and restaurants. Tourists stopped in small clusters to listen to the music floating over the town square from the gazebo stage, where an all-female zydeco band played joyous songs and sunbaked children and elderly couples in foldable camping chairs clapped happily along. Popcorn and tamale vendors pushed carts with ostentatious signage, and the early evening air smelled both salty and spicy.

Dana finished her burrito on a bench directly across from Dune Bloom, oblivious to the levity of the tourist trap and sunny dispositions of the passersby.

"Come on, *Phoenix*. Show yourself," she muttered.

The details of her plan ran through her head. Nick had gone back home, leaving Dana to wait out Ashley alone. Her backpack held her skates as usual, but also an extra T-shirt and socks, plus a bus ticket back home. Once Ashley appeared, Dana would threaten to expose her drug dealing in exchange for information on her—their?—mom's whereabouts. If Ashley refused, Dana would call the "police," which would actually be Nick impersonating an officer over the phone. If Ashley still wouldn't cooperate, Dana would proceed to beat some sense into her, at least until she gave up the information. She had not shared this last-resort option with Nick, but Dana guessed she was allowed to take a few liberties if necessary.

Dana adjusted her goggles, which she was using as a makeshift hairband, and checked the time again on the pendulous town square clock. Seven o'clock. Nell the cashier walked to the front of the gallery and flipped the placard on the door to CLOSED. After turning the bolt with her key, she appeared on the sidewalk below and merged with the handful of people heading toward the less populated end of the street. Dana stood and brushed away the crumbs and sauce drippings on her jacket. The end of day seemed to be set in motion, with multiple stores going dark almost in unison. Behind Dana, the band was packing up and the square was clearing out.

"Damn it." Dana sighed and extracted Laverne and Shirley from her backpack, clicking the shin guards and boot closures in place. She nudged the power cell into sleep mode, allowing the wheels to unlock and roll freely like traditional skates, albeit heavier and muddier. With short thrusts, she rolled down the sidewalk past the square and stopped at the closest crosswalk to wait as cars pulled out of parking spaces.

"You gotta be kidding me," said a voice on the opposite corner.

Dana looked over to see Ashley crossing her arms and pouting. She could see her hair clearly now—shoulder-length, light brown with blond highlights. Her white nylon vest and rainbow-striped leggings were stained with the red-brown dust of the desert. Her left skate was at a ninety-degree angle from her right one, keeping her steady on the curb as she licked her lips and lifted her jaw.

"What do you want?"

"I'm your sister! I think!" Naturally, the plan dissolved at step one.

"Look, *ma'am*, I don't know what you want—"

"Did you just 'ma'am' me? How old do I look?"

"Get the hell out of here and leave me alone!" Ashley pulled her helmet from her bag, set it on her head, and kicked off the curb, shooting into the path of a pickup truck. She swerved to avoid it and crossed to the far side of the street in a fountain of sparks, increasing her speed with each leg stroke.

"Yeah, well, I'm not going away!" Dana mimicked Ashley's push off the curb and launched into the street. She clicked her heels to activate the power in the tiny but mighty motors in the skates, creating a burst of sparkling exhaust from the wheels eerily similar to Ashley's. A second truck swerved to avoid colliding with both girls as they roared around the town square. A third vehicle screeched and swerved, smacking the fender of a fourth car. In reply, a whooping siren blast jolted Dana as a police sport utility flashed its headlights from a side street and pulled behind them.

"Shit shit shit! Hey, Ashley, I just wanna chat!" Ashley extended a middle finger behind her in response. "We don't have to talk about the drugs!"

Ashley stutter-stepped at the outburst. Dana took her chance and lunged but just missed grabbing her backpack. The police vehicle whooped again at the girls, and Ashley grunted.

"Hey, lady, you're not helping. We have to outrun them." She peeked over her shoulder at the approaching cop. "I *cannot* deal with the police right now," she said, patting her bag.

Ashley lowered her right hand to her hip and flashed her index finger toward the sign for the outbound highway. Dana followed the signal, and they accelerated in unison as the police SUV barreled closer. Ashley tucked into a downhill skier's crouch and flashed ahead with a burst of tiny burning stars in her wake. Dana chopped at the pavement with her feet and sprinted to catch up to her.

"Okay, *Phoenix*, he's gaining on us. Can you get us to a straightway?"

"Are you afraid of heights?"

"Maybe?"

Ashley waved at a passing sign for the Rio Grande Gorge Bridge stamped with a mileage marker. "Keep a straight line over the span or you'll slam into the guardrail."

"What? I can't hear you!" Dana barked into the rushing wind.

"Stay straight on the bridge!"

The road crooked to the left. The skaters leaned into the turn to maintain their speed while the high beams of the police SUV pushed chaotic dancing shadows ahead of the girls. Another sign for the bridge approached, this one with a one-mile distance indicator.

"Photograph, right? Once we cross the bridge, head to the right and punch it. Then it's no man's land, so whatever you got in those skates, burn it."

The tall arch supporting the bridge stretched over the deep narrow chasm carved by the Rio Grande. The water below looked like ink in the shadow of the cliffs. Dana spared a moment to glance across the guardrail as they crossed the expansion gap at the edge of the bridge. Before she could get a better look, the spotlights of two police cruisers parked at the opposite end of the bridge suddenly illuminated the fugitives.

"Stop and turn off your engines . . . or just stop," boomed a voice from the police loudspeaker.

"Ash, you ever jump in those?"

"Yeah." She adjusted her helmet. "Stay straight when we go over."

The two pairs of skates hummed and whirred a metallic chorus. Dana and Ashley raced closer toward the police blockade.

"Three. Two. ONE!"

Dana compressed her legs and bounded into the air. Ashley lifted her lead leg and stomped into the road, blasting her body upward. A rainbow of sparks pelted the cruisers' hoods as the girls glided over the blockade, leaving the bewildered state troopers standing dumbfounded beside their open car doors. Another explosion of light marked the landing of the skaters on the road beyond the bridge. Dana raised a thumb to Ashley as they flashed genuine smiles at each other.

"Turn it up, old woman!" Ashley crouched again and shot forward. Dana slapped her thighs and sliced her skates into the pavement, rocketing behind Ashley toward the dark-blue horizon. A coyote trotted across the asphalt, pausing to sniff at the burnt ember trail left behind.

Chapter 20

Take Your Mama – Scissor Sisters

The sign across from the truck stop entrance read TAOS 60 MILES in peeling reflective paint that partially shined with the passing traffic. Two semitrailers idled on the edge of the parking lot. Dana and Ashley slipped between the sleeping giants and squatted on concrete berms that straddled the empty lanes of parking spaces across from the service center and convenience store. In silent agreement, they removed their skates before heading inside the neon oasis of twenty-four-hour snacks and toiletries.

"That was fun, right?" Dana said, breaking the silence that had endured since the bridge crossing.

"Fun? As much fun as writing a term paper on Nietzsche." Ashley's gaze drifted slowly down and up Dana's body, sizing her up. "Too close for comfort, but it's risky for me always. One dumb move and the cops are asking to look in my backpack or interrogate me about my skates. You get that."

Dana nodded as she opened the door, an electronic chime announcing them. A man north of middle age stood up from behind the cash register and tipped his baseball cap. Ashley fluttered her fingers in his direction as a hello, then grabbed a burrito and placed it in the filthy microwave.

"So, real names?" Dana asked.

"Ashley. Ashley Walker."

"Dana Jefferson."

Dana grabbed two bottles of a sports drink from the cooler. She observed her possible sister moving up and down the aisles as the burrito cooked. Ashley slid a pair of socks from a spinner display into her vest pocket and rejoined Dana at the register.

"Hi, ladies. Is that all?"

Dana slid her hand into Ashley's pocket and dumped the socks, a pack of batteries, and two candy bars onto the counter.

"Not enough hands, am I right?" Dana smiled at the man and placed a pile of crumpled singles on the counter.

"Dang girl, you must be pretty bad at stripping," Ashley said as she feigned a smile at Dana. "Must suck to dance for eight hours and only make that much in tips."

Dana screwed her head toward Ashley, then back to the cashier as he leered at Dana.

"Eyes up here, creep."

Dana clawed at the pile of goods and hustled out of the store without her change. She dropped to the curb and gazed up at the mercury bulbs humming above on the paint-flaked lamppost. Ashley slid off her backpack and set it between them as she sat down.

"Stripping a sore subject?"

"Very funny—no. Nothing I've done, personally. I just don't tolerate creeps." She swigged her sports drink and ignored the lemon-lime drops dribbling down her chin. "You're too young to be a *gentleman's dancer*, so what else is on your felony list?"

Ashley laughed and unzipped her bag. She slowly pulled out an envelope clearly stuffed with bills to give Dana a glimpse before sliding it back inside.

"Look, my current gig is just a temporary thing. I just need enough to buy a car, maybe a sleeper van, and some startup cash so I can just get out of here. I'm just running cash for some bookies. Occasionally it's a big old bag of weed. I just take the envelope or box and deliver it, no questions, no sampling of the merchandise. I usually don't even look inside the packages."

"It's more than that, missy," Dana huffed. "Meth. Hard shit. You're dealing bad news, and people are suffering." Dana didn't care if she was sounding sanctimonious anymore. "You're hurting people who need help."

Ashley dragged her foot in a slow circle and looked down at her feet. "That's not what they told me I was carrying."

"Yeah, well, whoever 'they' are, they're bad people. Just stop it."

"You sound like my mom."

Dana paused, unsure if she should feel insulted or honored. "Yeah, well, you should think about bagging groceries instead. I know some people who are on the other side of what you're doing. You need to stop. Tell your dealer or whoever that the heat is on you, and you need to bail." Dana stared into Ashley's eyes, the light-brown irises mirroring her own. "Why do you want to get out here so badly?"

"You haven't been in New Mexico long, have you?" Ashley stood up and twirled with her arms outstretched. "There's nothing here! My mom thinks we're *better off* being around nothing out here. She's super paranoid. She's a mountain woman with a prepper lifestyle. You just don't understand. I'm . . . handcuffed, being with her until I'm eighteen. 'I am no bird, and no net ensnares me. I am a free human being with an independent will.'"

"You make that up yourself?" Dana crossed her arms and paced slowly. "That's heavy stuff."

"That's Charlotte Brontë, you uncouth illiterate. You try living hidden away, toiling in libraries in secret while your mother spends her time painting and cleaning her guns." Ashley mockingly kicked at Dana's leg. "So, yes, I'm doing something illegal to hoard cash until I get out of here."

Dana stood and lumbered across the pavement away from Ashley, her legs beginning to ache from their successful police elusion. She stopped under a malfunctioning parking lot light and watched the bulb flicker on and off.

"You know, girl, there are worse things than having an overprotective mother." She glanced back at Ashley and unzipped her leather coat. She slid off the sleeves and turned the jacket inside out, folding the tuxedo style tails carefully.

"Come here."

Ashley approached and squinted where Dana's finger was pointing at the coat tag. Under the flickering light, she read the name handwritten on the nylon in faded black magic marker.

"Who's Simone?" she asked.

"That's my mom. And I think yours, too." Dana traced the letters slowly to make sure Ashley got the point. "This matches the font style of the signature on the painting by your mom in the gallery, and the one on my mom's painting at home—from when she was Simone Jefferson, not Jessica Walker."

Ashley cocked her head. "I don't think so." She turned the label over before handing the jacket back to Dana. "Besides, wouldn't my mom—*if* my mom was your mom—come looking for you, or have told me about you?"

"I would've thought so, but things were complicated." Dana slipped her jacket back on and zipped the front. She tucked her nose into the collar. "I like to think this smells like her."

"She smells more like gun oil, paint, and lime," Ashley countered.

A fuel tanker lumbered into the lot and settled next to the diesel pumps. The driver turned off the grinding thunder of an engine on its last legs. Ashley lightly punched Dana in the arm. "You think we really are sisters?"

"Well, our eyes are the same funky color, but if that's not enough evidence, I think these are." She tapped her skates. "Do you know these were developed for a government project? Like, top-secret level. There are just too many coincidences."

The girls' conversation came to an abrupt halt when they spotted a state trooper car pulling into the back entrance of the truck stop and park on the side of the store's front entrance. The officers' laughter and muddy chatter echoed across the lot as they approached the front of the building. Dana glanced at Ashley, who replied with a nod. They picked up their bags and speed-walked across the lot to the gap between the trucks and into the tall grasses beyond the lights.

"So, what now, Phoenix?"

"I don't know, Photograph. Best bet? We split up and catch up later. I mean, I'm the one holding a bundle of cash in a backpack that will light up a few drug-sniffing puppies." Ashley held out her hand and Dana shook it. "No, idiot, your phone! Give me your cell. I'll put my number in it."

"Oh, right, right, right. Here."

"Thanks, dummy. So, text me tomorrow. I gotta do a thing first before I head home."

"Back to Taos?"

"No, we live—" Ashley smirked and shook her finger. "Ah, you almost made me say it." She winked at Dana and began walking through the grass toward the side road.

"Wait, where's the bus stop?" Dana shouted in a loud whisper. Ashley turned for a moment and raised her hands, flicking her middle fingers into the air before she sprinted toward her original trajectory.

"Jackass. Now I hope we're *not* related," Dana muttered. She walked back to the pair of trucks and sat on the step of the closest rig's sleeper cabin. She whipped out her phone and dialed Nick, but it went straight to voice mail.

"Hey, roomie, it's me. I'm at a truck stop somewhere north of Taos, I think. I gotta find the bus stop. I spent my last cash. I'll explain it all later. Anyway, I'll be back hopefully by the morning."

As she ended the call, she heard the cab door of the truck gently open. She looked behind her to find a woman in a gray flannel nightshirt rubbing her eyes.

"Sweetie, can you keep it down for just another hour or so? I'll drop you off myself if you let me just sleep another hour."

Dana flashed a toothy apologetic smile and nodded vigorously.

Chapter 21

Take It Uptown – Bill Champlin

The thing you two idiots don't appreciate is a little something called the gray man theory. It's critical when it comes to tracking."

Brian was facing the map taped on the aircraft hangar wall. He swigged the dregs of his beer and threw the bottle into the trash can with impressive accuracy. Agent Thirty-Seven clapped appreciatively as his brother, Agent Thirty-Six, rechecked his notebook. Thirty-Six raised his hand with hesitation.

"What's 'gray man theory'?"

"Ah, he speaks!" Brian spread his arms and clasped his hands together with fervor. "The theory of the gray man is to blend in, right in plain sight. You can't walk around in a ghillie suit at the mall or on an airplane. You go gray—you become completely unremarkable. You mute your colors . . . no logos, very generic." He strode over to the seated twins and grabbed a fistful of each one's braided beards. "*This* stands out." He let go and smoothed his thin moustache with his finger and thumb. "This does not and is easy to remove on the fly."

Brian ate up the attention from the two stooges assigned to him. Olsen had agreed to place the twins on the mission to bring in Dana on the condition that they follow every order from Brian or face dismissal from the group. Brian basked in the glory of being in command, even if it was only over a team of two. As a soldier of fortune, he rarely got to call his own shots for the group.

"As the gray man, you don't just put on your khakis and a polo shirt and follow. You need to have a plan." Brian placed a highlighter marker on the map and began tracing sweeping arcs across city names and roads. "These are all the pursuit routes I've taken when following the target. You find the target, you follow, then you depart. You can learn a lot discreetly in a half mile of tracking at a time, rather than risk blowing your cover trying to follow the target home in one shot."

Thirty-Six raised his hand and motioned to the board, silently asking for permission to approach.

"Go ahead, dummy."

Thirty-Six picked up a red marker and stood in front of the map. He drew a large bullseye in one spot, then replaced the cap and tossed the marker at Brian.

"She's in Alamogordo. And Brian? My name is Eugene." He sat down in his chair next to his befuddled brother.

Brian examined the map, tapping on the circle.

"How do you know that, *Eugene*?"

"If you look where all your lines intersect, you can clearly see where she's leaving and coming home. It's Alamogordo."

Brian crossed his arms and nodded silently, his face turning red—partly from anger, partly from embarrassment. He whipped his head back and forth between the map and his two students seated behind him.

"I guess we're smarter than you thought," Thirty-Seven remarked smugly. "And Brian, *my* name is Zeke."

Brian glared at him but didn't respond.

"Brian," Eugene said, "we have experience with this girl. You haven't had to deal with her and those skates. If you're running lead, we'll follow, but you need to listen to us as well. So, no more treating us like idiots. Okay, sir?"

Brian was about to set these two straight when Olsen appeared across the hangar and waved for him to come over. Nina stood next to him with an open laptop. The group converged next to a large crate of empty kerosene tanks. Brian kicked one and listened for the dull echo inside.

"What are these even for? To power the giant robot thingamabob?"

"The Atomic Juggernaut," Olsen corrected him. "And no, not now." He indicated for Nina to present the laptop. "This is an older schematic of the juggernaut. It looks like the power cell will go into the bod, and then line up with the targeting cell."

Nina closed the laptop and licked her lips. "My father did a good job keeping the pieces away from each other, but it looks like the components, the battery modules, will help to mostly automate the juggernaut." She glanced at Olsen for his approving nod. "*Mostly*. But the batteries, the prototypes, those will burn out quick unless we can locate the schematics for the near-zero energy atrophy plans from Samuel Jefferson."

Brian stared blankly at Nina. She shook her short blond bob. "The point is, Nails, we need to get those plans or this whole thing goes to rot. *Find that girl.*"

Brian had had enough tonight. He spoke firmly and with confidence. "I *know* what the mission is. I am *not* a rookie. I'm the *best* there is at what I do." To emphasize his point, he drew his sidearm and pointed it at a sign outside the hangar. He pulled the trigger and drove a hole through the center of the *O* in "NO PARKING." Olsen whistled. "Let me do my job. And when the time comes, just tell me who to erase."

"When the time comes," Olsen said, "you'll know."

Chapter 22

Words – Missing Persons

The reflection of scattered clouds drifted across the Lincoln Memorial Reflecting Pool, framed by packs of wild schoolchildren on class trips to the surrounding monuments and museums along the National Mall. On the south end of the pool, Joshua Green sat in the grass on his folded windbreaker and opened his plastic container. He stared down at the chickpeas and leafy sprigs, counted the allotment of each component in his salad, and ran the ratio of each ingredient to each other—one of his mathematical tics. Invisible to the schoolchildren, government agency employees in dull suits of blue and gray threaded through the crowds and landed upon various benches and grassy clearings for lunch. Joshua had planned ahead and left for lunch early to ensure his favorite spot.

His transfer to the Department of Homeland Security's secret and recently formed Counterterrorism Accounting Force had made his heart swell with pride. His work in preventing the hijacking of the Atomic Juggernaut in New Jersey, and his tidiness with sorting out the financial aftermath, had caught the eye of the top brass in the DHS. A professional recommendation by his mentor, Director Carmen Jameson, along with her personal blessing offered additional confidence to Joshua that this was the best move for his future in DC and for creating stability for his wife and child. As the youngest member of the CTAF, as insiders called it, he took on the task of generating terror financing bait drops—or more simply, placing deposits into flagged international banks and then tracking the recipients. The fun part for him was calculating the interest on the deposits and determining who received the funds when the operation resolved.

He was carefully spearing a piece of kale when he felt the vibration of his phone. Instinctively, he pulled his cell out of his shirt pocket, but the screen only showed the date and time. *No, the* other *phone*, a voice in his head reprimanded. Setting his salad haphazardly on the grass, he glanced over each shoulder before pulling his jacket from underneath him. Another scan of the crowd around him. No one stood out. He opened the black phone tucked into the lining and accepted the call.

"Joshua Green, CTAF." A lump formed in his throat, and he swallowed hard. Silence. He pulled the windbreaker over his arms and felt the reassuring stiffness from the thin Kevlar lining hiding inside. "This is Joshua," he repeated with as much authority as he could muster. A cough on the other end of the line told him that the connection was valid.

"The line is secure. Go."

"Okay, whew! Hey, Joshy!" a female voice blasted through the speaker. The perkiness and singsong quality immediately connected his mental files to one contact.

"Dana Jefferson, you got me. How are you?"

"Sorry, I had a mouthful of home fries when you picked up. The food out here in New Mexico is amazing. How are things?"

Joshua bent over and began the meticulous process of rebuilding his salad. "Good. Really good. I'd love to chitchat, but you called on the black box line. Are you in danger?"

"Oh no, nothing like that. Well, yeah, I am. I mean . . . let me start over—One Hundred Roads is out here."

Joshua spied a young woman, about the same age and height as his wife, running after a toddler as she headed toward the glassy water. His focus blurred at the mention of One Hundred Roads. "Dana, I thought we shut them down. Or you did—I just cleaned it up and locked up all the accounts we could find."

"I know, but they're out here, or at least a cluster of them, and they've got some money, that's for sure. They tried to buy mining rights on the Apache reservation in Mescalero. Palladium. Nick told me to say that. He's also pointing at my feet."

"Dana, I need to get this all down, hold on." He pulled out his standard work phone and opened his notepad app. "Okay, hit the bullet points again."

"One Hundred Roads. Major Olsen. Money. Palladium. Roller Skates."

"Huh?"

"That's why Nick was pointing at my feet. There's another girl out here with the same skates I have."

"Wait, who has the same skates?"

"A girl. Younger than me. Her name is Ashley Walker. Her mother is Jessica Walker." Dana's gulp was audible on the other end. "She also may go by the name *Simone Jefferson*."

A silent acknowledgment lingered between them. Joshua tapped in the names and stared for a moment at the screen as he formed his words. "Okay, let me see if I can find anything out. Simone Jefferson. Jessica Walker. What's the kid's name again?"

"Ashley Walker."

"Got it. Listen, Dana, I'm in a new role here so I'll be blunt. Do you need extraction?"

"Ha, you're so formal! No, not yet. I still have your magic credit card."

"That's good, but I can arrange some bigger things if needed now. Working on your case out in New Jersey put me in the good graces of quite a few people. I can get you out of there if necessary."

Joshua gave up on his salad, jogged to the trash can, and pitched the remains of his lunch. The children assembled around the park were rapidly funneling to the caravans of buses on one side of the Mall. The area around the pool emptied with the accompanying breeze. He rubbed his chin and scanned the trees on the edges of the park. With the children now gone, the remaining government agents stood out in their blue and gray. No one seemed to be looking at him directly, but anyone surrounding him could be listening or tracking him in plain sight.

"Josh, you still there?"

"Sorry, yes. Is anyone from local law enforcement involved?"

"I may have pissed off a few police here, but no one knows my name."

"But they know a girl on turbo skates is out there causing a fuss, whether it's you or this Ashley."

"Is this where you tell me to lay low?"

"That's exactly what I'm going to tell you." He paused before continuing. "Dana, when I did the research on your dad and the Atomic Juggernaut, there was something that didn't sit right with me."

"What thing?"

"Your mom's death. There was a bit of a long tail on the cashing in of a few life insurance policies. Most went into your trust, but some seemed to just vanish through cashier checks and money orders at check cashing places. I assumed this was your grandfather trying to keep some money from going into his taxable estate. But the conspiracy theorist in me thought that maybe your mom was not dead, but maybe in hiding, and that she needed a lot of money."

"Why wouldn't you mention that?!"

"I did debate doing so a few times, but I never had a real lead. Just tread carefully while I try to find some more out. Remember that if it is her, and she is still alive, she has been off the grid for a reason. Don't let that reason find you, because you could lead them to her."

"Got it. Thanks, Joshy."

"I'll call you when I have more info." He hung up and slid the phone back into his secure pocket, then juggled back to his personal phone and dialed his wife.

"Honey, I'll be home on time, but I'm going to have overtime coming up. And whatever you're thinking of for dinner tonight, make extra. I barely ate lunch." He paused to look at the monuments on each end of the pool. "I love you."

Chapter 23

Speechless — School of Fish

Lilly pulled her compact car into the driveway behind Nick's pickup. Dana stood beside it with a bucket of water and a garden hose. She waved excitedly, accidentally spraying a blast of water into her face.

"Hey, hey! What's up, roller rookie?"

Lilly skipped up the drive, swinging her tiny backpack. She wore baggy cotton shorts and a sleeveless tee.

"I feel overdressed," she said, eyeing Dana as she stretched over the hood of the truck in her soccer shorts and sports bra, her muscles and broad build a stark contrast to Lilly's slim frame.

"I should've told you to wear a bathing suit. Help me finish cleaning the dirt box here. Nick's been working in the basement all day. You can just whip off your shirt if you don't want it to get wet."

Lilly blushed as she pulled her shirt over her head to reveal what she thought was a far less flattering sports bra than Dana's. She grabbed a sponge and started to wipe down the wheels. A cold blast to her back made her gasp out loud.

"I'm sorry, I couldn't resist a sitting duck," Dana chortled, the hose pointing in Lilly's direction.

She hosed out the back of the truck bed as Lilly scrubbed the tailgate. Nick stumbled out the screen door into the blinding midday sun.

"A girl washing my car? Really? Am I in a teen movie now?" he yelled as he draped his arm over his eyes.

"Nothing you haven't seen before, and it's rated PG, roomie."

Nick stepped off the porch to tease Dana a little more but finally caught sight of Lilly.

"Hey, Lilly, didn't see you. Uh . . . just kidding there. Um, Dana? Can I ask you something really quick?"

Dana set down the hose and followed Nick up the stairs. He turned to face her, his eyebrows slowly knotted over his nose.

"Do you think it's a good idea having guests over right now?"

"Hey, it's just Lilly! It's cool. And just because I have one friend and you have zero doesn't mean you get to be jealous." She poked him in the arm.

"Alright, well, we need to be careful. That's my job, as usual . . . reminding you to be careful." He leaned around Dana and watched Lilly hose down the cab windows. Dana noted his interest.

"Nick, she is single, and yes, she is easy on the eyes."

He stepped back and grabbed the door. "I don't disagree, but I'm . . ." His voice trailed off. "I'm not interested right now." He avoided Dana's eyes. "I'll be in the basement putting the rest of those cables away. Your dad was a bit of a hoarder."

Dana hopped down the steps back to Lilly.

"It's silly to towel dry that truck with all this sun, so I think I'll hose it off one last time and call it day."

The girls tidied up the car wash supplies and happily entered the air-conditioning of the house. Dana produced two glasses of iced tea and sat on the couch next to Lilly.

"We have that convention coming up in a month. Twenty regional teams. Are you ready, Lil?"

"Yeah, I think so. Thanks for helping me out. It's a lot easier when you have someone watching out for you." She slid her finger down the condensation on her glass.

"You've got great fundamentals. Did you skate a lot as a kid?" Dana asked as she held her glass to her forehead.

"Yeah, it was kind of my escape. It's something you can do in a crowd," Lilly said, "and be alone at the same time." She looked down at the floor. "It's not easy when you're, you know, different than everyone else."

Dana put her hand on her shoulder. Lilly flinched at the touch but quickly relaxed.

"Hey, I know all about being different. I was pretty young when I lost my parents and grandfather. Then I went to boarding school on a trust fund. Do you know what it's like being in a girls' dorm on holidays all by yourself as a teen in crisis? Let me tell you, it was pretty lonely." She sighed, lost in her own thoughts. "It was the complete opposite and, like, totally overwhelming for me when classes resumed and it was full of girls."

Lilly smiled at Dana and took a sip of her drink. "Dana, you're the only person who's been nice to me out here."

"It's easy, 'cause you're a likeable person! I think you just need a little confidence. And you're showing that out there with derby. I love seeing that."

"You do?" Lilly placed her fingers lightly on Dana's wrist.

Dana looked down and then back up at Lilly. She could feel her pulse quicken beneath her fingers. After a beat, Lilly leaned in and gently pressed her lips to Dana's. Dana eased back, slowly pulling her hand away.

"Oh, Lilly, I'm sorry. It's not like that. I mean, *this*," she said, gesturing from Lilly's torso to her face, "is all good. You're a catch in a lot of ways, but *I'm* not. I have a lot of complications right now, and I just can't bring someone new into all that."

Pools of water filled Lilly's eyes. She quickly stood up, clutching her shirt to her chest.

"I'm sorry, this was a mistake—I'm sorry."

"Lilly! Lil! No, I'm glad you did it! You took a risk. Listen!" Dana grabbed her by both shoulders and stared unblinking into Lilly's teary eyes. "I *know* how hard it is to admit something like this to someone. Especially for people like you and me. Doing that's going to knock you down a couple times." She smiled gently and squeezed her shoulders. "It is not easy being us. You ask someone out, they say no for whatever reason, but you lift your head knowing you took a chance."

The basement door opened and Nick stopped short in the doorway.

"Everything okay?" He took one step back into the stairwell.

"We're okay," Dana replied. "Just girl talk."

Nick nodded and closed the door again. Lilly placed her hands on Dana's and forcibly removed them from her shoulders.

"You keep saying 'people like you and me,' but I don't think you *are* like me." She stared at the shut basement door. "I can see it, even if you don't. You don't know what it's really like, for *me*, in *my* family." The tears welling in her eyes finally burst before she ran for the door.

"Lilly, wait!"

But Dana didn't follow—she froze. Through the window, she watched Lilly's car reverse quickly out of the driveway and lurch into drive. The whine of the engine faded rapidly as the car accelerated in its retreat. Dana sat down on the couch and slumped into the cushions, craning her neck and following the lines of the exposed beams running the width of the room. The grain on each beam swirled in small circles around each knot, reminders of the trees that once grew somewhere north or west of the house. Footfalls in the stairwell and the squeak of the basement door announced Nick's return.

"What happened, Dee?"

Dana hugged her knees. "Oh, I just screwed up my one and only friendship. Guess we're even again."

"Was it a fight or something . . . else?"

"Something else. She made a move. She kissed me." Dana knotted her fingers into the flesh of her thigh. "And she's a shy girl, Nick. This was a big moment for her . . . I think it was *the* moment for her. I don't know how else I could have handled it." When Nick still looked puzzled, she added, "I don't think I can explain what coming out means to someone like you."

He nodded as it dawned on him. Silence filled the room until he cleared his throat.

"You're right. I don't know. But I do know that you can't be everything to everyone, no matter how you or they feel. Some people just won't be happy with who you are." She felt his hand on her shoulder and placed hers on top.

"It's okay. She's having trouble being happy with who she is. But she found derby, and the sisterhood that goes with it. I was helping her out of her shell, and she misread the signs." She looked up at him. "She misinterpreted my friendship."

"Do *you* like her? Or are you pushing her away because of the whole 'giant robots and roller skates and military dudes' thing?"

"No, it's not that. I'm ready to be with someone . . . I think." Dana's eyes twitched, and tears spilled over. "Why am I crying?"

Nick sat down and wrapped one arm around her. She nuzzled into his chest and bawled.

"Keep talking, Dee."

"She's a nice girl, she's . . . she's going to get there," she stammered.

"But I'm just a mess. I don't know why anyone would pick me. Some mornings, Nick, I walk around the house after you leave, and I just stare. At *nothing*. I don't know what to do—I just stare out the window with my mouth open. And when I go to the group meetings, I feel like I'm an imposter. There are people with some real shit there."

"*You* have real shit, Dana." He laughed lightly and pat the back of her head.

"Lilly shouldn't try to chase someone like me. I'm just damaged. And sometimes . . ." She pulled back and wiped her eyes. "Sometimes I feel like I don't even deserve you."

Nick looked out the sliding door and saw clouds overtaking the sky. Rain began to tap on the roof as they sat in silence.

"So much for washing the freakin' car," Dana said quietly.

Nick chuckled as Dana lay down and rested her head on his lap. His hand hovered over her dark ebony waves slithering down her shoulders, but he pulled his hand back and placed it on the back of the couch. Her knuckles rested on the floor next to his feet.

"Nick?"

"Dana?"

"Can we just stay like this for a little while?"

"Sure. As long as you want."

Dana let the white noise of the house's air-conditioning system and the rain outside calm her. She closed her eyes, but her thoughts kept coming. Her mother, if she *was* alive, hadn't come to find her. Nick had left his dad in New Jersey to be her sidekick, and now One Hundred Roads was somewhere looming in the background again. The only new friend she had met in New Mexico just walked out on her. Nothing felt safe except Nick's undying friendship.

It had never occurred to her that he might be feeling something else—

until now. As they sat in companionable silence, in the place they'd begun to craft into a home together, her heart told her that *she* may be feeling something else.

Her brain quieted, and suddenly she was dreaming. She was roller-skating through her grandfather's house with her mom, but her mother was wearing a mask, a bag with eyeholes. As they skated, her mother withered away until she disappeared, leaving young Dana in a house with no lights.

The sound of her phone vibrating on the kitchen counter startled her awake. The rain had passed, and the sun was streaming in the early evening sky. She tiptoed over, making sure not to wake Nick on his side of the couch, and checked the call history. The screen displayed several missed calls: one from Lilly, one from Joshua—and one from Ashley.

Chapter 24

The Ludlows – James Horner

Nick's truck rolled up to the Spartan bus stop where Ashley was waiting. The knot in Dana's stomach tightened in anticipation of the meeting ahead. She and Nick had barely spoken on the ride to the meeting point, only parsing a handful of words all morning. Dana jumped out of the cab, and Ashley jammed herself into the front seat next to Nick.

"So, this is fun, right?"

Nick nodded as he pulled back out onto the highway. "Nice to meet you. I'm Nick. Where am I headed?"

Ashley pointed down the road at a break between the guardrails. As they got closer, Nick could see a hidden driveway that rolled across the plain, tufts of dried and dead grasses all around. The road bent to the east a handful of miles later, blinding all of them. Nick pulled down his sunglasses that had been perched on his head as they navigated another lazy turn in the road.

"Is this property all your mom's?" Nick asked. "This is hard-packed dirt. Must have taken some real machinery to do this. Unless this was a fire trail?"

"Part of it was. I know she has a few acres, but honestly, I have no idea where it begins and ends. She does. Generally, anyone who crosses past that last bend is trespassing."

Dana spotted the tiny rancher in the distance. Behind the building, she could see a chicken coup and gothic-style red barn residing inside a timber paddock fence. A lone gray horse whinnied as it emerged from behind the house to observe their approach.

"You did tell her that I'm coming, right?"

"Not exactly. I thought it would be a fun surprise."

Nick slowed the truck to a stop.

"Well, then, that would explain *that*," he said with a nod.

A woman stood at the end of the formal driveway with a lever-action cowboy rifle aimed at the trio. She wore a long-sleeved smock smeared with dabs of paint and a scarf across her mouth. The exposed portion of her face was a brown hue darker than Ashley and Dana and showed signs of too much sun. Her light-brown eyes were stony, and her long black hair, flecked with auburn and silver strands, whipped in a long braid behind her. The revolver strapped to her thigh glinted in the sun.

"She doesn't look like she's ready for visitors," Nick posited.

"Get out of the vehicle!" the woman yelled.

The travelers obliged. Nick and Dana raised their hands instinctively. Ashley pushed past them both.

"Ashley!" the woman bellowed, not taking her eyes off Dana and Nick. "Are you okay? Are these people holding you against your will?"

"Mom, please, put that down. That's Nick, and this is Dana."

The woman's thumb slid off the hammer of the rifle. "I don't know them. Ash, step away from them and get in the house."

Dana stepped forward and lowered her hands. The woman's voice was like her mother's, but slightly lower with a touch of raspiness. Her memory strained to recall her mother's tone as she sang her favorite song or scolded

Dana for stealing cookies.

"Get back in your truck and turn around," the woman commanded.

"I'm Dana. I think I'm your daughter . . . *Simone*."

The woman held the weapon level and steady as she panned between the two trespassers.

"*My* daughter is Ashley, woman person." She flicked the barrel at Nick. "And who are you, man person?"

"I'm Nick. Nick Andrews. I'm Dana's—"

"He's my best friend." Dana smiled, trying to thaw her, and stepped closer. *This has to be her*, she thought. Her defiant posture made Dana think of the time she had demanded to speak to the manager at the local grocery store when the rude teenage cashier tried to overcharge them.

"Ashley, what's going on?"

The horse behind the fence snorted and dug a hoof into the dry dirt, matching its owner's energy.

"Mom, I think she really *is* your daughter." Ashley titled her head and looked at Dana. "So that makes you my sister? Half-sister?"

"Ash, walk on over." The woman continued to swing her rifle to point at each individual as she addressed them. "You two, get the hell off my property."

Dana's throat swelled. She took another two steps closer. Closer to *her*.

"Simone. *Mom*. It really is me. My dad, your husband, was Samuel Jefferson." The woman slowly shook her head. She squinted at Dana and adjusted her grip on the gun. Dana's breath quickened with each second that recognition eluded the woman she was certain was her mother.

"My name is Jessica, and I don't know any Thomas Jefferson or whoever you're blathering about."

"Mom!" Dana yelled. "We lived out here, in New Mexico, with your father-in-law, Sam Senior." Her eyes watered at the memory of family dinners when her father returned from his work trips. "Your husband got sick from his work for a top-secret program. Dad's program went out of control. You died . . . or, I guess, ran away." *Believe me. Please believe me.* Dana dropped to her knees slowly as the frustration took over. There was nothing left to keep her standing. Tears ran down her cheek. "Mom, *please.*"

The woman lowered the rifle's barrel an inch. She pulled down her scarf and revealed a grimace, one that Dana had seen before. It was her—her mother, *alive.* The fine lines on the corners of the woman's mouth twitched.

"Missy, I don't know what you want. Do you want me to *paint* you or something? I don't take walk-ups, and this is weird way to get me to agree. I have one daughter, and her name is Ashley. Now please, just go. *Just go.*"

Dana heard a waver in her voice. She lowered her head and exhaled. She had one card in her hand, and it was an ace. She rubbed the swollen bags under her eyes and grit her teeth. "Mom?"

"Please." The woman's voice cracked. "Go."

"Mom. When I was seven, we went camping and you forgot the toilet paper. I was so freaked out that I got constipated and you had to take me to the pediatrician for an enema." Dana couldn't help but laugh even as tears continued to roll down her cheeks. "Mom. At the doctor's office, I pooped all over the exam table . . . and the doctor, and the nurse. The nurse threw up. *On me.* And you still called me 'Star.'" She looked back at Nick and wiped her cheeks. "Nick, can you just forget that you heard that?"

"Already forgotten," he replied.

"That's going in the permanent file," Ashley muttered.

The woman stepped closer, lowering the rifle a hair more. The barrel shook slightly. "I have one daughter—"

"Mom!" Dana interrupted. "Why didn't you come find me?" Her chest heaved with each percussive sob. "Mom, it's me. *Star.*"

The woman finally relaxed her trigger finger and lowered the rifle's muzzle to the ground. She examined the girl in front of her from head to toe, then glanced at Ashley, who nodded an affirmation. Dana's mother's lower lip began to tremble as rivers of tears fell past her crow's feet and down her cheeks. The gun slid through her hands and clattered to the dusty driveway.

"*Star*," she said, clasping her hand over her mouth. "*My* Star. Oh, Dana, how did you find me?"

Dana leapt up and rushed toward her, catching her mother as she fell forward. Her hands tingled, her chest ached. *This is real,* she thought. The years of imaginary stories and anecdotes faded, and at last the real memories bloomed in vivid color. What she had dreamed for the future was wiped clean, instantly replaced with a blank slate. *This is my mom. Simone Jefferson.* Today was a day she had never dreamed was a possibility until the Atomic Juggernaut emerged and diverted her destiny. Mother and daughter clung to each other, sobbing and smiling. Her mom buried her face into her oldest daughter's locks.

"Dana . . . it really is you. Oh, God. Oh no . . . I'm so sorry. I had to run, Dana." Simone exploded in a wailing howl. "I *had* to. I had to run." She wiped her dirty hand across Dana's cheek. "It was for you. Because I loved you, Star."

Nick and Ashley stood by silently, giving them time and space. Dana looked up at her sister.

"I guess we're stuck with each other now?" Dana asked. She saw a sheen in Ashley's eyes, and Dana got up and stepped forward to embrace her, knowing they were true sisters. Simone stood and picked up the rifle, slinging it over her shoulder with one hand and grabbing Dana's hand with the other. She smiled broadly, and Dana could remember that smile from when her mom had tucked her in at night, the dimples that came out when they were roller-skating across the parlor floors. She pressed Dana's hand to her lips.

"We have so much to cover, Dana. My shooting Star."

Chapter 25

Mars Hotel – The Mayfield Four

Simone led her daughters and Nick up the stone steps to the porch and opened the thick oversized door. Dana crossed the threshold and examined the expansive room that smelled of light oak and traces of flowers and pollen. The high ceiling extended to the roofline of the rancher, and a long single step across the width of the house divided the living room from the kitchen. A long boxy couch sat perpendicular to two high-back chairs in the center of the room. Two easels holding blank canvases stood in the corner. Nick noticed no photographs in frames or any other personal touches—the opposite of his father's house, still haunted by portraits and memories of his mom.

"You have a beautiful hou—*ow!*" Nick was suddenly slammed into the wall, Simone's hand gripped firmly around his neck.

"Sorry, Nick. I had a moment where I let my guard down out there. Just a formality. Lift your shirt up nice and slow. No sudden moves."

Nick lifted his T-shirt up to his clavicles with a sheepish grin. Simone directed him to turn around, to which he obliged. She gently kicked the sides of each of his ankles and finished with a pat down of his back pockets.

"Just checking," she said, releasing him and winking at her daughters. She then flung her arms around him.

"You are *definitely* Dana's mom," he said, bewildered. "The mood swings are hereditary, I'm guessing."

Simone laughed as she picked up the rifle and placed it on a stand above the fireplace. After sliding off her smock, she stepped into the kitchen to get glasses and a pitcher of water. Her arms, now bare in a sleeveless shirt, were covered asymmetrically in a kinetic pattern of tiny square tattoos over her deltoids and triceps. A tiny contingent of runaway squares dotted her forearms. Dana cocked her head and addressed Simone.

"Hey, Mom, were those tattoos free? Did aspiring artists need to practice making squares?"

"Consider it digital camouflage. Multi-scale patterns to break up my silhouette on low-resolution and long-distance cameras. Every few months I add a square or two." She examined the pattern and ran her thin elegant fingers over her sinewy forearm. "You probably figured out that I'm over-the-top with my preparedness and paranoia," she added as she looked over at the untouched water glasses. "I think this calls for something stronger." She walked back into the kitchen and retrieved an open bottle of whiskey. "Shots, anyone? Except you, Ash."

Ashley slumped in her chair. "Mom, this may be the closest we've ever come to having a party. Come on."

Simone grabbed a can of beer from the fridge and flung it at her youngest daughter. Dana gasped and then smiled.

"Aren't you the cool mom?"

Simone laughed and poured three shots. "This is a one-time thing, Ash. Bottoms up, everyone!"

Everyone took a drink, and with that, any residual tension dissolved.

"Well," Dana started, "I guess I'll get right to these." Dana slid her backpack to her feet, which Nick had brought in during the mother-and-child entanglements, and unzipped the main compartment. She waited for Nick to nod before presenting the skates. "Mom, this is Laverne and Shirley."

Simone sat down next to Dana and tapped the battered ankle housing on Shirley with her thumb. She raised an eyebrow for approval before lifting the skate into the air. Her face screwed up as she attempted to spin the front wheel.

"You should change the standby mode to allow for free spin, rather than initiating the gyroscope locks," she muttered. "Ash, you do that on yours, don't you?"

"Yes, I do," she replied. "I like having the wheels locked so I can walk, but I added a dummy switch ring I can flick on or off when my foot passes the ankle rocker."

Dana swatted down Nick's raised hand. "Mom? Sis? Am I the dumb one in the family?"

"No, honey," Simone cooed. "We're pretty much a family of smart ladies. Ash has just had the benefit of home schooling, both traditional academics and more . . . unique subjects. She's had two articles published under pen names on Victorian-era linguistics."

Dana felt a pang of jealousy. Nick noticed the change on her face and jumped in.

"Mrs. Jefferson? Or Simone—Jessica?"

"Definitely not Mrs. Jefferson. I suppose you can call me Simone; I never got very used to Jessica."

"Can you give us more of the story? We—I mean, Dana has been under the assumption you were dead until after we found the Atomic Juggernaut and were told you may be in hiding."

Her mother stood up and reached once more for the whiskey, swallowing a mouthful right from the bottle.

"*The Atomic Juggernaut*. That's the whole enchilada." Her eyes traveled from window to window, her gaze paused on each. All of them were covered, the only natural light coming from the patio doors beyond the artist easels. The horse sauntered across the dirt path just beyond the doors and wandered back to the barn.

"*That* is a good horse," she said with a lowered voice. "Besides Ash, one of the only good things I've had since I ran from that program. Since I ran from Rhodes." She looked at Dana. "Since I ran from you. It was run, or lose everything. And I mean *everything*, Dana."

Everything. Right now, in the moment, Dana felt that she somehow had *gained* everything in the world. Her mother, with a ferocity for survival that was a little familiar to her, was right here in front of her. Her *mother*, who had helped her with her homework and organized the sixty-four crayons from the Crayola box in a color wheel pattern on the coffee table. Dana felt the quickening of her pulse and the pounding of her heart, a sign she now recognized at the onset of a panic attack. *It's alright, girl. You found her.*

Simone lowered herself to the couch and knotted her fingers behind her neck, suddenly looking tired. "Ash, can you do the loop? Check on cameras Mississippi through Florida, buzz-lock the inner fence, and send up Canada Dry?"

As her younger daughter bounded to a bookshelf and retrieved a small touchpad, Simone acknowledged the next layer of confusion painted on Dana's face. Nick mirrored the sentiment.

"What's 'Canada Dry'?" he asked.

"It's our drone, Nick. Just a fun little code name in case we're away from the ranch and need to enable security." Simone rubbed her knees. "It's been a long morning, kids."

Her eldest daughter opened her mouth to speak but paused, choosing her words deliberately. "Mom, who are you still hiding from? I don't know if you heard, but Rhodes is in jail."

"Dana, there are a lot of people who want to find me—dead or alive, but mostly dead. A means to an end, by their logic. It's been five years since the last threat, at our last place. But I got tired of running. So, I made this our home. And our fortress."

"Mom, you've got to start putting together some plot points for me here. I really feel like the dumb one."

"No, Dana. Not at all. You're just the raw one."

Chapter 26

Suddenly Last Summer – The Motels

Simone drew a long breath and reached out to Dana, palms up. Her daughter responded by placing her hands on top, and Simone squeezed them and smiled. She let out a long slow breath and looked at Dana and Nick.

"Here we go. Dana, Nick, as you both may know, my husband, Sam, and his father, my father-in-law, were brilliant military scientists. They worked on some very complicated, technical, and, if I may say so, *ridiculously* expensive projects. They spearheaded a program that was touted as a movement toward global peace, the greater good, the 'silver lining' of the military-industrial complex." She paused and looked upward to the high ceiling for a moment before letting out a small chuckle. "Some silver lining." She brought her gaze down to meet Dana's. "You've seen when the news shows the military coming out to help with natural disasters? That's the type of feel-good program we hoped to create."

"Wait," Nick interrupted, "'we'?" Were *you* in the program?"

"Yes. And even in the dawn of the current era, most women's contributions were placed in a tidy folder marked for later. But in *this* program, I was able to excel and even encouraged to run. The Atomic Juggernaut, those skates, most of the programs and designs were mine. *Mine.*"

Dana sat frozen, her curiosity surging with every word that passed from her mother's lips. Whatever notions she had had of the past, she prepared again to erase and rewrite them.

"Mom, I saw the blueprints of my skates. I built those from Dad's notes."

"That was one of the cleverest parts of the ruse. Everything was signed or attributed to 'S. Jefferson.'" She raised an eyebrow. "*Simone* Jefferson."

"Hidden in plain sight," Nick said.

"You got it. Samuel, as brilliant as he was—and he was *elite* in his intelligence—would run his most technical issues through me. I worked most of the time here in New Mexico on your grandfather's ranch, spending time with you during the day, then checking and correcting Sam's work at night. On a few occasions, I flew out to the lab in New Jersey for inspection. I was the only civilian member of the team—part of why everything was credited to your father.

"Anyhow, the Atomic Juggernaut was actually created as a recon and rescue vessel. In the case of a nuclear reactor meltdown, a category five on the Saffir–Simpson hurricane scale, or any natural or manmade catastrophe, there is a high certainty of losing communication networks. Lines and towers go down, and internet and satellite connections aren't reliable. We didn't want the juggernaut to be reliant on any of that, and the next best computer is the human nervous system. To start, we used fresh cadavers as navigators." She jutted her chin forward. "*Cadavers.*"

"And then you started using the people who got cancer from the program," Dana said.

"Right. Rhodes had found black market and enemy combatant buyers for the tech. As always, your grandfather and Rhodes could only see the military application of an idea. At that point, Rhodes cut us off, and he pushed to finish the program using the people who were already sick or offering payouts to volunteers who thought it was worth the sacrifice. It also silenced a few potential whistleblowers. But even that wasn't enough. He believed the giant robot could be run autonomously if it had a perfect navigator. Do you know what eugenics is?"

Dana nodded. Her mother returned the acknowledgement with a cold stare.

"Well, he wanted to develop the 'perfect' host body to run the juggernaut. If someone had a high-level nervous system, they could be the body and mind of the robot. He seemed willing to try anything to make that happen. And then suddenly, two of his top researchers found out they were having a baby . . ."

Simone looked in Ashley's direction, and Dana and Nick followed her gaze. Ashley stood at the far corner of the room, scrolling and tapping on the tablet as she switched from one security monitor screen to the next. She looked back at the three seated adults staring at her and waved hesitantly.

"So, I was pregnant with Ashley. We were afraid what Rhodes would do when he found out. We were losing any leverage to get out. Your father had just gotten his cancer diagnosis. You, Dana, were the apple of your grandfather's eye, so he was determined to keep you out of it. He knew all Rhodes's secrets and could hold them over him if it came to that. Rhodes didn't know that I was pregnant, and your father and I had to make a radical decision in a very short time. You have no idea how difficult it was, to choose between leaving one daughter or losing the other to a sociopath." She held her hands palm up, side by side, and looked back and forth between them. "And in both scenarios, my husband was still going to die."

Nick leaned forward and placed his hand on Simone's. Her eyes fluttered as she tried not to cry. Dana looked at Nick, the empathy for her broken mother so clear in his face.

"Simone, this is a lot to hold on to. You don't have to carry this alone anymore."

"And I thank you. I did what I had to do to protect my baby, and I knew your grandfather would keep you safe, Dana. But these were decisions that, once made, I could never walk back. And by choosing to fight to live, I died a little inside."

Ashley, who appeared to have been listening after all, entered their circle and sat down next to her mother, placing her head on Simone's shoulder.

"Mom's a badass, Dana. You don't even know about the thing in Alaska with the Russians. Mom went psycho on them. Dana, it was amazing—"

"Another time, sweetie. Let's save some stories for another day." Simone rubbed her neck. Nick stood up slowly, and Dana held his hand until he reached full height.

"Anybody need a water or something?"

"I do, young man. Too many whiskeys in a short window."

Nick presented her with a glass of water. "Simone, if it's okay, I have one more question right now. I saw some of the plans for the energy plant."

Simone scoffed. "Oh, that."

"It's truly brilliant. I mean, free energy is the dream! Why was it never built?"

"Because it's a lie," she said, laughing bitterly as she sipped her water. "It's not usable for providing free energy on a grand scale. The structures necessary to support a system that size, the energy *maintenance*, the energy to *transport* that energy—it's not realistic. If someone flipped the switch, it would do nothing or blow up. Either or."

He leaned back and rubbed his chin. "I thought for sure it would work."

"Nick, what if I told you I *can* get us to free energy, just not that way?" Simone surveyed the eager listeners fixated on her every word. "Let me demonstrate."

Simone dipped her finger into her glass of water and placed a large drop on the table. She spread the drop into a thin layer, then placed another drop next to it. She pointed at the two drops, side by side, then blew lightly across the tops of the drops until they moved close enough to combine into one larger blob.

"One single but bigger drop of water has been created from the two. Now, add a second drop again and . . ." She repeated the steps. "Another single drop is formed, this time a little bigger. And rinse and repeat, over and over."

Dana placed her finger into the glass and flicked a tiny spray of water at her mother's face. "Mom, is this the part where you draw a diagram of a flat earth?"

"I do practically live off the grid," Simone joked. She stood up and walked over to a black case on shelf, opening it up to reveal a battery about the size of a soda can. "Anyhow, using that theory, this is what I created. This one is a model; it doesn't work. It's meant for after a disaster when rescue workers need to power up dormant evacuation vehicles. For developing countries to dig wells so they can build hospitals. This battery can self-power into perpetuity. *But*," she emphasized, closing the case, "you can imagine what a free-energy battery cell that generates never-ending power could do if weaponized."

Nick had been listening intently, nodding along with his thumb on his chin in thought. "Simone, do you have the plans for this?"

"The only written plans were in New Jersey at the project bunker, which I assume were seized by the government if Rhodes didn't grab them first. But those were from very early on. Since then, everything has been hidden away in here," she said, tapping a fingertip on her temple. "It was only ten years ago I finished the math. Now, I know how to make it so the battery would never drain to zero. That's what your skates are capable of, Dana. Near-zero power erosion."

"Simone, we've got to get this all written down," Nick said.

"So, I probably shouldn't die anytime soon if I can help it, then."

Chapter 27

Sailing – Christopher Cross

Nick barely noticed as the hours ebbed from the early afternoon into the evening. Dana spent the time recounting to her mother the winding tale of her years at boarding school, the discovery of the plans for the skates, and her technical self-education to build them through trial and error. Simone periodically placed her hand on Dana's own as she listened to the account of Nick and Dana's adventure discovering the Atomic Juggernaut and the eventual showdown with One Hundred Roads and their victory. He enjoyed injecting polite corrections to the details as well as his own moments of technical prowess. Simone appeared impressed when he dove into the details of how he had improved Dana's skates, and he replied to her technical questions with pride. In return, she shared the clearly happy memories of Ashley learning to design her own mechanical wheels under her mother's tutelage.

When it came time for dinner, Simone prepared a hearty meal that made Nick long for a return trip home to see his dad. He missed New Jersey some days, but he knew for now he belonged here in New Mexico, with Dana. Steamed vegetables from Simone's garden overwhelmed the air with their sweetness. Pure delight radiated from Dana as her mother slipped easily into the role of a parent, correcting Dana's grammar and poking her to finish her plate and not waste food. The three women shared the quiet conspiracies of mothers and daughters from generations throughout time. Nick mostly was quiet, happy to bear witness and share in the infectious joy emanating from the reunited family.

After attending to the dishes so the women could continue to catch up, Nick stepped onto the back porch with what he swore to himself was his last beer of the day. The mountains in the distance bisected the red sun as long shadows stretched across the prairie, blanketing the barn and fences in stormy browns and blues. Ashley slid out the back door and stood next to him.

"Dick's here."

"Who?"

"Dick. Our horse. Mom named him after Dick Proenneke."

The stallion appeared on the edge of the patio, huffing once to announce his entrance. White and light-gray hairs added a brindle texture to his face, aging him beyond his muscular stance.

"That's an interesting name. He's a big fella."

"Yeah. Mr. Proenneke was a conservationist up in Alaska. He built an entire cabin by himself using only tools he *made* himself. Mom has used his books as templates for her life off the grid. I've read them all." She let Dick sniff her hand. "Interesting guy. The man, not the horse." Dick huffed. "Okay, I guess you too, fella."

Nick reached his hand out to the horse and felt his hot breath as he snorted in acceptance.

"So, are you and Dana going out?"

"What? No. No." He glanced over his shoulder and saw Dana and Simone chatting in front of a massive bookcase. Dana felt his gaze and waved. "We're best friends and roommates."

"I don't know. I think it's more than that. She's into you, from what I can tell."

"No," he scoffed, "she's not into me. She broke up with her girlfriend right before we met."

Ashley raised an eyebrow. "That doesn't mean anything. She *likes* you." In response, Nick took a long swig from his bottle and finished the contents. Ashley poked him in his ribs. "And Nick? I think you like her, too."

"What makes you think that?"

"Observational cues and evidence."

"Based on your own experience?"

Ashley glanced at her feet before jutting her chin at him. "Well, no. I can just see it, the way you two interact. When she looks at you, it's the way Mom looks when she talks about my dad . . . our dad." Her voice trailed off.

"We've been through a lot together," he said while therapeutically petting Dick's muzzle over and over. "She helped me get over someone. Helped me break out of my shell a little. And for that, I'm grateful to have her as a friend."

The patio door slid open. Dana stepped out to join them as Simone wandered around the living room holding the tablet and checking the camera feeds.

"Are you guys telling secrets?" Dana chimed in in her singsong way.

"Well, *sis*, we were just talking about you," Ashley said.

"I'm going inside to talk to your mom." Nick felt the blood rush to his cheeks and hoped Dana didn't notice.

"Well, don't get too comfortable. We should get going back home soon," Dana noted.

Nick closed the door behind him. Looking back over his shoulder, he saw the sisters poking each other in the ribs, clearly teasing each other. He smiled at the glow emitting from Dana. Turning back around, he cleared his throat as he approached Simone, careful not to startle her as she focused on the glowing tablet.

"Simone, I saw the solar panels on the barn. Did you wire those in independent circuits? They should be parallel or series circuits."

She smiled at his interest. "I did. It loses some power transfer through entropy, so it's less efficient, but it has a redundancy in that if one goes down, it won't affect the output from the others into the storage cells." She refocused on the girls on the back patio. "You're a clever boy. I can see why Dana likes you."

He slapped his hands on his face and huffed. "Is everyone here trying to ship us?"

"Hey, listen, it's alright. It's just kind of obvious." She sat the tablet down on its charger and gently laid her hand on his arm. "There's never enough time to properly enjoy the time we do have. I'll leave it at that."

At that point, the sisters retreated into the house and Dana began to pack up her skates. Nick interpreted this as his cue to get ready for the drive back home. Tomorrow, he had a lab day at the university, a check-in with Frank Irons in the evening, and a trip to the grocery store to fill their empty pantry. He was reflecting on their domestic situation when Dana bounded up to him.

"Ready, chief?"

"Yeah. Hey, Simone, what's the protocol when I come back to avoid being held at gunpoint and patted down?"

"Just give me a heads-up of at least an hour. Depending on the time of day, I may have to disarm the robot jackalopes."

"Very funny," Nick replied. "That is a joke, right?"

"Yes, I'm kidding. But I do need a heads-up. As you can understand, I don't take kindly to guests without warning, especially if I'm in the middle of an intense painting session. Ashley should know better."

"Understood."

"Nicky, ready?" Dana tugged on his arm after hugging her mother. Ashley widened her eyes at Nick.

"Yeah, I think I'm ready."

They walked out to the truck and heard the heavy front door close behind them. As they sat inside the pickup's cab, the outside lights on the house dimmed to a faint yellow haze. They drove down the dark dusty driveway in silence, each one of them smiling to themselves as the radio played in the background. Nick pulled onto the highway and aimed for home.

"Dana, I've got a funny feeling your mother isn't sharing something major. I can't put my finger on it."

"We're new to her, big guy. We gave her a big shock today. Give her time." Dana twisted and pulled her legs up onto the seat. "Everything and everyone is going to be just fine."

Chapter 28

Fascination Street – The Cure

The television in Lilly's apartment droned on in the background as she sat on her couch and scrolled aimlessly on her laptop, browsing roller-skating videos online. She tucked the edges of her robe under her thighs as she waited for her cup of mint tea to cool. At last, she dipped the decaffeinated bag three times before setting it on the saucer and taking a sip.

She had skipped roller derby practice, unsure how she would face Dana. She wished she had just handled things differently. *No . . . I wish the outcome was different.* She was staring at the array of nail holes in the wall, from paintings and pictures removed before she had become the tenant, when a rapping on the door startled her.

"One minute!" she called out.

She cinched her robe tightly and glided toward the door. Through the peephole, she spied a handsome man in jeans and a black button-down shirt flipping through a tiny notebook in his gloved hands.

"Hello, Miss Patel?" he asked loudly through the door. "My name is Ron Mexico, and I'm with the *Albuquerque Journal*. Do you have a minute?"

Lilly scratched her head and opened the door as far as the chain would permit. "That's me. Um . . . hi, I'm Lilly. Can I help you?"

"Yeah, I'm sorry to bother you so late, but I'm doing a piece on the derby scene in the area." He smiled as he smoothed his fingers over his thin moustache. "I've been told that you're a star member of the hot new roller derby team here, the Roswell Roses."

"Well, I'm not a star, but yes, I'm part of that team." She smiled back at him through the crack in the door.

"Got it, I see. If you're not *the* star, who is? The name 'Dana Jefferson' has, uh, come up in my investigation. Is she your roommate, by chance?"

Lilly gulped. "No, she's my *teammate*." Lilly eyed the man carefully and studied his appearance. *Why is he wearing gloves? It's certainly not cold enough.*

"Well, if she's the real star, I'd love to talk to her. Do you know where I can find her? I want to talk to you, too, of course. Trying to get some player profiles into the lifestyle section before Friday, so I'm on a tight deadline." He smiled with an open mouth. "You'd be a big help if you could just tell me where she lives."

Lilly flashed a weak smile. "I can give her address to you, I guess. I have all the girls' names and addresses, actually."

"Great. If you just let me in, I can get those and also ask you a few questions while I'm here."

Lilly stepped back from the door and drew the lapels of her robe close under her neck.

"You know what? I can email the addresses to you. It's kind of late." She peered over his shoulder to see if anyone was parked in the street waiting for him. He tilted his head into her line of sight.

"Yes, email the list. But can I have *her* address now? I can probably still stop by her house tonight."

"It's late," she repeated. "What paper did you say you were with?"

"*Albuquerque Times.*"

She swallowed hard. "I thought you said the *Journal*?"

The man's friendly demeanor quickly changed. He kicked in the door before Lilly could shut it, the chain exploding off the frame and smacking Lilly in the face. He stomped on her foot to pin her in place as he entered and punched her in the stomach. The impact forced the air from her lungs, muting her attempt to scream. His gloved hands clutched her throat as he forced her to the ground, slamming her next to her derby bag.

"It's not personal. It's just that I don't like to leave witnesses if they're not being helpful," he whispered. "And you're not being helpful, princess."

She gasped as he adjusted his grip. "Please, don't hurt me, please!"

"That's not your decision to make, sweetie!"

Lilly's head throbbed from the impact with the floor. Her hand scratched at the carpet and clawed toward her bag, one inch at a time. She could see the wheels of her skates peeking out the top of the unzipped main pouch. Another inch closer. Her neck throbbed and her arm burned as she tried to get closer to the skates. Her assailant laughed and nodded toward her bag.

"Oh, you're not going to get any help there." He extended his leg to kick at the bag, lifting some of his weight off his intended victim. Lilly took the opportunity to jam her knee into his groin and swipe the strap of her gym bag as he recoiled in pain. She swung the bag at his head, connecting the skates inside with his temple.

"You dumb bitch!" he howled, rearing back and clutching his eye socket.

Lilly sprang to her feet and grabbed her phone off the end table. She dialed 911 as she inventoried possible paths to the front door, but all of them required getting past him. She crouched into her skater's stance as she locked eyes with him. There was no use trying to get around him, and an operator had yet to answer her call.

Be brave, she told herself.

Lilly sprinted directly at him and jammed her shoulder into his chest as he drew his arms up. He fell back but righted himself after the impact, then lunged for her and caught the edge of her robe as she headed out the doorway; she let the sleeves slip off her arms. She tumbled forward as he pulled back hard, and suddenly she was free of her robe and on the porch. She ran into the street as he stumbled toward her with malice in his eyes under his bloodied brow.

"You should have just given me the address, princess!"

"Screw you!" she yelled back.

Suddenly, a blaring car horn and squealing tires diverted their attention. Lilly turned too late to see the car coming—her body was launched onto the hood and whipped back onto the pavement. The driver and passenger leapt out of the car, not noticing the man stepping back onto the porch.

"Shit," Brian whispered.

Lilly's phone rested in the grass next to the sidewalk, the screen still illuminated from the active call. Brian crept toward the phone and hung up on the 911 operator. The passenger stood over Lilly while the driver fumbled with his own phone. Brian glanced at the one in his hand, unlocked and able to be searched.

"Brian, you are a lucky dog."

He snuck down the alley next to Lilly's apartment building and thumbed through the apps until he found one for maps. He looked at recent locations. *Bingo, one in Alamogordo.* He clicked on the address and selected the satellite view, zooming in on the image of a simple rancher set back from the highway. The address was saved in Lilly's favorite places under two letters:

DJ.

"I think this trip may have been worth it after all." He looked back into the street and saw that the car's owners were still preoccupied with Lilly. Flashes of red and blue lights flickered off the building. Brian headed toward the back of the alley and out to a parking lot, where an idling pickup truck was waiting with Eugene behind the wheel.

"Nails, is this the part where you tell me I was right? That Dana doesn't live here?" he asked through the open window.

"No, but we know where she lives now," he said with a beaming smile as he presented his prize, Lilly's phone.

Chapter 29

Dirty Blvd. – Lou Reed

The dull thud as the hallway's double doors closed announced Dana's tardiness to practice. Her boots squeaked on the gymnasium floor of the Walt Whitman Community Center as she strolled over to the girls ending their pre-warmup skate. Kendra, standing apart from the group, frowned at Dana.

"Girls, bring it in!" Janice bellowed to the collection of athletes. The assembled skaters glided to the table where she sat with her hands folded, her lips pulled tight and flat. She scanned their faces as they stopped to create a semicircle around her.

"Sorry I'm late," Dana said. "Long story."

"It's okay," Janice replied. She cleared her throat and scanned the girls' faces, each looking inquisitive but at the same time bracing for some sort of bad news. "Ladies, there's no easy way to say this. I just got a call. Lilly was assaulted last night and hit by a car as she tried to escape." The silence was broken by gasps and sobs. "You're welcome to stay and freeskate, but this won't be a structured mandatory practice today." She covered her mouth with one hand and began to cry herself.

The pit of Dana's stomach gnawed at itself and tensed. Her hands shook and trembled. *This is not my fault*, she told herself. *This is not my fault.*

Her knees felt like they might buckle as fragments of thoughts swarmed and buzzed around in her head. Lilly trying to kiss her. Lilly running out of her house.

Dana needed answers. Her head snapped to attention.

"So, is she . . . alive?"

"I'm sorry, yes. I should have said that. She's stable. To be honest, I'm more worried about mental trauma once she's home."

A swollen chorus of sighs and tiny outbursts of tears continued to wash over the assembled team.

"Well, I know this sucks," Kendra interrupted flatly, "but does anybody know another skater? Hopefully with twenty or thirty more pounds on her than Lilly?"

Dana walked around the group and planted her feet as she squared her body with Kendra's.

"I don't think that's the appropriate reaction here, *Kendra*."

Dana's chest heaved. She tried to slow her breathing and her drumming pulse. Kendra cocked her head and wore a coy smile.

"I'm just being honest. Someone's got to keep focus on the team here. Don't get so uptight about it." With a flippant wave, she dismissed Dana. "Now get out of my face. Go grieve."

"You know, Kendra, I don't think you're a good presence on the team." Dana looked back to Janice for approval. The skaters had formed a circle around the conflict. "I think the best thing for the short term and long term is for *you* to go, Kendra." A quiet murmur bled from the crowd. Kendra pushed her face closer to Dana's unyielding scowl.

"I've carried this team. I put my heart into this," she growled, then looked around her at the rest of the team. "You're going to let the new girl call the shots because she's the shiny new thing? This is the problem I always run into with you selfish hotshot—"

Dana rammed her forearm under Kendra's jaw and pinned her by her throat against the nearest wall. Her teeth were clenched so hard that she felt a sting in her cheeks.

"You don't get to talk to me, or anyone, that way." She leaned in closer, her lips brushing the hair of Kendra's sideburns as she whispered into her ear. "And you are done selling drugs through Ashley. You don't talk to her. You don't answer any calls. If you see her, you cross the street. Because if you do talk to her again, I will call the police. And they will find you *severely* beaten and covered in *coyote piss.*"

She released the pressure on Kendra's throat and stepped back. Janice and the rest of the team stared at them, slack-jawed.

"We are a family here—that's what derby is. You're *not* family."

Kendra stood there utterly humiliated, rubbing her throat and glaring at Dana. She stomped out of the room, her footfalls echoing in the dead silence.

Dana pulled the keys to the pickup truck from her pocket. "Janice, I can't skate today. Can you give me the information for the hospital?"

"Understood, come back when you're ready. Here's the number for her hospital room." She handed Dana a piece of paper. "As for Kendra, we'll have to figure out how to do this all without her. And her finances."

"If I just jeopardized the team, I'm sorry."

"No, she had it coming. We'll figure it out somehow." She didn't sound convinced.

Dana turned to find the team looking as unsure as Janice. "Hey, I'm not the bad guy here for ripping out the tumor, okay?" A few girls walked away to pack their bags. "You'll see that. Janice, I'll be in touch."

She walked back out of the double doors with her head down.

Chapter 30

True Faith – New Order

The cashier at the Bighorn Mini-Mart sat slumped on the stool behind the register. He adjusted his red plastic name tag with MATTHEW printed in faded white letters while counting the packs of cigarettes in the display cabinet behind him. He found it annoying that he was too young to sell them without calling his manager. With a bored sigh, he leaned over to grab a month-old copy of *Hot Rods and Bikini Bods* from the spinning stand on the counter. The chime of rattling bells on the door indicated a customer had come in, but he didn't bother picking his eyes up from the periodical.

"Hey," Dana called out toward the cashier.

Matthew finally glanced up and promptly dropped the magazine with one look at Dana. "Oh, hey. Hi. You need anything, I'm your man." He crossed his arms and puffed his chest. His toothy smile drew the attention away from the handful of whiskers sprouting on his chin.

"I'll keep that in mind," she deadpanned. She headed toward the fridges at the back of the store and placed a finger on her wireless earbud. "Sorry, Nick. Go ahead."

"Dana," Nick buzzed in her earpiece, "you're telling me you threatened to have coyotes pee on her?"

"Not the best threat, I know," she replied as she flicked a fly off one of the glass doors. "But it was just, I don't know, my breaking point."

"I get it. But we have Ashley and Simone to worry about now. You can't just go off half-cocked on someone and end up with one more reason to look over your shoulder, you know?"

Dana grunted an affirmation. She was acting more like her ex, Angela the hothead, and not like the "rational one," as Angela had often called her. Of course, next to Nick, she felt like an aimless wrecking ball. She decided against a drink and instead eyed a box of donuts.

"You want donuts? I just want to sit and stew and eat garbage." She eyed the looming expiration date on the package. "I could eat this whole box. I'm getting two, Nicky."

Despite their well-stocked pantry, thanks to Nick's work at the reservation, the one item Dana found lacking was junk food. Nick never bought it. Back in New Jersey, she would frequent all the local bakeries and load up on regional snack favorites, but in New Mexico her sweet tooth was in a steady state of withdrawal. Sugar always made her feel better after she and Angela had suffered a frustrating derby loss. *I really should check in on her*, she mused, *after all this settles down.*

"You get what you need, Dee. I decided to finally sort out this kitchen utensil Pandora's box in the cabinet under the island." The earpiece hiccupped in her ear.

"Oh, I meant to get to that. I'll help you after I get home and call the hospital to check on Lilly."

She paused and felt the gaze of the cashier on her.

"Hey, creep, you keep drinking milk and going to parties in the woods with girls your own age. Plus, girls like me got baggage and issues."

Matthew froze and slunk back to his stool with his magazine.

"Sounds like you got a fan?" Nick chuckled.

"Yeah, this seems to be a thing out here. Too much space, too few people to look at."

She placed her acquired goodies on the counter. Her earpiece clicked and chirped again.

"Nick, can you hear me okay? My Bluetooth keeps crapping out."

"Yeah, the call's been a little wonky. Hold on a sec . . . someone's pulling up. Did you call the cable company about the crappy service you keep complaining about?"

"That would be the responsible thing to do, so no, it wasn't me." She laughed as she laid her cash on the counter and picked up the bag Matthew had filled. She bumped the door open with her hip on her way out. "I'm five minutes away."

"Dana . . ." Nick's voice trailed off. "They're here."

"Who?"

"One Hundred Roads."

Dana almost dropped the bag onto the pavement. "What?! Who exactly?"

"It's those two dopey twins, the ones from the airport in Jersey, and some other guy. Looks like a businessman jacked on coke. A discount-store Patrick Bateman."

Dana opened the truck door and flung the bag into the passenger's seat. Her backpack sat on the floor below. "Nick, get into the basement and lock the door with the bar. Start breaking shit! Computers, files, anything related to my dad's projects." She turned the key in the ignition, but nothing happened. "Shit, not now! Girls, it's go time!" she panicked, heaving her skates from the bag.

A loud crash erupted from her earpiece.

"I think they busted in the front door," Nick whispered. "I'm in the basement. I don't know if they know I'm here."

Dana had already secured each skate and shin guard and leapt from the truck's cab to the pavement, grabbing her knapsack and then slamming the door behind her. A burst of sparks skittered over the painted parking lines as she pushed off.

"Nick, I'll be right there."

Then silence. Just the crackling of the headset.

"Nick!"

"Dana, I'm here. There's a lot of noise upstairs—they must be raiding the house. Dana, I can hear them outside the basement door. It sounds like they're trying to peel the door of the hinge."

"Sixty seconds, Nick. Just hold on."

The skates clanged with a raging metallic thunder. Dana sprinted onto the two-lane roadway and hammered her toes into the accelerator pads. The pavement would've cried out in pain if it had the means, her furious strides gouging the blacktop as she outmaneuvered the thin traffic on the country road. Just ahead she spotted the side road that led to her house—*their* house.

"Hold on, Nick."

Chapter 31

Wait — White Lion

The house was finally in Dana's sight. On the driveway, a black jeep sat parked diagonally behind Nick's dirt bike. The double entry doors were splayed open, and Dana could see a lone figure moving inside, but it was too distant for her to ascertain any useful details. The driveway felt much longer than she ever recalled, curling through the edge of the arid mesa up to the front porch.

"Nick, I'm here!" she yelled into the earpiece, hoping he could still hear her.

She crouched as she got closer to the front porch steps and then launched herself over them, landing in the foyer in a cacophonic blast. At the edge of the kitchen, the twins turned in startled awe at her entrance. A well-built man with a wiry thin moustache glanced over his shoulder as he worked the hinges of the basement door with a large flat tactical knife.

"Eugene, take her out," he barked, refocusing on dismantling the door.

"I got this," one of the men responded. Dana recognized Eugene not by his name but by the 036 printed on his fatigue shirt. He reached into his shoulder holster for his semiautomatic pistol but Dana was already across the room, launching a heavy kick into his wrist and knocking the gun from his grip.

"Zeke, back me up!"

Dana spied the other twin—037, as his shirt proclaimed—with his pistol already aimed in her direction from across the kitchen.

Her heart beat faster. *Not now, not now!* she pleaded with herself. Her head filled with oxygen as time slowed around her.

"Nick, are you there?!"

A gunshot rang in Dana's ears. Instinct took over. She dropped into a tight ball as her wheels changed direction and swept her under the arc of the bullet. Her back hit the kitchen island, the open box of still unpacked utensils falling to the ground.

"I'm here!" he shouted back through the earpiece. "How many?"

"Three. I got this! Stay put!"

Dana stayed down behind the island for cover, searching the pile of kitchen tools next to her for something she could use. *Why do we have so damn many spatulas?!* Her fingers coiled around a black metal handle attached to a shining metal blade. Her lips curled into a sneer. She'd never been so happy to find a pizza cutter.

In one fluid motion, she spun on her knee around the corner of the kitchen island and slashed at Zeke's leg. He howled as he fell, clutching his thigh. Dana then twisted her attention to the athletic man with the moustache still working on the hinges with no success. Eugene had been on his hands and knees searching for his gun but gave up when he heard his brother's cries.

"I'll do without it," he grumbled as he pulled a jagged knife from his boot sheath. He beckoned Dana with his free hand. Her earpiece buzzed.

"Dana, the one by the basement is the boss. I heard them call him Brian."

"Not sure that helps now, but thanks for the info!"

Eugene glowered. "I'm gonna kill you slowly, girl."

"Didn't I kick your ass before?"

Dana looked above Eugene's head at the exposed beams. She charged across the laminate floor and leapt toward the joist between her and her adversary. Her fingers gripping the wood beam, she swung her right leg into the side of Eugene's head, then landed in a heap behind the couch.

Both of his men incapacitated, Brian gave up on his task. "Fine. I'll do this myself," he said coolly.

He turned his back to the impenetrable basement entrance and dug into his waistband for his pistol. Just then, the door flew open. Dana sat up in time to see Nick grab Brian's shirt collar and pull him back toward the stairs behind him. Before Brian could steady himself, Nick let go and Brian tumbled down. Nick slammed the door and looked around wildly. Without much thought, he clutched the refrigerator door handle and pulled the appliance toward the basement door, the contents erupting in a tidal wave of leftovers and half-filled plastic containers across the kitchen tiles. He stopped when it was close enough that Brian wouldn't be able to push open the door.

"Nick! Behind you!"

Zeke was lumbering around the kitchen island, clutching his leg wound. Dana pushed off from behind the couch, her skates taking her across the room in just seconds. She dove headfirst across the island's slick surface, crashing into Zeke and sending them both to the floor.

"Dana, move!" Nick had liberated a drawer from the main countertop and swung it at the twin's face, striking him flatly and knocking him out.

A low groan oozed from the other side of the couch. Eugene staggered to his feet and flashed a blood-soaked smile. He spat a pair of teeth onto the floor and held his gun up in the air.

"Look what I found."

Dana took one step forward, partially blocking Nick from the line of fire. "You know that's a gas stove behind us?" she panted. As Eugene stepped closer, she moved one of her legs in front of the other, toes pointed down, and shifted her weight to the back leg.

"Not sure if I care if we all go up in flames." Eugene lowered the gun and aimed.

Dana rocketed off her back leg and leapt with spinning wheels across the kitchen. Eugene raised his arms to brace for the impact, catching the full force of her body. She landed on top of him and landed a single punch to his nose.

"It's an electric stove, idiot. We're in the desert." She swung again, slamming her other fist into his cheek.

Her home had been torn apart. The few mementos of the life she had once had here with her family were now covered in blood and errant bullet holes. All the plans and files in the basement were no longer secure. Most importantly, she and Nick were safe no more.

She swung again, missing and hitting his collarbone.

"Dana!" Nick grabbed her arm mid-punch and held it.

"I HATE YOU!" she screamed into Eugene's face, not realizing he was unconscious from the last blow she'd landed. She broke free from Nick's grip and slammed one more fist into Eugene's face. "I hate you," she sobbed, her voice trailing off.

Nick pulled her off Eugene and pinned her in his arms. He glanced around at the remnants of mayhem. "Dana, we have to go."

She stared at the thug on the floor near her feet. Blood matted his beard, and his chest moved up and down slowly. Suddenly, a lump inside the front pocket of his shirt writhed behind the cloth. She pulled the vibrating phone out slowly. The color from her face drained as she noted the dozen or so unanswered calls on the display.

"Nick, they're coming."

Through the open double doors, Nick could see a serpentine cloud of dust rising from the road in the distance. Two large black Hummers emerged from the haze.

"Dana, they're here."

Chapter 32

Dig On This – Bedlight for Blue Eyes

L et's go!"

Dana shoved Eugene's phone into her pocket and pushed off, sailing through the open front doors. Nick was on her heels, his eyes looking instinctively for his pickup.

"Dana, my truck?! Where the heck is it?"

"I had to leave it behind! You're right, we should have used this to buy a new one." In her hand was the black credit card Joshua had given her. She pressed it into Nick's palm, along with the card from Joshua. "Get on your dirt bike, go over the hill, and pick up the road to the airport. Use the credit card and get on the first flight out of here to anywhere. There's nowhere safe for you to hide out right now." She gritted her teeth, scraping her plan together bit by bit. "I'll go to my mom's ranch."

"There's got to be another option! What about this?" He flung open the jeep's passenger door and ripped open the glovebox, tore down the visors, and ran his hands under the seats. Nick lifted a closed laptop from the passenger side and felt the seat seams underneath.

"No keys!" he shouted back to her.

"Nick, there's no time!" She ripped him from the interior as he clutched the computer to his chest. "GO!"

"But Dana . . ."

The mammoth diesel engines of the Hummers roared as they clipped the corner of the final turn toward the house.

"Nick . . ." Dana grabbed his shirt and wrapped the cloth around her knuckles. Her hands were bloodied and sore from wailing on Eugene, and fear and panic ebbed through her body. She wished for one moment for the right thing to say, what words to leave with Nick in case this was the last time they saw each other.

The edges of her vision darkened with panic.

She had to stop the fear.

She had to fight the paralysis. *I don't know what to do.*

Nick pressed his lips against hers.

She kissed him back.

She released her grip on his shirt.

"I just needed you to know," he said as his eyes welled. Turning away, he sprinted to his bike and revved the engine as it lurched across the driveway toward the backyard, the laptop still cradled under his arm.

"Go," she whispered. Dana whipped her head back to the drive. The lead Hummer drifted into the final straightaway as Dana dropped into a sprinter's block stance and then surged. Her thighs transformed into massive pistons as the skates accelerated with their internal engines and her locomotion. Each wheel squealed and sparked as she closed the gap between herself and the enemy. The faces of the driver and passenger in the first truck came into focus.

Olsen, Dana thought as she recognized the driver. A woman sat next to him in the passenger's seat.

The Hummer roared as the duelists moved headlong toward each other.

Dana sprung forward, up and over Olsen's oncoming hood. Her trailing skate caught the edge of the roof rack, which she used to propel herself over the second Hummer's roof in a flailing somersault, her legs attempting to run in midair. Her skates found the pavement as she clumsily landed and righted herself. The skidding screams of the vehicles now behind her ripped through her ears as she veered onto the country road past her mailbox.

Run, girl, run!

The words splintered the fear inside her mind. Each stride, each footfall, each breath synchronized. Her body responded automatically to the machine commands from her brain, her skates an extension of her very anatomy. The wheels turned with the flow of her blood. A muscle twitch and lean to the left adjusted her velocity so she could make the turn onto the main highway without decelerating. She was no longer a pilot or a driver; she was one with her machines, and the remaining shards of fear burned away.

She saw the sign for the upcoming entrance to the interstate. A glance over her shoulder revealed the Hummers finally swerving onto the deserted lanes behind her, but she held the advantage. *They can't catch me*, she thought, *until I wear out*.

In a low crouch, Dana swerved up the interstate entrance ramp and across the multilane highway. The road ahead lay barren with no traffic to hide behind or manipulate to her advantage. The only object of any note was a rise in the road about a mile ahead as the interstate crossed over a two-lane state highway running east and west. Below the overpass, she spied a lone tractor trailer approaching from the west. Her skates emitted a low undulating vibrato as she adjusted her speed to slow down. Another check behind her confirmed the two Hummers were entering the highway.

The two vehicles accelerated, Olsen's vehicle in the lead. She stopped at the apex of the crossover and stepped over the rail, then looked back at her pursuers.

This might hurt, but so would a bullet to the head or a bumper to the torso.

Dana made one final assessment as the truck approached and, before she could second-guess herself, stepped off the overpass. As she crashed onto the top of the tractor trailer, she heard gunshots, at least one sounding like it had ricocheted off the railing where she had just been standing. She lay on her stomach, pressing herself flat against the cargo container, and looked behind her. She saw the woman with Olsen leaning out the Hummer's window, a rifle on the sideview mirror. The curses she yelled rang audibly but incoherently as the Hummer crossed the overpass and Dana lay on the truck's trailer, heading east.

Dana looked back again and saw the Hummers rumbling down the embankment just past the overpass. She surveyed a slight bend in the road ahead and an oncoming truck traveling in the other direction.

"Crazy Dana, this is Sane Dana," she hissed to herself. "You are *not* going to do this."

The two combatants closed in. The dark stink of diesel exhaust washed over her.

White noise flooded her ears.

The edges of her eyes glowed until her peripheral vision narrowed. "Oh, Crazy Dana is going to do this, alright."

As the truck beneath her rounded the bend, Dana crouched into position. Again, her body's automated instincts acted before her mind could talk her out of it, and she leapt from the trailer to the roof of a passing cargo container in the westbound lane. She landed on the metal roof with excessive force, almost sliding off, her hands and feet clawing for any seam or rivet for friction to slow her from slipping over the edge. She squirmed back to the center of the roof, her ribcage once again pressed against the metal as flat as possible. The whistling wind rushed over her and the smokestack exhaust plugged her nostrils, but mercifully the drumming of the Hummer engines rapidly grew and faded as they passed her in the opposite lane, oblivious to her daredevil leap.

She lifted her head and glanced at the road behind her. Her heart pounded furiously as the pair of black vehicles disappeared eastbound down the interstate, pursuing her former chariot. Dana allowed herself a moment to smile and close her eyes before she rolled onto her back and stared at the sky and clouds passing above. *Just breathe.*

A white passenger jet bisected her view as it climbed steadily into the clouds, its contrails expanding and fading against the blue. The boil of adrenaline faded as the cool wind blew over her.

She pressed her earpiece and hoped Nick would pick up. It went to voice mail. She waited for the beep and simply said, "Nick, I know."

Dana hit her earpiece again to end the call, then closed her eyes and let the vibration of the cargo truck rock her to sleep.

Chapter 33

Konstantine – Something Corporate

Dana opened her eyes to see blues and purples draped over the evening sky, tattered with only the boldest stars that could outshine the setting sun. She counted twelve of the brightest stars in her line of sight as trailer under her back vibrated with the idling engine of the rig, but it took her a moment to realize it wasn't moving. She sat up carefully on her elbows and saw in front of her an immense sign high atop two sky-scraping poles for a twenty-four-hour truck stop. The driver must have pulled in for a break. She took her chance and rolled over, crawling carefully toward the edge of the cab and down the ladder to the parking lot.

Her body ached and her legs burned, but the hurricane in her mind dominated her pain receptors. She was hopefully still somewhere in New Mexico, but she was definitely on the run. Her new status as a sister and daughter weighed heavily on her heart as she rubbed her face, pressing the details of the past few days into her filthy skin. Her father's work, which had turned out to be as much her mother's, lay exposed in the house. Her mother was alive and trapped in a fortress of her own creation. Her sister was ferrying drugs just to find a way out. Lilly lay in a hospital recovering from a vicious attack because of her.

And Nick? Nick was carrying growing feelings she hadn't realized she had nurtured, feelings that were perhaps inside herself as well. *Nick had kissed her*, and now he was out there alone somewhere also on the run.

She sat down on a curb and unlatched her skates, pulling her sore feet out one at a time. Her left big toe waved through a hole in her sock, looking more purple than brown in the artificial light. The mega-sized truck stop beckoned to her with its food court and mini-mall where she could find surely sustenance and maybe some shoes. She had left her boots in the truck when she hurried off to save Nick, but thankfully she still had her backpack. She found some crumpled bills in the outer compartment.

"Clothing?" she asked the clerk behind the counter once inside. He looked at her a little strangely, looking down at the socks on her feet, but pointed to a back corner. She walked carefully to avoid the random puddles from spilled drinks, oil drops, and who knows what else.

She placed a six-pack of striped knee-high socks and a three-pack of underwear into the crook of her arm and chose a pair of blue slip-on casual sneakers. She set the items on the counter along with a protein bar and bottle of cola. The cashier rung up the order and smiled.

"Forty-two thirty-five."

Her hand unfolded to reveal a twenty, a ten, a five, and two ones.

"I'm sorry. Can I put back the underwear?"

"I got it, miss," whispered a low female voice behind her. A middle-aged woman wearing a large headset around her neck and a dirty yellow work shirt slapped a hundred-dollar bill on the counter. "We lady truckers stick together. You ring all that through with my stuff."

"Thank you, ma'am."

Dana walked out, her head hung low, next to her benefactor.

"Listen, I know you're not a driver, but you don't strike me as a prostitute either," the woman said, "but I reckon you're a lost lamb that wandered into the coop here. And lambs shouldn't hang out with roosters."

"I guess you could say that," Dana replied. "I've had a rough couple of days."

"Out here, it's just me and Big Joe." The woman pointed to a white flat-faced Freightliner with a light-blue stripe across the door. "He's the only partner I'll ever need. Do you have a Big Joe?"

Dana shook her head. "I've got a Laverne and a Shirley." The woman's eyebrows went up. "But not much else right now. Speaking of, please take this." She offered her the cash she didn't get to use inside.

"Just take a deep breath, sister. You keep that money and hitch a ride or get a bus ticket to the next town. You should be able to get to Vaughn from here. I'd take you myself, but me and Big Joe have to keep moving on." She playfully slapped the truck's fender. "Just take a moment to breathe and enjoy the road. You never know where the pavement ends."

She waved over her shoulder and disappeared around the cabin of her truck. Dana watched Big Joe rattle to life and roll out, then pull away. She lifted a dirty hand to wave goodbye, cringing with the effort. She sat down on the curb and put on a new pair of socks and the sneakers, placing everything else into her bag with Laverne and Shirley.

She took a bite of the protein bar and a swig of soda, then pulled her phone from her jacket pocket. The display showed three missed calls from an unknown number in the last half hour. As she stared at the illuminated screen, the number rang again.

"Hello?" she answered, her voice dry.

"Dana, it's Nick. Oh my God, I've been trying to call you. Where are you? Are you okay?"

"Nick! Where are you?" She coughed wildly. "Sorry, I still have road dust in my throat."

"I think I'm in Minneapolis? I'm on a burner phone I bought near the airport."

Dana felt happy tears stream down her cheeks as her heart burst. He was safe. "Nick, what the hell are we going to do? I'm at a truck stop near Vaughn. I guess I'll get to my mom's somehow."

"Dana, it's not all bad news. I still have the contents from the laptop from the jeep. I nearly crushed it holding it under my arm until I got to the airport. I knew I couldn't bring it with me to make sure they couldn't track it, so I found an electronics store first and bought a second laptop and a portable hard drive with Joshua's credit card, and I copied over the files before dumping it. The original owner had the password saved to the laptop, so I just got right on."

"You just dumped a heck of a lot of details, buddy. Wait. Original owner? Not One Hundred Roads?" Dana scratched her head, entangling her finger in one of the new knots of hair.

"Right. I don't think it was *their* laptop. I think they stole it—the desktop photo is of some guy on vacation with his family. But it's got all these train schedules, including a shipping manifest for one of the trains. And then there are some blueprints for high-tech military stuff. *Batteries.* Something your dad—or mom—might have worked on."

Dana paused as a pair of truck drivers strode by and nodded at her. She smiled politely to not arouse suspicion.

"Give me a minute . . . my head's still not firing on all cylinders. *Batteries?*"

"There's a power cell and some type of guidance component. Like the one your mom showed us."

"You could tell it was a match just by looking at the blueprints?"

"They were labeled pretty clearly. And here's the most helpful part: I was looking over the train schedules. One of the trains runs through the corner of the Mescalero reservation. The train containing the high-tech parts." Nick paused for dramatic effect.

Dana sipped her drink and scanned the parking lot for anything that could be labeled a threat. She counted the number of trucks and watched the main entrance between two large illuminated arrows. Gnats swarmed around the glowing markers.

"Dana?"

"I'm thinking. Okay . . . let me call mom and Ash. I'll touch base when I get there and we can figure out what all this means. Where are you going next?"

"So, the next flight I could catch is to Memphis. And only first-class was available, but it's on the government's dime, so I figured why not? Then maybe a bus back to Jersey. I'm paranoid someone is tailing me, so I'm trying to break up my travels."

She laughed. "You are such a clever boy. Clever boy."

"Thanks. I'm going to get into preboarding in a couple minutes."

"Gotcha." She bit her lip and shook her dusty, dirty raven locks. A tiny piece of asphalt fell out of her nest of hair. "So, do you want to talk about that thing that happened right before you left?"

"Uh, maybe not in the middle of an airport or while you're wherever you are hiding from psychotic paramilitary forces."

"Ok, well. Well. I just wanted to say—"

A horn blast from a truck thundered over her voice.

"Dana? I didn't get that."

"Just . . . have a good flight. And stay safe. I need you alive, okay?"

"You, too."

The phone clicked in Dana's ear as Nick hung up. She rested her chin on the heel of her palm and watched two truckers having an argument over a parking space. She silently thanked whoever had blasted the truck horn from keeping her from saying something poorly worded to Nick. Across the pavement just beyond the lights, a small dark form, much smaller than a dog or cat, darted out of the shadows.

A roadrunner.

The bird cocked its head. It glanced left and right, its feathers shimmering in the edges of mercury-vapor light rays as it flexed its wings. The roadrunner then titled its head again and seemed to look directly at Dana. Silently, it turned back to the brush and sprinted away into the shadows of the field.

Dana opened her phone and dialed Ashley.

"Hey *sis*, think you can talk Mom into letting you use the car?"

"What's up, *sis*?"

"I need a ride from Vaughn. And tell her to consider this my one-hour notice that I'm coming over, maybe for a couple of days. Nick's flown the coop. We kind of stepped into a giant pile of shit."

"Like that nurse after your camping trip?"

"Jeez . . ."

"I told you I was filing that away for later."

Chapter 34

Into the Dark – The Juliana Theory

F light 927 now departing for Dallas."

Nick ignored the latest announcement from the tinny airport speakers and flopped onto a couch in the first-class lounge. He placed his shopping bag containing his new laptop between his shins. He had no other luggage to speak of, which he hoped wouldn't arouse suspicions. The ostentatious wall art and modern furniture was in stark contrast to the homey feel of his house in New Jersey, and the minimalistic décor in the rancher in New Mexico.

He expected to see more middle-aged men in tailored suits as his traveling cohorts, but instead found the lounge comprised of families with children in white pants and pink polo shirts and young women in large sunglasses that covered half of their faces. A group of older men sat nearby, wearing golf attire that definitely cost more than Nick's jeans from the warehouse club and his plaid shirt bought on clearance at a sporting goods store near Roswell. He politely declined a drink from the waitress, a middle-aged woman with large hoop earrings who reeked of strong perfume.

As she walked away, a man in a blue suit sat on the couch next to Nick.

His hair was black and neat. He made no eye contact with Nick, instead looking out the window onto the tarmac at the taxiing carriers. Nick spied the handle of a gun poking out from under the man's armpit in a shoulder holster. He assumed he was an air marshal, perhaps, but made no acknowledgement.

"Sir?"

Nick realized the man was addressing him, although still not looking at him.

"Yes?"

"My name is Dan Sun. Please do not make another sound. Do not look at me. When I get up, please wait a few seconds and then follow me to the door next to the courtesy desk. Please remain calm. You're not in any danger or in any trouble."

Nick didn't wait to hear more. He stood quickly, tucked his bag under his arm, and walked in the opposite direction of the desk. The man was up and right behind him.

"Sir, please come with me," he whispered again with urgency.

A family rolled their carry-on bags in a caravan heading into the lounge. Nick increased his pace and leapt over the children's bags, sprinting out of the frosted glass vestibule and into the terminal. Two men in black windbreakers and tactical boots walked purposefully toward him. He spun around and spied a large pack of passengers exiting from the closest arrival gate.

"Sir," Dan called behind him.

Nick dove into the mob of people and shoved his way through the passengers. He targeted the escalator under a sign that read BAGGAGE CLAIM. He leapt down the first five steps and then slid down the handrail. The clatter of boots from his pursuers grew louder behind him. As he crossed the landing at the bottom of the escalator, Dan overtook him and wrapped him in a firm bear hug.

"Easy, buddy, we're the good guys," Dan calmly stated as another slapped a black baseball cap on Nick's head. The other man presented a gray sweatshirt.

"Put this on, please."

A fourth man waltzed up to their cluster and extended his hand. He wore a blue-striped dress shirt and khaki pants as generic as his short dark haircut.

"Joshua Green. Homeland Security CTAF. We need to get you out of sight now. Let's slip in here."

He gestured toward a door marked for authorized personnel and flashed his badge at the airport security officer. They all filed in, the last man shutting the door behind him.

"Joshua, what the hell is going on?"

"Nick, long time no see, right? Very relieved! I'm guessing you were the one who booked those flights using Dana's black card?"

"Um, yes. Wasn't it for emergencies?" Nick asked, brow furrowed.

"It was. And once the purchase of the airline tickets hit in New Mexico, that pinged our notification system. The airport cameras showed someone who *wasn't* Dana at the point of purchase, so we assembled to apprehend whoever was using the card. Sorry I didn't recognize you from the footage. Couldn't get a clear view of your face."

"No problem," Nick replied. Dan looked at his phone and nodded to Joshua.

"Car's pulling up. Let's boogie."

Boogie? Nick thought. *Is this how federal agents normally talk?*

The pack of men burst through the door back into the baggage claim and hustled Nick outside just as a pair of black vans pulled up, one jumping the curb. The airport staff were, not surprisingly, disaffected by the haphazard parking job. Joshua and Dan boarded the first van with Nick, and as soon as the door shut, it rolled back into the airport traffic.

"So, Nick, fill me in."

"Well, there's a lot of bad stuff going on right now. We got ambushed at the house in New Mexico by some guys from One Hundred Roads."

"What about Dana? Where is she? Is she safe?"

"I just spoke with her. She's good," Nick said. He bit his lip and reeled in his disclosures. "She's fine. She was trying to get to her mom's house. That place is pretty secure."

"And where is that?" Dan asked.

"I wish I could tell you. Honestly, she doesn't know exactly where, either."

Joshua checked on the driver as the van barreled onto the highway. The driver nodded once.

"Is that a positive scenario?"

"I think it is. I'm sorry, but weren't you with the GAO or one of the budget offices? I thought that's what you said when you gave all that stuff to Dana and visited me in the hospital after . . ."

"After the fight with the big, giant stolen robot? Yes. I got a promotion." Joshua slapped Nick on the knee. "Thanks to you guys! Well, it was more of a transfer and commendation type of thing. I'm with Homeland Security now, or under them." He unfolded his wallet so Nick could inspect his ID card and badge. "Counterterrorism Accounting Force, CTAF. I had to go to a special retraining through Quantico and everything!"

My God, this guy, Nick thought to himself. He used his foot to slide his bag farther under his seat in the van.

"Besides the plane tickets, we saw you purchased a laptop, hard drives, and a couple of cables at the PC Barn." He pointed under Nick. "Guessing that's what's in there?"

"Yeah. I swiped their laptop and copied all files to the hard drives before dumping it."

Dan smiled and took off his jacket. His shirt sleeves stretched over his large biceps. "You want a job with us when we're done?" he asked with a smirk.

Joshua ignored his colleague. "We have to find Dana, get you into a secure location, and then crack open those files."

Nick's gut said this was the best scenario, getting the feds to help, but his brain warned him to tread carefully, and his heart told him to do whatever was best for Dana.

"I'm going to be blunt here. Joshua, Dan, I need to check in with Dana before I tell you where she is, and unless you have a warrant or something, aren't the hard drives mine?"

"Technically, everything you bought belongs to the federal government since it was bought with our charge card," Josh said. "But I get where you're coming from. Okay. Let's do this: We're going to make sure everyone trusts everyone and is on the level. Look out the front window. If you see a hotel you like, we pull over and you check in. That way you know you have a private room that we couldn't set up in advance. However, we will post a rotating guard to keep you secure. You don't leave unless it's with Dan or myself."

"That one." Nick immediately chose an executive luxury suite hotel coming up on the right. "Right now." He hoped the immediacy of his selection would keep them on their toes. As much as he wanted to trust Joshua, he had to stay frosty, keep churning ideas, and buy Dana enough time to get herself, Ashley, and Simone safe and up to speed.

"Done. You want food? They have these great cheese-stuffed burgers here in town."

"Two, with fries. And a new pair of jeans and a shirt."

The van rolled into the parking lot of the hotel and stopped under the entrance awning. Joshua gave Nick's shoulder a gentle pat.

"You're good, I promise. We got this. Let's check in you in. You look like you could use a shower."

Chapter 35

The Bomber – The James Gang

Let me get this straight. You let yourself get tossed down a flight of stairs, these two clowns got their asses whooped and one of their phones lifted, *and* they managed to steal the laptop?"

Olsen paced as best as he could on his canes, wobbling with a menacing ferocity across the hangar. His legs ached more from driving the Hummer than from his lingering injury. He huffed as he reached the far wall and turned around to glower at Brian and the twins.

"She was fast," Brian tried to explain, "and he was stronger than he looked."

Olsen stomped one of his canes on the ground. "That's not the bloody point!" he hissed, his accent biting more sharply through the syllables than usual. "Unbelievable."

"Listen," Brian pleaded, "this wasn't like us mowing down those kids in Indonesia—"

Olsen whipped a stern finger to Brian's lips to shush him. "Indonesia was a mistake. A miscommunication. A complicated mess. *This* was a simple operation. This was supposed to be a milk run, mate."

"She surprised us! I've never seen anything like those skates." Brian gestured with an open palm. "I'm sorry, I know I let you down. This is on me."

"We did get *something*," said Eugene as he adjusted the sling holding his arm in place. "We at least got what we could in the basement. Although the guy sabotaged quite a bit of it while Mister Moustache here was trying to finish his lockpicking internship." He fumbled in his pocket for a piece of new wadding for his mouth. "I'm the one who lost *two* teeth."

"Hey, that was a reinforced bunker door. Could you have done better?"

"You're the big-deal tracker!" Eugene countered "But apparently, you only got the job because you two were buddies in the bushes back in the day."

Brian stomped over to him and shoved a finger in his face.

"You two got your asses handed to you by Roller Girl. Apparently for the second time!"

"ENOUGH!" bellowed Olsen. "That's enough." If there was one thing he had left to steady the team, it was his air of authority. Nina emerged from the shelves of supplies that had been categorized and assembled over the past several days: gasoline containers, ammunition pots, propane tanks, and a dozen other types of explosive and illegal materials to support an arsonist's workshop.

"We're fine," she cooed. "We have the copies of all the files from the laptop. We can still intercept the train and grab the assets."

"That's not the point," Olsen said. "Who knows who has access to the laptop now? And Dana Jefferson is still at large!" He swung his cane and pointed it at Eugene. "That idiot's phone isn't even traceable. The only way we could leverage it now would be to call her on it and ask, 'Hello, love, want to get together for a pint or two?' Christ!"

He guided himself into a folding chair and dropped his crutches angrily to the floor. He fumed, thinking of the planning, the time, the hours, all the risks they'd taken, and now they were potentially exposed. The crown of leadership seemed to be slipping further off his head. "Everyone just get out. Except you, Nina."

Brian and the rest of the assembled crew slunk into the far corners of the hangar. A smaller group of men that had been watching the confrontation left together out the side door. Olsen ran his hands over his face.

"Nina, I'm not sure I'm the right man for this job. I'm just barely able to make sense of the plans your father left. I know he's a better strategist than I am, but I'm missing something, or the pieces aren't fitting together." He expelled a dramatic sigh. "I have no real idea why we're actually trying to get the palladium mining rights, truth be told." The thought of burning the reservation as a last resort soured in his mind.

Nina waved him off. "Perhaps he expected you just to keep the ball in play, rather than score the touchdown."

This certainly didn't instill confidence. He leaned over to retrieve his canes and struggled to his feet. He walked over to a large shipping crate and pulled the lid off with a concentrated effort. Inside, the large metal husk lay on its back, with four holes where limbs would attach to the body. Olsen leaned over and ran his fingers over the seams. He was aware of Nina standing behind him, craning her neck to watch his movements.

"The infamous Atomic Juggernaut," she trumpeted.

"The Atomic Juggernaut . . . or what's left of it. Or, rather, what's left of the one we salvaged from that barn." *Stole*, he admitted to himself.

The device. The machine. The thing that had taken his mobility away. The juggernaut prototype obtained from Hardy Farms lay in pieces inside the shipping crate built around it. The atomic power source had been removed, most likely years ago, leaving only a cavity that would hopefully accommodate the new battery and guidance system. Olsen placed his fist inside the opening, imagining the power surging through his arm and powering his dulled legs.

He wondered if the second juggernaut now resided somewhere in a government warehouse, or if it had been destroyed and auctioned off for scrap to make file cabinets for the IRS. *Is this the best I can do to protect this country? Collect the curios and rubbish to build a snare and lie in wait for our enemies?* He frowned. He knew he could do better. False flags and black ops were Rhodes's way of doing business; he had just been his hired gun. Now that he had some power and authority, he could dream a little bigger. *Dream a little different.*

"We *are* going to get the components—the power cell and the guidance module."

Nina flipped through her laptop and opened a file. "Yes, we will. Finding that train schedule was serendipity. We'll get everything done in one shot, and then we'll have some clarity on the next priorities."

"Nina, get in touch with our contact at the supply depot. I think we need to change some dates." He opened his own phone and ran his shaking thumb over the Kevlar impact-resistant case, purchased after dropping his phone one too many times as he attempted to direct his broken hands. He scrolled through the call history and stopped at a frequently called number.

"What dates?" She leaned over his phone. Her musk of leather and oil filled his nostrils. "Are we going somewhere?"

"We're not going anywhere, but I want the juggernaut out of here and on the way to our manufacturer as soon as we liberate what we need from that train." His fingers twitched as he worked through his call history.

"Olsen," she said soothingly, "let me call Silver. He gave me these." She presented her ungloved hands, skinned with metal rings that quietly clicked and whirred as she rotated her wrists. "He can fix your back. Your legs." She traced a metallic finger down his forearm. "He can fix everything."

Olsen pushed her away.

"No," he scolded her. "I'm not getting in debt to anyone else, especially someone powerful enough to push *your* father around. We do not need to get anyone else involved."

"I don't owe Silver anything for getting my limbs back."

"No, but your father does, and that led to some compromised allegiances, Nina."

"Fine, suit yourself," she said coolly, turning on her heel before he could respond. The echoes of her steely footfalls faded as she walked out the hangar doors. Olsen leaned on his canes and stared at the juggernaut's damaged carcass.

"Damn you, Dana Jefferson."

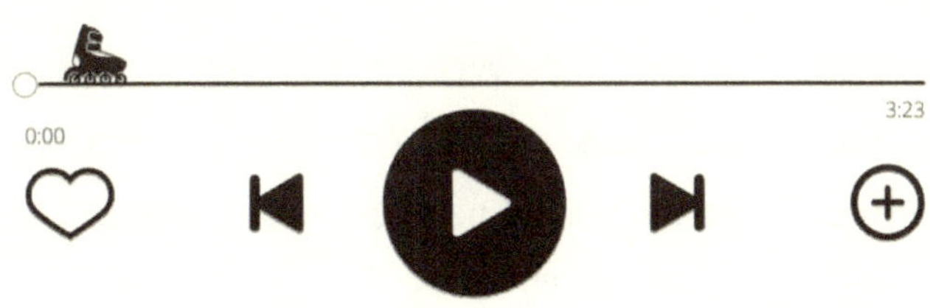

Chapter 36

Mother Mother – Tracy Bonham

Dana pushed her fork through the remains of her scrambled eggs and sweet potato hash browns. Her mom was a better cook than Nick, although he was still quite formidable with a stocked pantry and full refrigerator. She scraped the final pieces onto her fork and savored the warm, peppery flavor. Her mother's stare burned a path across the table, forcing Dana to look up.

"Dana, they did *what?*"

"I told you, they ambushed the house but got their asses kicked. Nick and I outran them, and he got on a plane and I woke up at a truck stop."

Simone pointed the spoon from her oatmeal at her daughter.

"So, they have all the files and plans now?"

"Well, no, Mom. I don't think so."

"You don't *think* so, sweetie? Do they, or don't they?" Simone's agitation escalated.

"Ok, then I don't know, *Mom*. Nick said he wiped the computers in the basement as best as he could and destroyed the model. I also took one of their phones, although not really on purpose. It's dead now, but maybe we can get something from that."

"The moment we turn it on, they'll know exactly where we are!"

Ashley, seated between the two, gingerly wrapped her fingers around the handle of the glass pitcher at the center of the table. "*Would you like some more juice, Ashley?* Yes, I think I would. *There you go.* Oh, thank you." She filled her glass and held the pitcher between mother and daughter. "Do we need a whiteboard or something?"

"Or something," muttered Simone. She stood up from the table and marched to the mantel in the living room. She grabbed the lever-action rifle from its stand and slung the strap across her shoulder.

"Mom, where are you going?" Dana didn't know the proper reaction to her mother grabbing a gun.

"I'll just get the dishes, then," Ashley monotoned to the kitchen table.

Simone stopped beside the couch, her arms tensed up to her shoulders. Dana noted that the woman in the middle of the room, although still her mother, was a changed version forged by nightmares and darkness. She was always aware—and made sure her daughters were, too—of the shadows surrounding them.

"So, Dana, you're telling me these guys, Rhodes's crew, almost caught you? And we don't know for sure what they pulled from the house?" She kicked at the side of the couch. Dana thought she was just taking out her anger but then a recessed latch clicked under the fabric, followed by a spring-loaded drawer expanding out. Simone pulled out a tall but thin rectangular backpack and a thin camouflage poncho. Ashley dropped the dishes into the sink loudly.

"Mom, another lockdown?"

"You bet your ass, Ash," she replied. "Dana, you two are *staying put*. That's the short version. Supporting details? I'm taking Dick and we're going to a cache of supplies I have buried out on the mesa. It's one day out by horseback, but maybe two days back given the weight and poor Dick's age. I'll have to run parallel to the creek so he can get water on demand."

"Wait," Dana said, "we're grounded?" Her mother's glare told her the answer.

"That would be an oversimplification, but yes. This is for your safety." Simone reached into a kitchen drawer, produced a revolver and its holster, and strapped the latter to her thigh. Dana noticed the pearl handle of the gun engraved with the outline of the state of Alaska.

"Is that a novelty lighter shaped like an antique gun or the real thing?"

"It's the real deal." Simone turned and wrapped her arms around Dana in a tight bear hug.

"Manic much, Mom?"

"Dana, Star, you think you know how bad these people are, but you don't know the half of it. They're not just killers—*they are monsters*. I need you to keep Ash in line, and vice versa." She released her grip and steadied her gaze at her elder daughter. "I literally just got you back into my life, and these people are the biggest threat to separating us again. I will *not* let that happen."

She kissed her on the forehead, the smell of clean soap and lilac enveloping the two of them. Simone turned to Ashley and repeated the ritual.

"Ashley, I know we made an exception with driving when you picked up Dana, but you are still not licensed. No running into town. You are both here for the next three days." She clipped her backpack's last buckles and straps and nodded at each girl. "I love you both . . . Phoenix. Star."

Simone jogged to the barn, where Dick obediently awaited her. Seemingly without words or even hand signals, the horse followed her lead and knelt awkwardly for his saddle blanket and gear. The gate outside the barn swung in the breeze, unlatched overnight. Simone pressed her head to Dick's and stroked his dark mane. She mounted him expertly, and he turned toward the vast emptiness beyond the property.

"Shouldn't they be galloping off or something?" Dana asked as she observed Dick's meandering walk.

"You've seen too many movies. He certainly can't sprint if they're going to be walking for two or three days. And carrying back fifty pounds of guns." Dana raised her eyebrow.

"How many guns does she think we need?"

"Well, really it's just three guns. But one of them is big." Ashley allowed herself to smile. "*Really* big."

The silhouette of Simone on Dick faded slowly into the surrounding landscape as the daughters watched from the back patio. As soon as they disappeared over a small hill, Dana punched Ashley in the shoulder.

"Okay, where are the car keys?"

Chapter 37

Smile – Flickerstick

Ashley rolled down the window of her mom's compact car and spit, hitting the sidewalk. Dana scowled as she pocketed the keys to Nick's truck. Their first objective was completed: retrieving the pickup from where it had sat abandoned at the convenience store, followed by parking it at Frank Iron's office trailer on the reservation. Dana was grateful to have made enough of an impression on Matthew the cashier to persuade him into jumping the truck's battery. The long car ride permitted the sisters several hours of discussing their mother, sharing anecdotes about her quirks, and filling in the gaps of each other's timelines. Dana hung on Ashley's every word as she recalled fragments of memories of moving from state to state as well as Simone's addiction to tattoos.

"Do you have any ink?" Ashley asked as they sat in front of the hospital visitor entrance. "Mom says I should wait to get a tattoo. She said once you commit to some skin real estate, you have to be sure."

"Nah, nothing on me." Dana rolled up her shirtsleeves as proof. "Nothing in the unseen areas, either. Never really thought about it."

"We should totally get some fake ones and not say anything when Mom gets back, see if she notices."

"I'm starting to really like how you think." Dana sucked her teeth and opened the car door. She eyed the blue and white letters of the trauma center's visitor entrance. Her feet felt like mud inside her shoes. "Thanks for coming with me, by the way. I'll be right back."

This was her second objective. She knew it was risky being out in the open, but after this was done, it would be back to the rancher. Dana owed her this much.

She stepped onto the sidewalk and entered the hospital lobby. She grudgingly signed in at the visitor desk and confirmed the room number provided by Janice, the pit in her stomach growing as she rode the elevator up to Lilly's floor. She cleared her mind of any expectations on what Lilly would say or do when she arrived. She decided to let Lilly steer their reunion and would accept whatever daggers came her way.

The door to Lilly's room sat propped open. She had been given a private room due to the nature of her assault. Dana was relieved she would be able to speak freely without a roommate overhearing her. Tapping her knuckles on the glass window of the door, she wandered inside.

"Hey, Lil."

"Hey."

Lilly's face displayed discoloration from a set of healing bruises; a small patch of scabs on her cheek and jawline created the only other imperfections on her smooth hazel skin. Her dark-brown irises, ringed by broken blood vessels in her sclera, contrasted with the dull blue of her stiff gown. Her right leg sat stonelike in a cast that covered it from her ankle to upper thigh.

"They say I got lucky," Lilly said bitterly. "Lucky that the car was already slowing down when it hit me."

"You're a tough kid. That's what the team likes about you," Dana said as she pulled up a chair to the bedside. "That's what *I* like about you. You're going to be okay."

Lilly turned to the window. Her shoulders began to shake. "I'm not okay. When I close my eyes, I see *him*."

"That's what's going to happen for a while. But it gets better."

Lilly turned back to Dana. Tears slowly dripped from each eye and rolled down her cheeks. "You've been assaulted?"

"No."

Dana hesitated. This wasn't the time to discuss her friends who had been assaulted or abused, including Angela. She loved that Angela was a survivor, a warrior, but this was not the right moment to reminisce about Angela's physical and emotional wounds. She refocused on Lilly.

Dana handed her a tissue from the bedside box. "But I have been through some really bad stuff that really screwed me up." She placed her hand on Lilly's. "You got to see it firsthand the day we met. PTSD—or, rather, PTSD *symptomatic*—but it's part of me now. And it may part of you now, too."

Lilly cried harder. "It's not fair," she whimpered. "It's not fair . . ."

"I know, honey. I know." Dana firmed her grip on Lilly's hand.

Lilly blinked slowly. "He was actually looking for you."

Dana closed her eyes and balled her hands into fists.

"Don't worry," Lilly continued, "I never gave him your address like he wanted. He was so creepy, with that icky skinny mustache—"

"Mustache?" *Brian*, Dana thought, and her own tears sprang from her eyes. "Oh Lilly, this is all my fault. I'm not trying to be a grief narcissist here, but if it wasn't for me, you wouldn't be here."

Lilly stretched her arms out to Dana and pulled her lightly to her chest. Her body shivered as she bawled, eventually followed by Dana's own heaving as they sobbed in their shared grief.

"I'm so sorry," Dana whispered into her ear. "You are such a good person. Such a wonderful person. And I will die before someone hurts any of my friends again." She pulled back from their embrace. "And you, you are so amazing. You fought your way through. I am so happy you're alive. We need more people like you."

Lilly wiped her cheek with her forearm and smiled. Dana wiped her cheek with her palm.

"And Lil, I mean 'we' as in 'people like you and me.' Never be ashamed of your heart." Dana leaned in and kissed Lilly on her forehead. "Never."

She reached into her pocket and placed a folded slip of paper on the table next to Lilly's bed.

"That's a number for a woman I know named Tara. She leads a group counseling that I go to. I don't know if the hospital provides anything, but this is what I got. For when you're ready."

Lilly nodded and smiled. "Thank you." She reached out and clutched Dana's hand. Dana tightened her grip around her small delicate fingers.

"And Lilly, I swear, when I track down the son of a bitch who did this, *I will kill him.*"

Dana strode out of the room calmly, but her brain was an inferno of rage. She reran the details of Brian standing in her house with his stupid thin moustache. His oversized teeth. His button-down dress shirt. Nick pulling him down the staircase into the basement.

Nick.

The blood on his shirt at the airport in New Jersey when he was shot by Olsen.

Angela.

Olsen's knife plunging into Angela's side.

Her legs softened as the script ran on repeat in her head. Dana slumped against the wall next to the elevator doors. A passing nurse grabbed her arm and lifted her back to her feet. "Miss, are you alright? Miss?"

The words floated in and out of Dana's ears. She processed them slowly until the vowels and consonants finally formed distinct sounds, a pattern of recognizable speech.

"Yeah, I'm okay. Just a tough visit."

"Are you sure?"

She imagined kicking her skates right into Brian's face.

"Yeah, I'm good."

Chapter 38

Midnight Blue – Lou Gramm

Nick folded his arms and leaned over the speaker phone on the desk. Joshua sat in another chair across from him while Dan slowly paced the room, hands on hips, adjusting his gun in his shoulder holster.

"Nick? Hello?" Dana chimed through the speaker.

"It's me. Hey, Dee."

"Nicky, oh my God, where have you been? I tried leaving a message on the number you left me. I—"

Nick cut her off before she could share anything too revealing. "Dana, I'm here with Joshua."

"Joshy! Hey! Nick, smart idea to call him."

"Dana, I didn't. They found me after I used the black card. And I'm also here with Dan Sun. He's an agent with Homeland. He's cool."

"Hey, Danny!"

Dan smiled but stayed silent.

"He says hi. Dana, we've got a list of problems. We've been putting together some pieces, and the short story is, there's a train scheduled to run through the reservation on a resupply to White Sands and then up to Florence, Colorado, to the supermax prison. It's carrying two components, a battery cell and a targeting device." He paused and confirmed with the agents to continue. "Dana, it's the ones your mom designed."

"Dana, Joshua here. We're getting a task force assembled en route to New Mexico, but there's problem. The train schedule was changed."

"And?"

"It's now coming in tomorrow."

"Okay, what am I supposed to about that?"

Nick looked at Joshua, and then Dan, who each nodded.

"Dana," Nick continued, "they're going to need you to rob that train."

"On the record," Josh jumped in, "we are *not* telling you to intercept the train and locate the two components. They are classified government property. But if we provide you with the details, and the components disappear . . ."

"I'm a fast learner, Joshy. I get it—I'm in. So how do I find these things?"

"The train is going to cut across the reservation at three o'clock in the afternoon. Write this down: Cars A127 and B243 are the ones listed on the manifest. The components are small canisters that fit in your hand, no bigger than soda cans, but each will be in a heavy-duty black equipment case. Ever see one of those fire-safe briefcases that people use to store documents? Similar to that."

Dan took over. "We are assuming they want them to look inconspicuous and not stand out, so there should be no padlocks or keys."

"That seems a bit careless, even for the government," Dana remarked.

"Not if you have people on the inside who set this up and are confident they'll get into the right person's hands."

"Got it, guys. So, how am I getting on this train?"

"I'll text you an official overhead map of the rail line and the beats of where to intercept it. Any other questions, call me back tonight and I'll walk you through it one more time." After Joshua sent the text, he inhaled deeply and added one last thing. "Dana, if you're flagged by base security and taken in, I don't know how quickly I can help, if I can at all. That goof will be on you."

"*Goof?* Are you sure you're with Homeland Security?"

"I ask myself that every day, Dana."

Dana laughed. "Okay, big guy, so we are not doing this *officially*. And I'll call Nick once I'm done *not* doing this. And speaking of Nick, can I please talk to him in private, if there's nothing else?"

Dan nodded at Josh and stood with his hand on the doorknob of Nick's hotel room.

"We're done. Dana, be safe."

"Drive fast, take chances, Joshy!"

Nick picked up the receiver and clicked off the speaker. He waited for the two men to close the door behind them before speaking.

"Okay, they're gone. How's things?"

"We're all fine. I saw Lilly in the hospital today. It was pretty rough, but I made it through. I had an incident when I left."

Nick's stomach churned. Her attacks had become a growing concern after their move out west, but so had Nick's anxiety each time she fought through a spell.

"How bad? Give it to me on a scale of one to ten."

"About a six. Maybe seven, but it was short. Listen, Nick, it was *Brian,* the guy who was in our house, who attacked Lilly. So yeah, we need to shut this shit down before anyone else gets hurt. Ashley and I are back at Mom's ranch now. Technically, we're grounded as much as you can tell an adult and a teenager to stay put and then literally ride off into the sunset. Mom's on some secret walkabout with Dick to go raid some weapons cache she has buried in the desert. Anyway, we're back here and safe, and we're fine."

"That's a lot to unpack in a few sentences. Your mom must be worried, then?"

"Apparently. But confident. I dig that about her."

"You get your moxie from her," he said admiringly. "And I'm sorry about Lilly, but you couldn't have known, Dana. That's just crazy they went after her somehow . . . just crazy."

"I'm trying to tell myself that."

"If it makes you feel better, I'm basically under house arrest here. Today I watched a certain sci-fi trilogy we discussed just the other day. All nine hours of it."

"Was I right? About the fight in the second movie being the best part?"

"Ha, yes you were. Yes, you were." He cleared his throat and stared at the menu for the local Italian restaurant lying on the desk in front of him. The words and prices blurred into nothingness as his eyes unfocused. Her voice came back over the line, a little fainter than usual.

"Nick, I miss you."

"I miss you, too."

"No, I mean *I miss you.*" Her voice fluttered through the handset into his ear. "It's taken me a long time to think of what I wanted to say. And I don't know what to say, so I'm starting with that."

"You don't have to say anything else." He got up and lay on the bed, remembering their nights in New Jersey under the stars, talking in the bed of his pickup truck. Now, instead of the tops of pine trees and the deep-blue sky, his field of vision contained the popcorn ceiling and mandatory fire sprinkler heads of his hotel room. "Don't say anything unless you want to."

"I want to, but I don't know if I'm ready."

Nick listened to the faint buzz of her breath through the phone. "'I miss you' is enough."

"Okay."

"I think the guys are going to get dinner here soon. I'm going to jump off the phone in a sec and put in my order."

The phone rattled as her deep sigh distorted the speaker in his ear. "Alright. Good night."

"Good night. Be safe."

Nick held the phone for a moment after she hung up and smiled. He glanced around his room. A bag of clothing from the local discount store sat on the dresser, next to the new laptop and a notepad left behind by Dan. The top sheet had the train's final destination, Florence, Colorado, written on the top. Underneath were the letters "ADX." Nick recognized these as the designation for the highest-security prison in the United States, the supermax in Colorado. It popped up often in the news as the place where notorious killers or terrorists served their sentences. He pondered the possibilities. *Why would the components be on a train that stops at a supermax prison? And why such urgency?*

His attention snapped back to reality at a knock at the door.

"Nick? Got a delivery for you." Joshua called out before letting himself in. He presented Nick with a box of significant weight and girth.

"For me?" His eyes widened.

"Yep. That's the latest console, some games, and two controllers. I put it under 'miscellaneous' in the budget. I'll have it delivered to a rec room in a barracks somewhere when we're done. We'll fire it up after dinner!" Joshua beamed from ear to ear. "My wife keeps telling me it's a waste of money for us to buy one at home, but heck, let's make it a boys' night in!"

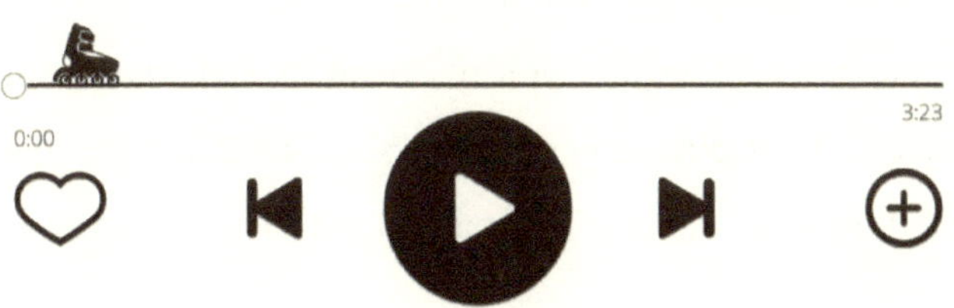

Chapter 39

Oath – Cher Lloyd ft. Becky G

Dana glanced at her notes. She memorized the car numbers A127 and B243 but stared at the assignments one more time, scratched in red ink on a notepad decorated with kittens and hearts. The rundown made sense, but her enthusiasm deflated with her growling stomach.

"Hey, Ash, what do you want for dinner? I'm not a great cook, but I'll do my best with mom's stash of grass and herbs and dirt."

Instead of answering, Ashley stormed into the kitchen alcove, phone in hand, and pushed Dana off her stool.

"What the hell, sis?"

"Yeah, I was going to ask *you* that!" Ashley frothed as she smacked her sister down on the floor. "What did you say to Kendra?!"

Dana got behind the stool and used it as a shield. Her sister, despite her diminutive size and typical teenage fashion, demonstrated a formidable speed and power in her attack. Dana slowly stood up but stayed behind the stool to maintain a barrier between them.

"I told her you're out of the game. You can't do that anymore."

"You can't just walk into our life and assume the crown, *princess*," Ashley snapped. "You're screwing things up for me!"

"I told you to knock it off with the illegal stuff! And I followed through on the other side and told Kendra you're off limits. Oh, and what, pray tell, am I screwing up? Your plan to get a car?" She turned her shoulder but kept her eyes locked with her sister's. "Get a real job. You're ruining lives with this crap."

"No, you idiot. I can't get a *real* job, you jackass! Mom won't let me get a job that requires tax forms or running a cash register under surveillance cameras. I transport her paintings, which is a nice high-dollar cash business for her, and I get a delivery tip for it. I used to run other odd jobs, courier for cash businesses, but that didn't make me enough money."

Ashley's features softened. Her upper lip curled and her chin began to twitch. "Do you know what school was like for me? I was switching schools twice a year until Mom just decided to homeschool me. I graduated at thirteen with a printed-out degree at a community center. Mom made me a cake with *vanilla* icing and that was it."

Dana relaxed her guard and sat back down on the stool. "Hey, you two have a different life. So what if you can't have a graduation party at the bowling alley and a chocolate-frosted red velvet cake or whatever?" She waved her hands dismissively. "Your situation isn't going to be like this forever. You know, getting your high school degree at thirteen is an amazing thing."

"I didn't, you ass. I got my *bachelor's degree* at thirteen. I graduated *high school* at eleven."

"Wait, *what?*"

"High school equivalency at eleven, and then an online degree at thirteen in liberal arts. It's easy to cram in all your credits when *you're not allowed to do anything*. I'm in a master's program for literature now. About halfway so far." Ashley raised an eyebrow. "Do you know what it's like to be a weirdo?"

"Actually, I do," Dana said. "And now, not only am I a weirdo, but I'm the stupid one in the family."

Ashley shrugged and lifted her lips into a half smile. "You read Mom's blueprints and built your own skates. I wouldn't say that." She held up a finger and jogged to her bedroom, returning with a cigar box covered in stickers from various clothing and shoe brands, closed with duct tape. She opened it and revealed multiple tightly wound rolls of cash.

"When I'm eighteen, Mom will have no say in what I do. This money all goes into the bank. I get to apply to a real college and move on with my advanced degree, a doctorate or two. If I can get into one of the Ivy League programs, I'll have access to some of the rarest books in the world. *That* is what I'll do with my money, however I have to make it. I'm buying my ticket out of here as fast as I can." Dana picked up one of the rolls with her finger and thumb, rolled it between her digits, and placed it back in the box.

"Ash. Sis. Just because you hit the genetic lottery and got to take the short route doesn't mean you can keep cutting corners, especially, *my God*, by delivering drugs. Maybe some school will give you a scholarship so they have a weirdo girl genius to parade in front of the alumni. Listen, when things calm down, I'll talk to Mom. And I'll help you figure out how to make money—legally—somehow." Dana laid her open hand across the table. "I promise."

"It won't be that easy. Mom's been looking over her shoulder the whole time I've been alive. She's paranoid. She's *broken*." She rubbed her nose with her wrist. Dana watched her sister alternate between adult and child, the unfortunate side effect of their mother's chaotic life. "And I don't want to turn out like her."

"Wow. Just . . . wow. Guess you had to grow up pretty fast."

"Not by choice." Ashley placed her hand in Dana's. "I love Mom, and she is amazing and fun, and so smart, you wouldn't believe it. But . . ."

Dana leaned over the table and grabbed Ashley by the back of her neck. She pressed her forehead into her sister's brow.

"Listen, if you swear to me no more drug mule jobs, then I swear to you, I will *always* come to your rescue. When Mom won't be a mom . . ." Dana paused. "You've got me."

"Okay, no more drug jobs . . . but I'm going to hold you to what you just said. I'm leaving the nest one way or another, so don't let me down."

Dana leaned back and allowed herself to smile, pleased with her first counseling session as an older sister.

"Done. Alright, now for dinner. I'm going to make some kind of burrito filled with whatever is edible—I think I can handle that—and then we'll put on a crappy movie while we clean our skates. As for tomorrow, any chance you want to help me rob a train for the sake of national security?"

"I thought you'd never ask."

Chapter 40

Voodoo Child – Tom Morello

The dust devils flooded the plain, whirling and spinning through the brush before just as easily dissolving with the changing winds. The soft tones of the breeze yielded to a train's engine droning in the distance, finally breaking up the monotony of the past hour as Dana and Ashley had sat hidden in the brush deep in the reservation's heart.

"Is it three yet?" Ashley asked. She flicked her skates' fasteners open and closed.

"Just about time." Dana held a pair of binoculars pilfered from their mom's house up to her eyes to look for the train. "I think I see it."

The overcast gray skies of the morning had surrendered to the afternoon sun, which helpfully glistened off the black steel as it barreled through the desert in the distance. The cars rattled in unison as the beast approached the bend where, just as Joshua had told her with his text instructions, a maintenance road reached out from the dry soil and ran alongside as the rail's companion.

Squinting through the binoculars, Dana searched for the supply cars, which were indistinct from one another save for the yellow markings of letters and numbers on the bottom edge of the gray panels. She quickly spotted the ones she was looking for.

"A127 is mine—looks like it's up near the front," she told Ashley. "B243 is a little more than halfway toward the back. Keep pace, read the cargo markers, and get in and out."

Dana tapped her earpiece to make sure it was working and nodded at Ashley to do the same. Her sister nodded back, and without a word, they sprang from their lookout to the pavement. The train's roar concealed the clang of their skates as they accelerated to catch up.

Ashley looked at Dana and gave her a three-finger salute, which they agreed was the sign that she was good to go. Dana soared ahead. The cracked pavement provided a rougher ride than most of the country roads in the area, baked in the sun and relatively unused. She effortlessly took small leaps over asphalt chunks and debris from trains long forgotten without losing velocity.

The roar of the engine twisted into a two-part harmony, a second source of pistons and exhaust wavering up and down in pitch. *That's not coming from the train,* Dana suddenly realized. She glanced between two cars and saw a cloud of dust erupt. She advanced another car length and caught a large black object moving just ahead of her on the other side of the train. Dana surged ahead, careful to continue hopping over cracks and train scraps, and saw the black blur on the other side of the train again through the next gap.

"Ash, we got company. It's moving toward the front, other side."

"Got it."

Another break between gave Dana the clearest look yet. It was a jeep accelerating in fits, and certainly outpacing Dana toward the front of the train. She arced to the shoulder of the maintenance road and pressed her toes onto the control pads, rocketing up the embankment. She stretched her arms, reaching for the railing between cars A129 and A128, and successfully grabbed it. Her feet dangled for a moment before she brought them up to the platform.

"Ash, make your move if you haven't already. I'm a car back from where I need to be."

"I'm heading into car B243 now," her sister's voice crackled over the Bluetooth earpiece.

Dana pressed her back to the door of the car and tried to catch another look at their uninvited companions. A woman with short blond hair was standing in the back of the jeep, her coat whipping in the wind as she squared her stance. She slipped off her jacket and then, in a single leap, bounded from the vehicle into the gap between two boxcars.

"Who in the froggy bottom is that?" Dana sensed that she had to get to car A127 before whoever that was. She tried the door of the car in front of her, but it wouldn't open. *Guess I'm going up.* Dana pulled herself onto the roof and lay flat, inch-worming her way forward. She reached the end and peered down.

"Nina, heads up!" came a shout from the jeep keeping pace with its former occupant.

The woman whirled around and looked up. Dana saw a gun tucked in at her waist and immediately retreated farther back on the roof of the train car, crawling backward as quickly as she could. The woman's torso rose above the train car roof, her eyes boring into Dana's, her lower half still on the ladder below.

Dana's eyes widened. *What in the hell are you?*

Silvery steel bands covered each of the woman's arms from wrist to bicep, glinting in the sun. She held the pistol in a gleaming metallic hand and pointed it directly at Dana.

The shots flew over Dana's head as the car bounced along. The metallic woman shouted unintelligible words at the jeep and disappeared again below. The driver accelerated, moving ahead of the next car. Dana waited a few seconds and then crawled forward again and, with no sign of the woman, leapt down into the gap at the rear of car A127.

"Ashley, how's it going? I got company up here. Very weird company."

"Dana, I'm in the right car, but there are two cases here. They look the same, and both weigh a ton. Which one do I take first?"

"I don't know, can't you open them?" Dana grabbed the handle for the train car door.

"I tried. They're locked. Bad intel from your fed boys? I'll see if I can grab both."

"Keep me posted, baby girl!"

Dana pushed the handle and muscled the door open. Once inside, she took a moment to wipe the sand from her goggles. A cell came into view, reaching from floor to ceiling, flanked by two armed guards. Before Dana could process the details before her, a flurry of gunshots tore through the compartment. Dana dropped to her knees and slid back into the alcove next to the door but kept an eye on the mayhem. One guard dropped to the floor, clearly wounded. The woman with metallic arms stepped out and reached a steely appendage toward the other guard, who cringed in fear, and tossed him into the wall.

The woman pointed her pistol at the cell's lock and pulled the trigger, but her face knotted into a frustrated scowl as the firing mechanism failed. She tossed it aside and grabbed the cell door with two hands. Her forearms and biceps bulged, accompanied by a whizzing and whining squeal. Bolts and hinges yielded to her inhuman strength as she ripped it open. With a giddy laugh, she reached inside and yanked out a man in an orange jumpsuit, his face covered by a black canvas bag. Dana peered farther around the corner, almost completely exposed as she watched the incomprehensible scene.

The woman's metallic claw crushed the handcuffs fastened around each sleeve of the jumpsuit. The prisoner reached up with his freshly freed hands and pulled the bag off his head. He shook out his hair, mostly gray but flecked with the remains of black hair dye. His square jaw framed his smile as he looked admiringly at his liberator. His voice pierced the silence with a sinister purr that Dana recognized.

"Hello, Nina."

"Hi, Daddy."

Colin Rhodes embraced his apparent daughter. He ran his hands down her steel biceps, admiring the minutiae of the elbow joint, laughing as his fingers touched her dainty metal gauntlets. He observed the two motionless guards and the resultant glee on his daughter's face.

"Well, they look dead. You did good, girl. Now get me the hell out of here."

Dana slunk back into the alcove until she heard the door at the opposite end of the car slam close. Her heartbeat pulsed into her throat. A rush of blood flooded her forearms; her legs felt numb. Her fingers trembled as she pressed her earpiece.

"Ashley. Get. Off. The train. Now."

"Sis, what's going on?"

Dana's muscles tingled at the memory of her last encounter with Rhodes—the exhausting battle at the airport in New Jersey. Any empathy inside Dana for the mad patriot she last saw broken and defeated had disappeared the minute she saw him smiling at his murderous bionic daughter. And right now, Dana and her sister were in more danger than either of them could have anticipated.

"Get off the goddamn train!"

Chapter 41

Miracle Man – Ozzy Osbourne

Dana had to will her limbs out of their paralysis, pushing herself up from her crouched position to retreat out the door she had come through. The wind whipped her hair back from her face when she glanced around the car toward the front of the train just in time to see Nina literally launch Rhodes into the jeep's bed. He almost bounced when he landed, assisted by two men in matching fatigues and masks. They stabilized him as he stood up, spotting Dana immediately. She saw Rhodes madly waving and pointing at her, the whites of his eyes bulging from his skull, and yelling back toward Nina. The jeep surged away from the tracks and raced off perpendicular to the train's course. In the distance, the tiny fencing from the military base came into view.

"Dana," Ashley crackled over the earpiece, "are you coming?"

"Don't wait, for the love of God, just go! Don't wait for me! *Go!*" Dana's heels clicked and whirred in concert as she prepared to jump off the train. Suddenly, the train car door to A127 burst open and Rhodes's daughter lunged at Dana, missing the moving target and falling to her knees with a clang. Dana grabbed the ladder behind her and climbed, clamoring onto the roof. She pushed her skates against the metal and sprinted to the end of the car. As she approached the gap, she propelled herself forward and onto the next car. She looked behind to see Nina's superhuman legs negating Dana's speed advantage. She decided to just focus on the number of cars between her and the tail of the train. The rocking movement, the whipping winds, and the wheels on her feet challenged her balance each time she soared over another gap. She counted just a handful of cars left to the end of the train when she heard Nina's voice just behind her.

"Dana Jefferson! Let's make this easy," the bionic woman yelled. "Give up, little girl!"

"I can't right now!" Dana yelled as she cleared the next car.

Dana's feet slipped as she landed, and she fell to her side. Nina landed on the car with a thud as her feet dented the metal roof only a few feet away. They were only one car away from the back of the train now. Dana feigned immobility as Nina strode up to her.

"You took my advice, I see?" Nina cackled, standing over Dana's crumpled form.

"Nope!" Dana shouted as she kicked her skate into Nina's shin. There was a loud metallic sound as her wheels impacted the seemingly steel limb. Nina stumbled backward, falling onto her backside.

Dana exploded onto her feet and soared over the last gap to the final boxcar. The paved access road that ran parallel to the line had long disappeared back into the desert. She whipped around to see Nina once again had caught up to her.

"Jesus. What the hell did your dad do to you?'"

Nina plodded closer. "I blame *your* dad for all this," she replied, holding out her arms and looking down at her legs. Her knees and ankles emitted short whirrs and clicks as she balanced on the rocking train. "I never expected to punish *him* for it, but his daughter is a decent consolation prize." She lunged forward but was stopped short, her face contorted with surprise, before landing face-first on the roof.

Dana saw Ashley's head just above the gap between the cars, her arm stretched out and gripping Nina's ankle.

"I'm definitely glad you didn't listen to me!" Dana yelled.

She slid forward and swept her skate into Nina's chest, heaving her off the train and into the desert chaff and weeds. Ashley waved her hand for assistance.

"Pull me up, sis!"

The girls settled next to each other, elbows linked for stability, and scanned the surroundings. Behind them, they could see the black jeep cut back across the plain on a path to retrieve Nina, rapidly fading farther away from the rumbling train. Ahead, the train approached a long fence lined by a single-lane paved track.

"That's the border of the base," Dana said. "We gotta get off, now."

Ashley panted. "How do we do this?"

"We go over the end of the caboose and hang on to the edge. We'll lower our skates to the rails, and just let go. You ever do a rail slide on your skates or a board? Like that. I hope."

"That should be less painful than just jumping." Ashley shrugged. Dana nodded to convince herself that her plan would work.

"Let's pretend that's true."

The siblings lowered themselves over the lip of the car, gripping the edge of the roof and dangling their feet just above the metal tracks. Dana dropped first, a cloud of sparks erupting around her. She slid, stumbled, and tumbled into the weeds. Ashley mirrored her actions and landed in the grass several yards away. She crawled on her belly toward Dana, both siblings breathing hard in the dirt.

"You good?" Ashley said.

"I'm good. I mean, yeah, I'm not hurt too bad. I don't know where that jeep went . . . I'm guessing they're not heading toward the base with a jailbroke prisoner."

"What are you talking about?" asked Ashley.

"Our new friend, the iron maiden back there, she just freed her dad from the train. Wait. What about the components? Where are the cases?"

"I could only get one. I tossed it off the train. Do you know how heavy those things were? It felt like they were lined with lead or something."

Dana stared incredulously at her sister. "So you don't know where the case is?"

"Not exactly. We'll find it. Give me your phone. I'll figure out where we are."

Dana slapped her handset into Ashley's palm. "Wait, where's your phone?"

"I dropped it when I came to save your ass. You're welcome, by the way. We'll ping it with your phone on our way back." She held the phone up to check the signal and began a confident stride into the desert. "This way— come on. Did you bring any snacks, by the way?"

"No," Dana snapped, "I did *not* bring snacks. This isn't a class trip."

"Class trip? What's that? Why, I'm just a simple homeschooled girl," Ashley replied with an affected Southern accent. Dana giggled and smacked Ashley on her arm.

"I hate you."

"I hate you, too, sis."

Chapter 42

High Hopes – Pink Floyd

Dana peeled off a sock and shook out another handful of sand onto the rancher's back patio.

"Here she comes, Ash. Should we help her?"

"Yep, might as well."

The girls stepped off the rear veranda of the rancher toward the silhouette of their mother walking her horse beyond the barn's fences. Dick stepped carefully, balancing the weight of two large black canvas bags strapped to each side of the saddle. Simone held his bridle with one hand, the other supporting a long thin rectangular gun case strapped across her back, almost as long as her full height. Ashley jogged ahead.

"Thanks, girl," Simone huffed. "Dick is getting too old for this, I think. But he did a good job."

Dana met the group at the fence and grabbed one of the horse's cargo parcels as Simone unloaded the other. Dick walked to the barn without any verbal orders and began to drink from the water trough. Simone smiled.

"He's my good old gentleman. Let's get all this inside."

The sisters laid the bags on the living room floor as Simone grabbed three beer bottles from the fridge. She uncapped each and handed them out. Ashley paused before taking a sip.

"Are you giving me carte blanche now to drink, Mom?"

"Might as well start. If I'm breaking open *these*, we're living day-to-day." She opened the first bag and spilled the contents on the floor. "This is the M27 IAR, or infantry automatic rifle, and here are the magazines." She placed four black rectangles next to it in one neat row. "Gas operated, low maintenance—the ideal characteristics for being stuck in an airtight barrel buried in the desert." She laid a scope and grip handle next to the gun. "I'll attach these tonight."

"Jesus, Mom." Dana drew a long sip from her beer. "Where the hell did you get this stuff?"

"The same place I got this," she said as she opened the oblong rectangular gun case. "This is Barry. He's a Barrett fifty caliber rifle used by snipers. This bad boy can be used to shoot something at a range of two miles." She hoisted the long black heavy rifle into the air, admiring all forty-eight inches from end to end, almost two feet of which was just the barrel. "I reassembled it before the trip back. Just in case." The weapon glistened as she wiped a fine cleaning cloth along each section. Simone looked up and saw her daughters' matching looks of disbelief. Ashley's beer hovered in mid-draught at her chin.

"You ever use that?" Dana said.

"Girls, your mom was a good shot a few years ago. An *excellent* shot, if I may say so. Plenty of time to practice. I think about sixteen hundred yards was my personal best. Almost a mile." She ran her hand across the stock and smiled as she admired the textured grip. "I'll sleep better with these in the house now that we know Rhodes's crew is out there."

"Yeah, about that . . ." Dana said as she sat her empty bottle on the counter. "So is Rhodes himself."

Simone lowered the sniper rifle and glared at Dana. "He's out?"

"Yeah. So we, uh, went out while you were gone." She smiled sheepishly with a reluctance not unlike when she had had to tell her mother that she spilled her finger paints on the floor. "Sorry."

"Go on." Simone folded her arms and frowned at Dana.

Dana quickly recapped the call from Nick, the unofficial request from Homeland Security, and their interception of the train. "The good thing is, we got this." Dana walked around the couch and produced the black case Ashley had thrown from the train containing one of the components. "Anyhow, turned out the train wasn't only carrying the components. Apparently, Rhodes was on the train, too, being transported to the supermax prison. His daughter, Nina Rhodes—Mom, she's like half robot—broke him out." After she finished, she tried unsuccessfully to read her mother's expression.

Ashley put her hands together in a mock prayer gesture and pressed her fingers to her chin. "It was totally Dana's idea."

Dana's eyes flung daggers at Ashley.

"Mom, Ashley's a drug mule."

"What the hell? You're ratting me out!"

"Hey, you just ratted me out, so I went for the nuclear option!"

"Girls, stop. Sit down. I have had a couple of very long grueling days, and need I remind you that not only am I am the only *armed* person in this room, but I'm also your *mother*, so again, sit down and shut up."

The sisters slumped into opposite ends of the couch. Simone sat on the coffee table facing them and laid the Barrett across her lap.

"Let me clarify a few things. One: I know you guys went out. You don't think I can check the monitors from anywhere I go? And I know it wasn't only the one time, either. I thought maybe you'd come back with a pizza, but I know you came back with *that*." She glanced at the closed black case from the train. "That is not a pizza box."

"That is true," Dana chimed in.

"Two: Ashley, I know what you've been doing. I have ears out there who have been keeping tabs. I don't approve, but I also have an 'unconventional' income stream, and I accept that." She turned to face Dana. "Art is a wonderful way for criminals to launder money. Some of my most expensive pieces are in the homes and offices of some very prominent local *business* people." She clawed her fingers into the shape of air quotes for additional emphasis. "*Business* people helped me buy all of this shit."

"*Mom,* how can you be okay with Ashley doing this? Running trash to the reservations and in the neighborhoods?"

"Dana, if you haven't figured it out, I have one goal: keep us safe for one more day, every single goddamn day. If something happens to me, Ashley needs to know how to make money and survive. It's not ideal, but we don't have the luxury of ideal." She squared herself to her younger daughter. "I acknowledge that you want to get out of this lifestyle. I know that. And I know I can't protect you forever . . . but I will for as long as I can."

Simone sighed deeply. Dana felt her mother had aged twenty years with that single breath, her eyes bloodshot above permanently set dark bags.

"Mom, I love you," Ashley replied. "Tell you what, you look exhausted. I can go start cutting up some veggies for dinner."

Simone nodded appreciatively. She placed the rifle on the floor and walked out to the back patio. Dana remained still, watching her mother rummage through the barrel of sticks next to the firepit and arrange them in a crucible, then went out to join her. She stood at the edge of the sitting area as her mother lit the fire against the backdrop of the evening sun dropping to the horizon. The fire quickly rose and glowed orange as the kindling and paper ignited, flashing light and shadows against the back of the house. Simone stared into the pyre and exhaled slowly.

"Dana, I know this reunion is a dream come true for you, but for me it's a shuffling of nightmares." She rubbed her forehead and pointed at the house. "Get yourself another beer and bring me one."

Dana glided inside. Ashley was leaning over a cutting board of chopped peppers.

"We'll talk later," Ashley monotoned, not looking up.

"Gotcha." Dana grabbed two bottles and returned to the patio. Simone stood at the edge of the concrete, her back to the house. "So. Mom. I have a couple more questions."

Simone, still facing away, replied to her daughter's query by pulling her shirt over her head, her muscular back flexing in the light of the fire. The tattoos up and down her arms flanked a faded image that ran down her back. A set of curls and swirls, reminiscent of hair. *A mane*, Dana thought to herself. *Like a horse . . . or a lion.*

"Dana, you need to know."

Her mother turned around. She stepped closer to the fire, exposing her bare torso to the flickers of light from the flames. Her chest muscles stretched bare, devoid of any hint of a mammary or nipple. Along the side of each pectoral, a large scar outlined the anatomical shape and ran partially underneath. A faded tattoo of a shooting star ran across her left chest and up to her collarbone.

"This is what the program took from me. I wasn't correctly diagnosed until after Ash was born, and we were on the run, so I didn't have the money or resources for real treatments." She ran her fingers across her right chest, indicating where an areola used to exist. "I had to take the hard-and-fast method to remove the cancers. Doctors who accepted paper bags full of cash." She looked up into Dana's horrified face. "Anything to survive, to live one more day. A mother will do anything. Fight. Kill. Hurt herself." Her features softened. "Lie to her own children for their protection. That's the hardest one."

Dana stepped closer and reached out her hand. Simone nodded and placed it over the tattoo on her chest.

"Dana, my shooting Star. Every single day we were apart, I looked at this as a reminder of you, instead of what was taken from me." Her eyes blinked through a sheen of tears as they formed. "*Every day*, Dana. I thought of you every day. I've had to do some terrible things to survive, to keep your sister safe, but you helped keep me going. If I had lost the memory of you, I would have lost everything."

"Oh, Mom," Dana whispered, "I'm so sorry." She ran her eyes down each jagged mastectomy scar. "I'm so sorry."

"This is why I'm so scared right now. If Rhodes is back, so is all this pain that he caused me. And I swear, if the stars align, I will kill him." Simone picked up her shirt and covered her scars once more.

Dana handed her mother the bottle of beer, now soaked in condensation from having sat on the edge of the firepit. Simone tipped it back and released an extravagant gasp of refreshment.

"Yeah, we're not a normal family," Dana remarked.

"No. We are not." Simone smiled.

"Mom, about Ashley . . ." Dana gulped.

"Yes?"

"There are some things, a *lot* of things, that she's missed out on. Not by her choice. Or maybe, you know, she's choosing some things because that's what she thinks she needs to do to keep you happy. But she's not happy. She has dreams." Dana reflected on the right words she needed to use to make her point, to keep her promise to Ashley. "She's saving money so that she can go to school, get her doctorate or whatever."

"I take it you want her to stop running narcotics so she can get a job at the mall with a name badge and a price gun to pay for school?"

"In a word, yes."

"It's not about running away?"

"I don't think she'd want to skip town the moment she turns eighteen *if* you supported her. I think you can have it both ways."

"Dana, someday you'll understand this." Simone finished her beer. "Actually, I hope that you never have to understand this: a mother will do anything for her kids. Sometimes that means holding back their dreams if it's for their own safety."

"Or letting them think you're dead?" *There, I said it.* She stared directly into Simone's eyes.

"Like I said, the hardest thing a parent can do is to lie to their children. I'm sorry, Star, that it had to be that way, but I hope you understand why now."

"I do. Try explaining it to Ash then like you explained it to me. Talk to her like a grown-up." She leaned over and stroked her mother's knotted hair, inhaling the dust and sweat buried in the strands.

"I will," Simone said, "but not until she's done making me dinner."

Dana allowed herself a quick smile before swallowing hard to announce a new request. "Mom. You have to let me leave, too. I mean, not forever, but I need to sneak out to meet with my counseling group."

"Absolutely not."

"Mom, I just saw the same guy who gave me a lifetime supply of panic attacks escape from prison. I am sitting on a powder keg here." She jammed her finger into her temple. "I need this." Her mother stared back, unblinking. "Mom. For my mental health." Dana furrowed her brow. "Just one night, only a couple of hours. Or you know what? Just my counselor. Just Tara. I'll call her and meet up with her, but I need to talk to someone right now who isn't a Jefferson. *I need to do this*."

Simone glanced back at the mountains instead of replying. She traced a slow circle around the firepit before wiping her cheeks. "So you don't turn out like me."

"That's not what I'm saying!"

"But it *is* what I'm hoping." Simone slid her hand into her pocket and tossed her car keys to Dana. "Ask Ashley to swap the license plates on the compact and fill the tank using our gas reserves. No stops, no idling. You drive the speed limit, you use your turn signals even if no one is around, and do not give anyone the finger or honk at them if they cut you off. Just go there and back."

"There and back home."

Simone smiled. "*There and back home*. I do like the sound of that."

Chapter 43

Wasted Time – Skid Row

Olsen had organized the papers on his makeshift desk into two neat piles, one on each side of his laptop. He placed his sidearm on top of the left stack and returned to the files on his screen, but his focus kept getting pulled away by the scene at the open hangar doors. There, a tiny parade of mercenaries greeted Colin Rhodes as he marched into the center of the room.

Dressed in fatigue pants and an army-green uniform shirt, he showed no signs that age or incarceration had abated his energy. It was a cruel contrast to Olsen's immobility as he staggered to his feet with the assistance of his crutches to greet his former boss.

"Mr. Rhodes, pleasure to officially welcome you to the operations center," he said, his hand trembling in an extended handshake. "You can see I'm not quite back to normal. Yet."

Rhodes declined the gesture and pointed at a shelf loaded with arms and munitions. "Stocking up, I see. We'll need to talk about recruiting. I have some ideas." He looked with obvious disapproval at the informality of the space. "Olsen, I'm surprised you've been able to run even basic operations out of here. For God's sake, Eugene doesn't even have a new phone yet. I guess I know why the train heist was a failure. Sure, I was extracted and one of the components was retrieved, but the other one was already gone, and I'm assuming it's in the hands of that damn Jefferson girl."

"Sir, my apologies. I've been doing my best," Olsen offered, spinning the laptop to face Rhodes. "It's just that I've had a lot of questions. We've been doing as best as we can with the outlines you left, but it seems something is missing from the project plans we were able to recover."

Brian and Nina approached at that moment. Nina leaned her chin on her father's shoulder and kissed him lightly on his cheek. She pointed a metallic finger at the screen.

"We're not where we want to be with the palladium. We couldn't get the reservation to play nice," she whined. "I would guess we're going the hard way next."

"Nina, you're right as always," Rhodes said. "Where are we with the crop duster?"

Brian pointed through the open hangar doors where a single-engine propeller plane and a small helicopter sat parked across the tarmac.

"Those are what we've got, boss. We just need to install the sprayer arms and the kerosene tanks."

Rhodes rubbed the silvery stubble on his chin and scanned Brian from toe to head. "And who are you?"

"Brian Nelson, sir." Brian crossed his arms and flexed his shoulder muscles under his polo shirt. "Tracking, target removal, and dirty deeds done dirt cheap," he said with a smile. "People call me Nails."

Rhodes stared, unblinking. "*I* didn't hire you, *Nails*." Rhodes glanced back at Olsen. "Is he one of yours?"

"Freelance mercenary." Olsen stood as straight as his back allowed. "One of the best. We worked together back before my international incident.

No one I trust more."

"And," Brian interjected, "I'm best damn chopper pilot for this kind of thing."

"If you ever fly an F-15 through twelve batteries of surface-to-air missiles," Rhodes barked, "then I'll call you a pilot."

Olsen shook his head. "Can we get back to business, sir?"

"Yes. I want those filled up and ready in two days so we can light up the reservation."

"About that," Olsen said. "I think we can go back with a second offer, maybe dangle a carrot on a stick. We grease the wheel by offering them a payment for the *right* to counter any other offers. Once they have cash in hand, they may feel more likely to sell. It's how it's done sometimes with cellular towers and water rights."

"Negative. If they don't want our price for the palladium, we're going to burn them out so they have no choice but to sell. They need motivation? It's easy to persuade a reservation full of widows and orphans. Parents who lose their children are *very* malleable."

Olsen slowly contracted his fingers into trembling fists. He dug his knuckles into the tabletop and lowered his head. His newly reinstated boss was showing more ruthlessness than cunning. "I thought, as a last resort, we were going to burn the crops and kill the livestock to pressure them to sell." He dug his knuckle into the laminate. "Not murdering children. Your suggestion seems a bit too swift and a bit too extreme."

"Olsen, are you going soft on me? You have a body count greater than this entire team combined." Rhodes placed a hand on his shoulder. "Collateral damage never bothered you before."

"What you described wouldn't be collateral," he growled, "it would be *murder*. I've killed enough people to know the difference. We're fighting to protect the United States, not wage war against its citizens."

Rhodes smiled wide, displaying teeth yellowed from a lapse in cosmetic treatment during his short time in federal prison. "Olsen. *Aaron.* These dogs in the desert may not even be *real* citizens. The American government is always looking the other way when things go down on reservations. Speaking of not being a real citizen, perhaps you need to be reminded how *my* legal connections obscured your status and kept you out of prison, you dingo. That cost me quite a bit of money." He slapped Olsen on the back and turned away from the desk. "The *citizens* aren't our concern, anyhow."

"Come again?" Olsen twisted his torso and lumbered behind Rhodes on his canes. "What's the whole point of this? We're the false flag. We set up the reason to attack the enemies of this country, and then we profit from it. I know it's not the same now that One Hundred Roads is no longer a favorite son, but that's how we've always worked." He pointed a cane at the laptop. "That's why I need you to explain how this whole plan is going to work. Who, exactly, are we rebuilding the Atomic Juggernaut for?"

Rhodes spun on his heels and faced Olsen, his nose inches from his face. "This isn't a false flag. There isn't a buyer. I rotted in that prison because of our failure in New Jersey. *Rotted!* We were going to be heroes—I still *am* a hero! I fought tooth and nail, *blood and bones*, for this country!" His mouth frothed, and then he shifted to a whisper. "My daughter is a freak because of what I did for this country." His nostrils flared. "For all this, my country threw me in prison."

Olsen stepped back. His retreat was matched by an equal advance from his superior.

"Rhodes, you're a dozen pints deep into your own brew."

"We're getting the palladium rights, whatever it takes," he spat. "I have manufacturers already in production waiting for my word. And we will unleash punishment, as true patriots, against this misguided country." Olsen wiped a stray drop of spittle from his cheek.

"This country," Olsen retorted, "*saved* me. I was persona non grata in my birth nation for the things I did. *America* gave me a chance. *You* gave me a chance." He adjusted his crutches and leaned forward. "I've done the things I've done for a country that had no reason to love me, but did anyway. And I would *die* for this country, do the *darkest of deeds* for this country—but I will not deliberately murder innocent people because you want revenge."

Silence hung heavy throughout the hangar as the assembled crowd of mercenaries watched the confrontation from afar.

Rhodes paced in a slow circle around his first in command, wringing his hands as he slowly nodded.

"Well, it appears we have a breakdown in ideology. Between that and your other failures, I have decided that the team has no use for you—a cripple with a broken body—anymore." He reached for the gun on the desk and handed it to Brian. "Thumbtack? Please."

Brian blinked rapidly. "It's Nails, sir."

"Whatever. You want to keep your job? Take him out past the airfield and put him out of his misery. Too much stuff in here for a stray bullet to ignite."

Brian took the gun and placed it into his waistband. Olsen clutched the handles of his crutches and grit his teeth. His face flushed with heat as he glared at Rhodes. "You can't be serious, sir."

Rhodes ignored Olsen and stared at Brian. "Do you want to keep this job, or should I ask someone else to shoot both of you?"

Brian's eyes flashed between his new boss and his friend.

"Sorry, buddy. You always knew I was a hired hand. The mission comes first and foremost." He slipped on a pair of black gloves from his back pocket. "I follow the paycheck. But I truly am sorry."

He put a hand on Olsen's back and pushed him to the hangar entrance. Olsen did not resist but struggled to keep pace on his crutches. He refused to look at anyone he passed. Only Eugene tried to meet his gaze before Olsen was marched out into the heat of the daytime sun.

Olsen and Brian crossed the tarmac in silence. At the edge of the cracked concrete, where the wild weeds invaded the crevices and desert sand obscured the painted lines on the runway, Olsen stopped and looked up at the blue sky. *Betrayal, failure*—these words filled his thoughts as he looked for some way out. There was none, by his own assessment. He could not overpower an armed Brian in his current state. He couldn't even run. He felt like a sitting duck with broken wings.

If he was going to die, he at least needed to make it count for something. *Rhodes must be stopped.* If he had any options remaining in the minutes before his own execution, he had to take them.

He cleared his throat, giving Brian pause as he prepared for the task.

"Mate, can you do me a professional courtesy? I just need to get one affair in order." He reached into his pocket and pulled out his phone. "A payment. To my mum's nursing home."

"I get it. Make it quick, and I'll make sure this is painless." Brian pursed his lips. "I owe you that, buddy."

Olsen's trembling fingers moved across the screen. He glanced at Brian, who was looking back at the hangar to see who might be watching this play out. Olsen slipped the phone into his chest pocket inside his coat.

"All done."

"Alright, let's go out to the runoff gulley." Brian pushed him several yards into a shallow ravine past the runway. A dusty-brown hare leaped away, catching Olsen's eye. He watched it scurry a few yards toward the desert.

"Knees." Olsen dropped slowly, and Brian leveled the gun at his head.

"I'm not going to beg. Just do me a solid, one last time. Not the face. If, by some miracle, my mum gets to see her boy buried, let me give her that.

For my mum, Brian. Aim for my heart." Olsen looked up into Brian's face with a quivering lip. "Just please do it quickly."

"Hey, better me than some plebe with bad aim doing the deed, right?" he snickered.

"Keep that sense of humor, Brian. When it's three in the morning and you, Nina, and the four other blokes on night watch are tossing empty beer bottles out the open hangar doors, finalizing your plans to burn down the reservation, just know I'll be waiting for you in hell."

Brian cocked his head and raised an eyebrow. He lowered it to Olsen's chest. "Whatever you say."

"And if you find Dana Jefferson, thank her for me."

Brian pulled the trigger, unleashing a direct shot at Olsen's chest. He fell back into the dirt. Brian turned to the hangar and marched back without a second glance or thought. The dusty-brown hare raced into the open fields.

Chapter 44

Descending – The Black Crowes

Dana looked down at the contacts in her burner phone, just the few she thought important enough to transfer from her old phone before she destroyed it, like Tara. She slumped in her folding chair in the community center under the faint glow of the emergency lights, arms crossed, and glanced around the empty room. Dana's restless left leg shook and tapped the floor quietly until the door creaked open, announcing Tara's arrival.

"Dana?" she said as a faint echo explored the corners of the room.

"Right here, Tara. Thanks for meeting me. No lights, please."

"Hi, Dana, glad to hear from you. Everything alright? You haven't been to a meeting lately. When you called me, I guessed it was something . . . sensitive."

"I really was hoping for a one-on-one session. I don't know if you do that, but I don't know who else to talk to, and your voice is so calming, and most people stop listening to me as soon as I start ram—"

"Dana, it's okay. Go ahead."

"Okay, so hi, I'm Dana, and I have PTSD symptoms."

"No need for that." Tara chuckled warmly. "Just tell me what's on your mind today."

"Oh, boy. Well, I haven't actually shared my whole story with the group, ever. See, my dad is dead, I watched my ex-girlfriend get stabbed, I saw my best friend get shot, and my mom is essentially a doomsday prepper. She's not exactly stable. Oh, and my new friend hit on me and then was assaulted at her apartment."

Tara blew out a long breath.

"Well, that was a lot. But thank you for sharing, Dana."

Dana hadn't even mentioned her and Nick being attacked in their home. She wondered if it was still standing or if it had been reduced to a pile of lumber by Olsen and his crew. Or, worst of all in her mind, if it had been taken over by the remnants of One Hundred Roads. She planted her feet under her steel chair, steadying herself as she leaned over her knees with her arms folded.

"That's some blatantly defensive body language after laying yourself wide open. You seem more distracted than usual. I acknowledge your challenges and ask permission to explore your feelings." Tara fingered her long necklace and silver roadrunner pendant.

"Yeah, I think I need that." Dana glanced at the pendant and then out the window into the blackness to make sure no one was outside.

"Ok, then, how about you identify one failure and one success in dealing with your anxiety? Or, more broadly, your feelings this week. Just start there."

"Well, I think one failure is that, as usual, I thought some people in my life were more than they turned out to be." She laughed and felt the echo reverberate in her ears in the otherwise silent room. "My mom, who I'd always had on this really high pedestal, has laid out all her flaws. I felt like I could lean on her, but she's more frail than I thought she was."

"What do you mean by frail?"

"She puts on a tough girl image—and I do the same, I get that. But my mom, she doesn't trust people *at all* and she's, I don't know . . . broken."

"Did she volunteer this to you?"

"Yeah, basically."

"Well, then, I'd also call that a victory. Someone is showing trust when they can reveal their shortcomings and hope you accept them for who they are. That was probably a big moment for her."

Dana's eyes widened as she met Tara's stare. "Whoa."

"Yeah, 'whoa' is right," Tara responded with a laugh. "And you just did the same thing, opening up with me. You don't usually mention your father."

Dana felt her eyes water with pride and humility as she considered this revelation.

"Hey, Dana, that's good work. Remember, one decision, one *feeling* at a time. Don't forget, we're all roadrunners. Let's pause there for a bit."

"Yeah, let's just pause there."

Tara leaned close. "If you don't mind me asking, any luck finding that girl on skates? The suspected dealer? I actually thought that's why you might be calling. You may not have heard, but someone in the group lost their battle with drugs just a couple of days ago."

"What? Who?"

"It was Christina."

Dana's mind drifted back to her first meeting. She may not have walked in at all if Christina hadn't been there to gently nudge her.

"What happened?"

Tara placed her hand on Dana's knee, then pulled back to relocate it to her shoulder. Her eyes flickered.

"She had a relapse, as is wont to happen, but she got some bad stuff. Apparently, there have been similar overdoses over the past week." Her fingers tightened on Dana briefly. "She was the only fatal one. The rumor is her dealer is using a new supplier and a new mule."

Dana swallowed. "That's horrible," she replied as calmly as possible, "but, no, I don't know anything. Never figured it out." She fumbled for her the keys to the compact. "Tara, I have to go. This is a lot to process."

"Dana, you know how to get in touch."

Her fingers felt cold.

"I have to go."

She jogged to the car, not looking back to see if Tara was following. As she hurled herself into the driver's seat, her lungs contracted. The thickness of her ribs pressed into her sides.

"Not my fault. It's not my fault." Dana turned the rearview mirror to confront her own gaze. "It's not my fault."

Her arm tingled in memory of pushing Kendra up against the wall. Her ears rang with her demands to leave Ashley alone.

"Not my fault."

She felt the impact of Ashley's headbutt from their first chase.

"Not my fault."

She heard herself yelling as Nick's body lay on the tarmac.

"Not my fault."

A ring of white surrounded her field of vision. She saw Angela's blood pulsing from her stab wound.

"Not my fault."

A new scene entered the script: Her father's mummified body falling out of the cockpit of the Atomic Juggernaut—his hollow eyes staring into hers. Gray skin pulled tight over his cheekbones, the dull brown hair plastered across his forehead, every stitch of his name tag frayed and tattered, the thin dry hands that had once held hers as she rode a bicycle without training wheels for the first time. He was barely recognizable. He had died a horrible death, alone, and she only learned that truth when she saw his body.

"Not."

She slammed her fist into the armrest. Her father was dead.

"My."

She slammed it again. Her mother was alive.

"FAULT!"

She screamed and laid her head on the steering wheel. Every strained breath pulled more air into her lungs. Her hands tightened on the wheel, knuckles ablaze. Everything that happened to her, around her, was part of her, but she was *not* the cause. *People make choices. Just because I witness their choices, I am not responsible for their choices.* She knew that now.

"Just breathe, Dana." She straightened up with a deep breath. Setting her hands on the wheel, she aimed the car toward the road. "Just. Breathe."

Chapter 45

Do You Believe in Love – Huey Lewis and The News

Nick smashed the buttons on his game controller with extreme prejudice. Joshua fell backward, his controller rattling to the hotel carpet.

"Touchdown, Andrews!" Nick exclaimed, pumping his fist in the air. "And that, my friend, is how it's done!"

Joshua collected his controller and placed it on the dresser next to the box of room-temperature pizza. After a grueling three hours of gaming, the duo conceded to their hunger and dove into the remaining slices.

"Alright, alright, you continue your undefeated streak," Joshua said through a mouthful of pizza. "I'm probably going to have to call my wife in a bit to check in."

The days in protective custody passed faster than Nick had imagined they would. Dan had provided a software patch to block Nick's IP so that he could log on to his school's site and check in on his courses. Joshua proved to be a formidable, but still beatable gaming opponent whenever he showed up a couple hours before his and Dan's daily briefing. Nick even found himself to be a valuable member of the meetings with Joshua and Dan, as he could chime in with his own insights from his encounters with One Hundred Roads. On time tonight, as usual, Dan knocked and entered to begin today's briefing.

"Guys, we got problems." He checked the hallway and closed the door. He slid the chain bolt into place and hopped onto the dresser next to the pizza box. "One Hundred Roads is screwing with us somehow."

"What's up now?" Joshua asked.

"Ever hear of Roswell, Georgia? Don't answer. That's where our tactical team got sent on their charter, and apparently their gear as well."

Nick grabbed his laptop and opened the browser. "How does that happen?"

"I'm guessing a hacker. If they had a real inside man, we'd already be located. Dana, too. Anything that goes into operations requests, they seem to spoil or change." Dan glanced over at Nick as he clicked on the keyboard. "What are you looking up, sport?"

"Directions. If the tactical team can't get to Roswell, *New Mexico,* then we'll go. I've overheard you mention regional field offices near there. Can't they supply us with what we need?"

"Yes," Dan said, "but to be clear, there's no 'we.' We're not taking you with us to Roswell. We will deposit you at a secure waypoint outside of New Mexico."

Nick had really come to trust and admire Dan. His ability to assess and execute was formidable, and Nick found himself often agreeing with him most of the time. In this case, he was hoping to change his mind along the way.

"So, sounds like a road trip?"

"It's going to be a full day of driving, but we can do it. Joshua, you're the accountant, so figure out how we can expense this without tipping off OHR as to what we're doing. Nick, draft a route that will get us there the fastest with some options in case we need to improvise. No tolls, if possible, to avoid license plate cameras. I'm going to my room to start packing."

"Fine. Can't wait to tell my wife all this when I call her," Joshua replied, giving a thumbs-up to Dan before he left. Nick rechecked the lock on the door.

"Hey Joshua, do you think—and I know this is crazy—that maybe there's no hacker? That maybe Dan is an 'inside man' for OHR?"

Joshua laughed as he folded the pizza box in half to stuff it into the absurdly small garbage can.

"Absolutely not. Don't think we told you this, but we overlapped for a year in college before we got hired to work for the government. He was only a freshman, but a genius. Got recruited early. But, nah, we know things about each other—things you only know the morning after an epic party." He laughed and pantomimed zipping his lips.

"I honestly can't remember the last one of those I was at."

"Maybe we'll have one when this is all over." Josh sat down on the edge of the desk and crossed his arms. "You talk to Dana today?"

"Not yet." Nick fell back on the stiff rough blanket covering the bed. "I think she's been helping her mom on the ranch today. Maybe they're tuning up the robotic jackalopes or something." He craned his neck and saw Joshua smiling broadly.

"You guys are a thing, aren't you?"

"I don't know." Nick shrugged his shoulders. He had convinced himself that their friendship was changing, and although he was curious to pursue something more, the current situation made it impossible. "It's hard to explain."

"Try me."

"You know, sometimes you just really work well with someone. You speak each other's language, you help each other out, you defeat a giant robotic engine of destruction, and then you find out you really enjoy being together. You want them to be the best person they can be." He smiled. "And you hope they think the same things about you."

Joshua fiddled with his wedding ring. He removed it and looked at it against the light.

"Do you know what I have engraved inside my wedding band?" He held it out to Nick, but as Nick reached for it, Joshua snatched it back. "Something very special that my wife said I am never allowed to say to anyone but her." He slipped the ring back on his finger. "It's the lyrics to a Beatles song."

"So, you *can't* tell me what it is?"

"I can tell you, but you wouldn't understand the significance. Only my wife does. If you and Dana share anything like that, then what you have means something. I hope that makes sense." He spun his ring on his finger. "From what I can tell, you two have something special."

"I think maybe we do."

Joshua held up his right hand. "I promise, my friend, that I will do everything and anything possible to keep her safe and get you two back together—whatever 'together' means."

The two men shook on the vow.

"And I promise, Joshua, that I will try not to snore on the car ride to New Mexico. Now go call your wife, and I'll call my . . . not-girlfriend."

Nick's phone vibrated on the bedside table, the screen flashing Dana's name.

"Looks like you guys really are mentally connected."

Joshua excused himself and left Nick to pick up the call.

"Hey, Derby Girl, what's up?"

"Hey, buddy." Her voice sounded upbeat but tired. "Just spoke with Tara."

"Wait, was that wise? I'm holed up here for a reason, you know."

Her voice was silent for a moment before she replied. "I'm being safe, Nicky. It's just something I really needed to do."

"Alright. How did it go?"

"It was a really good talk that somehow ended with me in a bad place, but I got out of it." She blew into the phone on her side. "I had a memory flash in my head today when I was starting to spiral, something I now know I never processed: the moment when I finally saw my dad's body. I just haven't even wanted to think about it. I'm sure now that I've acknowledged it, it's easily fixed with ice cream and a good sad movie. Or years of therapy and shock treatment."

"What a relief," Nick said kindly. "I'll get a pint of rocky road and some jumper cables."

"Ha, yeah." Her voice faded.

"Everything else alright?"

"I had some heavy moments with my mom. It's a lot to unpack. Did I mention how surreal this all is?"

"I'm sorry, Dana."

"So. Anyway. Anything you can tell me about what's going on with the fed side of things?"

"Well, plans are underway to head to New Mexico, myself included."

"Don't make any promises you can't keep."

"I won't," Nick replied. He tucked the phone under his ear as he folded the small assortment of newly acquired clothes and placed them inside a backpack Joshua had left for him. He held up a Minnesota Twins T-shirt before adding it to the bag. "But you have to promise you are not going to steal all my sweet new threads funded by the hard-earned dollars of the US taxpayers."

"I'm going to guess my mom is not one of those. Most likely, tax evasion is on her rap sheet just under murder and assault charges."

"Are you sure you're talking about the same woman I met? That woman seemed nice. Rugged, but nice."

"Same woman, but her prequel is a different story."

Nick heard two raised female voices in the background.

"Gotta go. Mom and Ash are coming in for dinner."

"Alright. Stay safe."

"I will."

He swallowed hard. "I miss you, Dana."

"I miss you, too."

Chapter 46

Banditos – The Refreshments

Dana sauntered into her mother's living room, bleary-eyed from tossing and turning. The clock in the kitchen noted the time was just after two A.M. Simone and Ashley were kneeling over the coffee table and staring at an unfolded map of the state while her mother rubbed the back of her neck and drank from a bottle of beer. She'd had a lot those since she got back.

"About time you joined us, Dana," Simone remarked. "Take a seat."

"Ok, what did I do now?" Dana smirked. *Just add it to the list.*

"That burner phone you took from Rhodes's guy? It started buzzing today. There was a voice mail." Her eyebrows rose. "For you."

"The phone you told me *not* to turn on?"

"It occurred to me that, much like myself, people like them would never use phones that could be easily traced, so I charged it yesterday and turned it on. Figured if they could trace it, they would have been here within the hour and the floor would be littered with shell casings. Anyhow, listen."

Simone pressed the speaker button so they all could hear it.

A voice slightly familiar to Dana spoke first, although it was so muffled and far away, she could only make out certain words.

"'Alright, let's go . . . the gulley.'"

"Knees."

An Australian accent floated into the air next, this one much clearer, and one that she recognized immediately.

Dana leaned over the phone and twisted her neck to listen. "That's Ninety-Nine," she whispered. "Olsen."

The other speaker answered, and when Olsen responded again, he clearly identified him as Brian.

The hair on the back of Dana's neck stood up as their words took shape. The talk of burning down the reservation sent chills down her spine as she immediately thought about Frank Irons and his kindness, reminiscent of Nick's father. Any potential harm that came to him was, in her mind, her responsibility. But it was the final thing Olsen said that stayed with her.

"And if you find Dana Jefferson, thank her for me."

Dana jumped from her seat at the sound of the gunshot that ended the recording. She stared at the phone in disbelief.

"Why did he mention *me*?"

"I listened to it a few times. I think Olsen knew you'd have *this* phone and I think he was trying to—hear me out—get your help or warn you of something."

"Why would you think that?"

"Because he texted this right before the call."

Her mother handed her the phone with the last text message that came through, only seconds before the voice mail's timestamp. It contained an address and a location tag for GPS coordinates.

Dana sat, slack-jawed. "What the hell? He dropped a pin for us?"

Simone pointed to the map on the table. "The coordinates are right here. That's an airport—looks like it's a private airstrip. There are a few around here like this that rent space or the entire location for a time period, usually to companies that need to shuttle materials or manpower for contractors. And, if you find the right one, they'll take your cash and look the other way."

"I see," Dana said hesitantly. "But I don't see. Ninety-Nine was there?"

"I think 'was' is the operative word," her mother noted. "I think he was being put to pasture and he was throwing a lifeline out." She paused. "To you."

Ashley grabbed a sheet of paper from the printer across the room and started writing.

"Sis, we think he's giving you details in his message."

Dana nodded slowly. "Right, like telling us to come at three A.M. when they're likely to be drunk or asleep?"

"That's what I think," Simone said. "And saying specifically that there are usually *six* people there during night watch. He didn't say 'a couple' or 'a few'; he counted out the personnel. *Six*."

She walked back to the kitchen and opened the freezer door. "What the hell did I come in here for?" Simone grabbed a chilled pint glass from behind a stack of frozen food and set it on the table. "We're out of cold beer, by the way." She poured one into the frosty glass and drank half before coming back into the living room.

Dana glanced across the map and tried to figure out the distances in her head. She rubbed her eyes and looked at the clock. "Alright, I'll get my skates on."

"Not tonight," her mom admonished. "Logistically, I need a little more time, and we're going to need our full energy for tomorrow night. We're not doing this without a plan, a backup plan, and a worst-case-scenario plan. Does that make sense to you two? I'm a tired mama bear, but I'm awake enough to listen to holes in my thinking."

"Let me run this by Nick in the morning. He's good at this stuff." She wished he were here to listen and tell her what to do. "We work well together. And he really needs to know about the reservation part. I don't know if that's true, but I think Rhodes is probably capable of anything."

"You are right about that. But tell Nick no feds. If this is all lining up the way we think it is, this is my chance to steal back my invention and dole out some outlaw justice, all while getting in some quality time with my girls." Simone leaned her head back and closed her eyes. "Just no feds . . ." She began to snore.

Dana poked Ashley in the arm.

"Does she usually fall asleep that fast?"

"Only when she's been drinking," Ashley whispered. "And she only drinks like this when she's about to engage in some bad mother behavior."

"What does that mean?"

Ashley nodded toward the pile of bags Simone collected from the cache. "She's going to shoot first."

The next day, Dana, Ashley, and Simone sat on the same side of the kitchen table, each daughter flanking their mother while she laid out a series of images taken from online satellite maps. She flicked the cap of her yellow highlighter with her thumb repeatedly and stared intently at the phone on the table, waiting for something to happen. Nick finally appeared on-screen and smiled.

"Okay, this is just insane," he declared after they filled him in. "There is no way we're going to pull this off. You're talking about infiltrating a highly trained team of mercenaries and ne'er-do-wells who have no qualms about killing anyone in their way."

"Nicky, don't say 'ne'er-do-well' ever again," Dana said. "You sound like a film noir detective."

"Right. Got it. Simone, run this by me again. I'm looking at the photos and maps Dana emailed, but I'm not seeing how this works."

Simone grabbed the phone and held it over the map. She nodded at Ashley to take over and maintain an aerial view for Nick.

"Okay, this is all based on Olsen, our dead information broker. Here's where we go in." She drew a thick line with the highlighter across the map. "We're going to head right up to the hangar door, assuming it's open at three A.M., and I'll set up a kill cone." She drew an *X* on each side of the hangar. "We're planning on six people being there. Assuming two are outside, they'll likely be on each side of the opening. I should be able to take out both of them right off the bat."

"Okay." Nick followed along mostly. "But that leaves at least four more people inside. We assume."

"Right. Once I take out one or both goons at the opening, I move the cone of fire." She drew a triangle on the map and an arrow to indicate a pivot to the left. "That opens up a hole for Dana to block for Ashley, since she's the weakest—"

"Hey!" Ashley pouted at her mother.

"You're a teenager, baby. You're at a disadvantage going against people experienced in hand-to-hand combat. Dana will be your blocker. Think roller derby. You're on the jam. Follow her, and she'll keep you protected so you can then loop through whatever structures are inside. Shelves, crates, lockers, whatever. Look for the same case you retrieved from the train. We have to assume it's there." Simone drew a circle counterclockwise on the map. "While you girls are doing that, I'll keep engaged with the rest of the group."

"Simone, if I may," Nick interrupted, "are you going to be the only one with a gun?"

"Yes. I've taught Ashley to shoot in self-defense, but engaging in offensive fire is different." She glanced at each daughter. "This isn't the movies. And I'm not going to put you in any moral dilemma if you have to kill someone."

Dana exhaled. She hadn't thought about choosing to kill, even though she wanted Rhodes, Brian, and Nina dead.

Nick's voice broke through her haze.

"Simone, I know you have security cams around the house. Any chance you have a GoPro lying around? You know, a camera you can mount on your shoulder that I can tap into and have eyes on things? I could help you remotely then."

"I actually have a GoPro," Ashley interjected. "I used to wear it when I started skating, back before everything got better with cellphones." She glared at Simone. "When Mom finally let me get something made in the current decade."

"Great idea, Nick," Simone commented, ignoring Ashley's snark. In a less-than-subtle whisper, she said to Dana, "I like him. You should definitely ask him out after this is all over."

"Mom." Dana slapped her hands over her cheeks.

Simone winked at Nick's image on the screen. "So, there are just two variables that worry me. One, if there's more people there than we were told, and two, if the hangar doors are closed."

Nick scratched his head. "If there are many more people, that should be obvious when you get there because there will be extra vehicles, extra gear outside. Then it's on you to advance or bail on the mission."

"And if the door's closed?" asked Ashley. "Ideas?"

"A hangar door that big is most likely opened and closed via a keypad or a set of buttons. Having to use a physical key to unlock it and relock a massive door like that every time would be cumbersome, especially for long-term renters. We used similar doors at the electric company's work center back in New Jersey. I can help troubleshoot whatever it is once you're there.

If it's closed, most likely there won't be anyone to greet you outside. We'll have time."

"Okay. We'll eat, get some more rest, and call you when we're on our way. Ashley will send you the log-in details for the GoPro. Anything else?"

"I'd like to go on record again and say this is insane. Why do you think this tip from Olsen is a change of heart and not a trap?"

Dana was resting her chin in her hands and looking over the map and aerial photos again. She traced the yellow lines from start to finish before feeling her mother's eyes on her, waiting for her to respond to Nick.

"Well, Nick," Dana concluded, "because we heard the gunshot at the end of the recording. And, if it was a trap, I think they would have given us a clearer trail of breadcrumbs to follow. They'd have given us a clearly defined time, date, and place." She bit her upper lip and exhaled slowly through her nose. "And he said my name. My full name. He wanted to make sure I knew he was counting on me."

Nick nodded. "Well, then, I think we should take the comment about the reservation seriously, too. I'll have to find a way to warn Frank Irons. I'd really like to tell the feds that piece."

"No," responded Simone firmly. "If we complete our mission, there'll be nothing to talk to the feds about."

"Understood. Good luck, and please be safe," he said to everyone, but Dana knew it was meant for her.

Simone hung up the video call. She placed her hand around Dana's pulsing wrist. "We got this, honey," she said in a soft voice.

Standing up, she walked over to a weathered duffel bag next to the gun cases, produced a small tan bulletproof vest, and tossed it to Ashley. She followed up with another slightly bigger vest of the same color and tossed it to Dana.

"This should fit you. Ashley, yours might be a little snug now, but it'll do the job."

Dana ran her hands over the stiff material of the vest. "Mom," Dana asked, "what about you?"

Simone smiled unconvincingly. "I'll be okay. We have two things working to our advantage. Number one, the element of surprise."

Simone walked past the long container for the sniper rifle and the box with her smaller guns to a third case nearby, which she picked up with great ease and placed on the coffee table. With a coy glance at Ashley, Simone unlocked the two latches with a slow and seductive flick of each wrist.

"Number two," she said in the same singsong manner as Dana, "we have speed."

She reached into the case with deliberate movements. She tugged back at the fabric and slowly revealed two matte black shin guards, weathered and gouged, attached to matching black roller skates. The wheels on each skate were wrapped in the same metallic coils as Dana's, oily and dirty from their time in storage. Dana extended her hands as her mom lifted one out, accepting the left skate like a newborn baby and cradling it to her chest.

"Oh, Mom, they're beautiful. They look like little baby demons." She laughed as Ashley pet the shin guard and mockingly cooed at the boot.

"They are demons," Simone announced with a smile, though her eyes brimmed with anger. She placed a hand over her left pectoral and patted the scar tissue underneath her shirt. "And with their help, I am sending a few of those bastards to hell tonight."

Chapter 47

Run Runaway – Slade

A comet of glittering sparks weaved over the two-lane road approaching the airport. Dana, bookended by her mother in the lead and Ashley in the rear, spied a lone coyote paused at the end of the airport driveway, watching their approach. It tilted its head with the changes in pitch as the skates turned and slithered in its direction. Abruptly, the coyote turned and sprinted over the plain as they closed the gap.

"Good boy," Dana yelped.

"Alright," Simone chirped into her headset, "stay tight. Nick, keep your eyes on the dead spaces." She tugged on the strap attaching the GoPro to her vest. "You got me? Night vision on your side is good?"

"Copy that, Mama Bear."

Simone entered the driveway, and Dana and Ashley accelerated to catch up. They huddled together to get their bearings. The hangar stood at the center of the runway area, flanked by a small single-prop plane on the right and a tiny bubble-shaped helicopter farther away on the left. Beyond the helicopter was a double-wide trailer with the words AIRPORT OFFICE over the door in large letters. Two Hummers and a jeep sat askew in their parking spaces next to a dumpster. The bay doors rested wide open, and only one guard stood outside next to them.

"That's one thing in our favor," noted Simone.

"And there's our cover, Mama Bear," Dana said, pointing to the Hummer closest to the building. "Ready to go?"

Simone swung the assault rifle that hung off her shoulder to the front of her body. Her old revolver clung to her thigh in its leather holster.

"Girls, stick to the plan. I will shoot to incapacitate if possible, but I will kill if I need to. Just trust me."

Both girls nodded their agreement.

Dana usually enjoyed the adrenaline that surged through her when she got ready to hit the derby floor, but this felt different—there was so much at stake here, real risk. She had observed her mother carefully on their way, her movements relaxed and graceful as she skated, but her skates looked militant compared to hers and Ashley's. Dana might even say "ruthless," an adjective she found herself applying to her mother as well. She had no doubt that Simone would kill if it came to that.

Ashley grabbed Dana's hand and squeezed. "Ready for launch, Photograph?"

"Ready, Phoenix."

"Okay, Nick, we're going in," Simone said into the earpiece.

"Copy, Mama Bear."

"Going right!" she barked and then pushed off.

The roar of the grinding skates filled the tarmac. The single guard leaning next to the open doorway looked up at the sound and promptly dropped his cigarette. Simone broke left and dropped to one knee, gliding on the power of her leading skate as she leveled her gun. A quick burst of fire into his shoulder dropped the guard before he could grab his sidearm.

"One down," she barked. "Nick, I need a real-time count as we plow through. Don't wait for me to ask to give me an update."

"Copy. Two coming from around the back on the right."

Dana pumped her skates and roared toward the two mercenaries as they rushed to see where the gunshot came from. They each took the brunt of Dana's elbows as she plowed in between them. Ashley followed with a stomp to each as she bounded off their bodies.

"Clear to the right, girls!" Simone fired a shot into each of the stunned mercenaries laying on the ground.

Ashley and Dana cut a wide arc to come back toward the opening in the hangar but held back when they saw two more soldiers emerge with handguns.

"Leave them to me!" Simone yelled as she headed behind the Hummer nearest the hangar door, pulling their focus.

Dana tapped her headset.

"I've counted five guards, right? Nick, anyone else visible?"

"Nothing yet, Photograph. Take Phoenix inside."

Dana reached her hand back and grabbed Ashley. Together they soared through the open hangar door, past the gunmen engaged with their mother hidden behind the truck.

"Phoenix, time to crack the whip!"

Dana swung her arm forward and shot Ashley into the hangar. The gunmen turned their attention toward the two younger skaters long enough for Simone to zone in on her targets. She stood and fired a shot into the shoulder of each man, felling them within a single breath.

"Ash," Simone yelled into her headset, "anything yet?"

"Nothing. Lots of boxes and shipping crates, but nothing that looks like a suitcase."

Dana skated in a loop near the hangar door, keeping her eyes on Ashley as she moved.

"Lights on in the trailer office," Simone chimed in.

"It's gotta be Nina or Brian. Ashley's fine in here. I'm coming."

"Dana, wait!"

Ignoring her mother's command as well as her better positioning, Dana flew back out the hangar opening and arrived at the trailer door just as it swung open. A short man with a shaved head and beard stumbled out, his arm in a sling.

"Oh, not you again," Eugene sputtered. Dana spun on her skate and landed a roundhouse kick to his face, smashing his nose with her shin guard. His unconscious body fell to the concrete next to a bloody tooth.

"Dana, stay on mission!" her mother called from behind her. "Let me take them out!"

"I got this, Mom!"

"Dana, pull back *now!*"

She had barely registered Simone's command when a metallic fist connected with the side of her head. Dana shook it off best she could and looked back to see Nina ready to swing again at her stunned adversary.

"You guys don't give up," Nina fumed.

Dana shot backward on her skates, and Nina's punch missed by a few inches. She lunged and caught Dana's wrist in her mechanized grip, then swung her into the side of the trailer. Dana's Kevlar vest under her jacket took the brunt of the force but it still stunned her, forcing air out of her lungs.

"Dammit, that hurt, you robot bitch!"

"So will this!"

As Nina swung again, Dana kicked high with her skate to block her, creating a burst of sparks as her grinding wheels connected with Nina's metal forearm.

"Hands off!" Dana pressed her skate into the artificial limb with all her might, trapping Nina's arm between the trailer and her skate, the impact of the whirring metal slowly slicing through the artificial limb. Nina screamed in disbelief as the flying embers scalded her face. Dana released her skate and, as Nina looked down at her mangled arm, swung a fist into Nina's cheek, knocking her back onto the concrete.

Dana glanced back at the hangar and sprinted toward the opening, but thought better when another guard stepped out from the other side. She dove behind the truck with her mother.

"Phoenix, where are you?"

"I'm going in circles! I don't see it anywhere!"

The guard fired his pistol at their location.

"Nick, is that six now? Seven?"

"Six guards."

"Plus Eugene and Nina."

"And now I see a runner. Simone, look right!"

A lone man sprinted from behind the back of the hangar toward the prop plane. His salt-and-pepper hair shone as he passed under a light pole. He tossed a small black case into the cabin and leapt inside.

"Rhodes!" With a primal scream, Simone erupted from behind the truck and fired an angry hail of bullets toward the plane.

Dana heard the propeller start before she saw the plane jerking and rolling onto the taxi strip perpendicular to the runway. The plane turned ninety degrees and accelerated. She sprinted across the tarmac.

"Mom, hold your fire! Nick, he's in a single-engine plane with the wing above the cockpit, maybe like two seats."

"Hang on," he buzzed back in their earpieces. "Probably a Cessna. Takeoff speed is sixty knots according to what I see here. That's about seventy miles per hour, I think? You can catch it."

"Done." Dana roared onto the runway behind the plane. There was no way she would allow Rhodes to escape, especially not with that component. This was the man who had torn her family apart—she would tear apart with her own bare hands if she was given the chance.

She funneled her anger into her legs and pumped harder. The blast of air from the propeller stung her face as she raced behind it.

"Closer!" she yelled, stretching toward the tail of the plane. "Shit, shit, shit! Come on, girls!" she barked at her skates.

"Dana," Nick yelled through the earpiece, "if you can grab onto the tail, just press down on the elevator!"

"The what?!"

"The flap on the tail! That will keep it from taking off!"

With a sudden surge, she got close enough to grab hold of the tail and secured her arms over the flap on the right side. She pressed her body weight onto it and held tight. The plane jerked wide left, then back right, as it reached the end of the runway and turned around.

"Dana," Simone shouted into the earpiece, "if you can hear me, he's turned around to take off. Hold that elevator down!"

"That's the only plan I've got, Mom!"

The propeller's roar intensified as Rhodes opened the throttle for takeoff. Her mother and Nick continued to shout commands through the earpiece, but she couldn't discern anything over the deafening decibels of the engine's intensifying whirring. She squinted behind her goggles as she gripped the tail and dug her skates into the concrete. The plane continued to buck forward against her effort, speeding faster and faster. She titled her head and shoved her ear into her arm, and could finally hear her mother.

"Dana, dive right!"

The plane attempted to lift off the ground as Dana let go and dove, rolling and tumbling to the side of the runway. Simone charged from the opposite end of the runway, skating head-on toward the plane. She dropped into a knee slide as she brought her rifle to her shoulder and fired into the propeller. The landing gear skipped on the ground as it lost control, turning sideways and rolling over in a raucous cacophony of shattering fiberglass and aluminum.

Simone slid over to Dana. "Star!"

"Jesus, Mom, a little more warning next time!" Dana sat up and shook her hair free of dirt and debris.

"I'm sorry, it was loud. Stay behind me. Phoenix!" she yelled into the earpiece. "Stay wherever you are! The case is with Rhodes."

The pilot's door clattered to the ground as Rhodes crawled out, his forehead bloodied, his pant leg tattered. He dragged the black case out of the wreckage behind him.

Simone crept toward the overturned fuselage and leveled her gun at Rhodes.

"Sit, you piece of dog shit."

"I know something you don't know," he sneered. Simone leveled the gun at his head. "Look up, sweetie." Rhodes began to laugh.

A motorized chopping noise rose behind them as the wind picked up. A spotlight from a helicopter blinded Simone and Dana, its draft blasting them with a storm of sand as it touched down with a thud on the runway next to Rhodes. A man jumped out and, to Dana and Simone's horror, he was holding Ashley, her arms pinned behind her back. Brian sat in the pilot's seat, smirking. Simone raised her gun.

"You have something I need," Rhodes said calmly. "Give me the component you stole from the train, and you get this little girl back."

"Don't touch her," Dana yelled. "Ashley, stay calm!"

"You'll shut up and listen!" Rhodes snarled. "You *will* bring me the other component tomorrow, six P.M. at the Hoover Dam. Better get going if you're going to get the part and make it on time. And come alone—or else."

Simone gritted her teeth and snarled back at him. "I'll be there, you bastard!"

Rhodes pursed his lips in disgust. "Oh, you poor old woman. All those brains gone to waste. I was talking to Dana. *She* comes alone. You won't be able to."

He waved to the chopper. Nina leaned out of the cockpit with a gun in her useable hand and fired at Simone, hitting her square in the chest.

Dana could see Ashley screaming, but she could only hear the ringing in her ears. Simone fell back.

The sound of the helicopter blades contorted into a high-pitched white noise in her ears as the man shoved Ashley inside and Rhodes jumped in, clutching the black briefcase. The helicopter lifted up into the blackness of night and disappeared.

Simone's cough pierced the sudden silence.

"Mom!" Dana dropped to her knees and grabbed her mother by the shoulders.

"Easy, girl! Mama Bear may have a cracked rib." Simone remained on the hot concrete and began to slowly unbutton her shirt. A weathered bulletproof vest was revealed, dented and tattered.

"Mom, I thought you were dead!" Dana cried.

"I'll be alright." She exhaled slowly through her mouth and wiped another tear from her eye. "I found this old thing before we left, thankfully." She coughed and wheezed as she carefully stood up. "It's been around the block . . . a block the size of Alaska."

Nick's voice broke through Dana's earpiece. "Dana, what is happening?! The camera went out!" He sounded panicked.

"They *kidnapped* Ashley, Nick, and Mom was shot but she's . . . fine? Mom, I don't know how you can be so . . . so . . . *fine* right now! Rhodes has Ashley!"

Simone picked up her rifle and slung it across her back. "I've been here before. We can't panic. We have a new objective: get Ashley back. He won't hurt her as long we have something he wants."

She started to skate toward the driveway out to the highway and motioned for Dana to follow, grabbing her hand when she got closer. "We've got a very hard thing ahead of us. But we still have each other, and that means we've got a chance. Come on, Star."

Chapter 48

The Gambler – Kenny Rogers

Simone went about getting supplies together as though it was like any other morning. They had only returned from the airport just before six A.M., and they had to get on the road ASAP. It was almost an eleven-hour drive to the Hoover Dam. How her mother could be so calm when her daughter had been taken by a group of terrorists was something Dana had failed to wrap her head around. Simone's life in hiding had clearly warped her perspective.

"Dana, I need to show you something. Or rather, you need to hear something." She walked over to the pantry and retrieved a box from underneath a case of freeze-dried meal packs. Dana itched her armpit and scrunched her face at her own sweaty odor, but there was no time to shower. She fell into the seat at the head of the table as her mom returned and set the box on the table. "There's something I need to play for you. This isn't going to be easy, but it's something you need to know. It's about your father."

Simone placed a microcassette recorder on the table along with a tiny box of tapes. She thumbed through the cases and retrieved one labeled "Ashley." She placed it into the recorder and hit Play.

The first voice on the recording pierced Dana's ears. It was her father, but his tone was tense and agitated, not smooth and soft like she had known as a child. Dana closed her eyes and shut out everything but the sounds of the cassette so she didn't miss a thing.

Samuel: So, what is it now?

Simone: The doctor said he needs to know what I'm on. He said there are cell masses in my chest cavity that concern him. This has to stop. We can't do this. *I can't do this.*

Samuel: We're so close! And this pregnancy couldn't have come at a better time.

Simone: I regret this, Sam. We can't do this to her. You saw what happened with Nina. Her nervous system went into atrophy from the shock. Her limbs aren't growing, and Colin said they might have to amputate her arms and legs because of the tumors and fissures.

Samuel: But we *know* she had too much of the formulas. We don't have to make that mistake. We've made so much progress in neurological and DNA studies since Nina's experiment.

Simone: Experiment? She's a goddamn child, *not* a test subject! *Our daughter is not a test subject!*

Samuel: You know they couldn't use Dana. She wasn't good enough, and definitely not smart enough.

AUDIBLE SMACK

Simone: Don't you *ever* say that.

Samuel: You know what I mean. She's not right for the program. She wasn't given any of the formulas or growth hormones early enough. Sure, her reflexes are in the ninety-ninth percentile, but we need a superior neurological base for the machine. And you and I both passed all the tests for the optimal gene and nerve maps for the proposed interface with the Atomic Juggernaut. This baby is it!

Simone: Bastard. Listen to yourself! You're blinded by the science. You didn't tell me this was next. You didn't tell me that my baby was going to be given up for the perversion of this invention. *My* invention. I don't even know you anymore. And if the doctor's right, I might not know you much longer.

Samuel: What does that mean?

Simone: It means I have *cancer*, Sam! That's the point he's talking around. I'm going to have this baby while I have cancer. They can't do radiation treatment, or it'll kill my baby.

Samuel: Our baby.

Simone: She's not your child anymore, as far as I'm concerned. I need to go. I have a follow up with another specialist.

Samuel: Are you going to tell him about the treatment?

Simone: How can I? I don't even know what's in that cocktail you've been feeding me! I can't even begin to synthesize it, and yes, I have already tried.

Samuel: You know that whatever it is, you can't tell them about the program, right? That needs to be clear.

Simone: You have no soul left.

Samuel: Simone, we all signed their waivers. When a person dies, the government takes care of their family. You know that—

Simone: That was supposed to be the worst-case scenario! Six men have died!

Samuel: Seven. Rodney died yesterday.

Simone: Oh my God. You're inhuman. I don't know you. Get out of this house. *Get out!*

The recording stopped. Dana stared into the recorder, her eyes glassy and unfocused. Her chest felt hollow, her fingers frozen as they clutched her coffee mug. The echoes of her father's words faded into the early morning air. Simone reached her hand across the table.

"I needed you to know how far I'd go for you girls. He's not the father you remember. I needed you to know that. I made these recordings starting after the third death in the program. At first, I thought I'd use them to get through to him, but instead they just found their way into the things I took for insurance when I went on the run. I knew they'd never touch you—you weren't 'good enough' and your grandfather would watch out for you. Ashley became the prize I could never let them win."

Dana's jaw quivered. "He said I wasn't 'good enough.'" The words cut her throat as she said them. Her own father. Her eyes stung.

"Hey, now, you know that's not true. *You know that, dammit*. I held on to that, Dana, while I was on the run. I knew that you *were* good enough, would be able to figure things out, be a good person, and do good things, even without me." Simone wiped at her eyes with her free hand. "I had to believe that."

"Does Ashley know that she was intended to be a lab rat?"

"I think she's figured it out to a certain extent. But I promise, when we get her back, I'll tell her the full truth just so she hears it from me."

Dana gripped her mother's hand tighter. Simone matched her grip.

"Dana, I may not be the best mom, but all moms, they just do the best they can. And sometimes as a mom, you have to make hard and painful decisions, even if it's with the best intentions. And like I said, the hardest thing that a parent can do is lie to their children . . . even if it's how you save their life."

Dana kept replaying the words uttered by her father in her head. Everything about him was now run through a dirty filter, her memories mutilated by his self-centeredness. He was nothing like Mitch, who had raised Nick with honesty and strength and love, no matter how hard it got. Now, Dana doubted if her father had ever truly loved her. But she would have to ponder this all later, after they rescued Ashley.

"I'm sorry I doubted you. And I'm sorry for when I disobeyed. And for not looking for you sooner."

"Later. We can all talk later."

"Right, sorry. We'll talk more later. Right now, we have a tight timeline."

Dana picked up the cassette to place it back into the box and paused; another tape underneath the pile caught her eye. The label was in her mother's hand, crisp and clean: ZERO ENERGY.

"Mom? What's this?" The tape glinted in the light as she held it up.

"My brain on tape. Just in case."

"Let's go over this one more time."

Simone and Dana stood in the studio and stared at the large painting on the easel. They turned the frame into the light from the single window in the room. The five-by-eight-foot canvas shone with the bright colors of the Colorado River as it carved through the Black Canyon and pooled behind the Hoover Dam. Simone's strokes added texture and life to the immense concrete structure, and subtle tiny specks of brown and blue paint decorated the walkway, representing pedestrians. Simone placed her thumb on the far-left ridge on the painted scene.

"Mom, this is beautiful. When did you paint this?"

"Years ago, right when we arrived back here and bought the ranch. Never thought it would be useful. Anyhow, this is where I'd set up," she said, pointing to a spot near the walkway. "At six o'clock, the sun will be setting in the west. That position will be backlit and blinding for anyone looking up." She traced her thumb across the canvas to the other ridge. "Remember, they think I'm dead, and you're supposed to be there alone. You'll come across here from the access road, on the same side."

"Why on earth do you think they picked the Hoover Dam?"

"Because it's on the way to their exit plan, or their rendezvous with their buyer? Maybe so that we'd lose prep time and resources just *driving* out there. I really don't know, and at this point that's immaterial. We have to leave now. We don't have the luxury of a helicopter."

Dana nodded and glanced once more at her mother's painted landscape. The size and scale of the dam, even in a painted representation, both impressed and intimidated her. "Seven hundred twenty-six feet, you said?"

"Yep, and I've got about eight hundred feet of rope in the barn with my climbing gear. It weighs about fifty-two grams per meter, so converting feet to meters, times grams, and converting to pounds, we're good. We're looking at under thirty pounds."

Dana blinked at her mom.

"You did all that in your head?"

"I designed a walking robotic tank and a near-zero energy power cell, sweetie."

"True. Do you think this will work?"

Simone placed the palm of her hand on the center of the dam. "It has to. Did you call Nick?"

"He just sent a text, said he's still hours away. He said it looks like we're not going to have any backup in time."

Simone snorted. "Maybe that's why they picked the Hoover freaking Dam. Anyway, what's the nuclear option if they capture you, too?"

"I offer them all your project plans and the whistleblower tapes." Dana leaned into her mom's face. "But I'm not going to do that, Mom. I can't."

Simone pressed her lips to Dana's forehead. "Then we can't screw this up."

Chapter 49

Freedom! '90 – George Michael

Dana drew a long slow breath to steady her nerves and mentally reviewed the details of what she had to do. The long curving walkway stretched a quarter mile across the lip of the dam with pedestrians and tourists milling around benches and plaques, pausing for selfies and snapping photos of the river and sinking sun above the far side of the canyon. The noise of the river choked by the dam's inlets echoed faintly. While she had only been to the Hoover Dam's observation walk once on a road trip when she was younger, she knew the powerplant building itself was patrolled by officers and marked off-limits to tourists.

Dana cinched the straps on her backpack, grunting as the weight of the coiled rope shifted and rested on her hips. She rechecked the clasps on her shin guards.

"I'm ready to roll, Mom. How's it looking?" She placed a finger on her earpiece to raise the volume.

"All clear here, Dana. I see Nina and Ashley at the far end. Looks like they're waiting for you."

Dana clicked her heels to disable the wheel lock without engaging the motors and began to roll slowly forward. Two men in black canvas jackets glanced at her before looking away.

"Mom, hold up. You said you saw Nina, not Rhodes?"

"Affirmative."

Dana scanned the tourists ahead of her on the concourse. A man in aviator glasses and a short-brimmed tan hat talked to another man wearing khakis and combat boots. Both wore plain navy-blue sweatshirts. Another man with a brown crewcut wearing jeans and a puffy varsity jacket with no school logo walked past her. Everywhere she looked, small clusters of relatively fit men between the ages of twenty and forty dotted the path.

"Mom. There are no women or children, only men. I feel like I'm about to skate into a hive of hornets."

"Dana, hold up. Someone just rolled up on the far ridge. Pull off to the side, look casual."

Dana did as she was told, then sheltered her brow and studied the crest of the hill on the opposite side. A black jeep sat parked alone. The driver was obscured by the distance and sun.

She assumed that by now her mother was now lying on her belly and staring down the barrel of her long gun, the Barrett.

"Who's up there?"

"I'm using the spotting scope to see now. It's a little challenging to pivot thirty pounds of sniper rifle on the fly." Another sigh followed a pause. "Looks they got a sniper here, too. I've got company."

"Details?"

"Moustache, well-built. I think he was the chopper pilot from the airport."

"Shit. Brian. Can you take him out?" Dana coasted a few steps closer to the center of the dam.

"Possibly, but once I do that, all our plans get thrown out at that point.

The gunshot will tip them off that you're not alone and make all the tourists panic. I'm beginning to think that's why they picked this place—we can't try anything too risky since there are witnesses."

"Then we stick to the plan for now. But keep your main focus on him."

"Don't worry, babe. Momma's got your back."

Dana rolled slowly toward a bench. Yet another man, this one with a short beard and oversized sunglasses, glanced at her as she passed. She noticed his hand was in the pocket of his coat.

"Not suspicious at all," she whispered out loud. "I'm having a good day, just roller-skating along. Nothing to worry about."

"Nina must have spotted you. She and Ashley are heading your way."

Dana was suddenly very aware of the bulge in her leather jacket pocket and tapped on the component canister for reassurance. As she skated toward Nina and Ashley's direction, she looked over her shoulder at the men behind her, each one trying not to be obvious with their observation of her movement.

"Excuse me, miss."

While looking the other way, Dana had bumped into the gentleman in front of her. He gently caught her by the shoulders as he attempted to step out of her way. His face was kind and unsuspicious compared to many of the men she had encountered so far on the pathway. His dark hair snuck out from under his hat, and he winked at her without breaking a smile.

"Joshua," she whispered.

Joshua nodded as he continued on his way, meandering over to the railing. Dana skated a few steps before talking into her earpiece.

"Mom, the good guys are here."

"Feds?"

"Yeah, but a friend."

"Okay. It's not in my nature to trust them, but it's nice to know you've got backup. I'll keep my focus on taking out Brian so he doesn't take out you. The feds can deal with Nina."

Dana finally spotted Nina and, more importantly, Ashley. They had come to a stop in the middle of the walkway, next to the large marker designating the state line between Nevada and Arizona. Nina wore a black waistcoat, although one sleeve just dangled loosely, fluttering occasionally in the crosswinds. Ashley stood in front of her, looking distraught with her eyes puffy and cheeks streaked. She bit her lip as she spied Dana slowly approaching.

"Hello, Nina, I don't think we've been formally introduced. I'm Dana." She paused as her pulse increased. "Photograph. Will your father be joining us?"

"He's not here," Nina replied. "You won't see him again. Just like I guess you won't be seeing your mother again, either. Give me the component and your sister is free to go."

Dana pulled out the small round cylinder and held it in front of her. She passed it from one hand to the other, locking her eyes on Nina's own.

"Do we need to go through the whole dog-and-pony show?" Nina grit her teeth and grimaced. "Hand it over, Dana. *Photograph.*"

Dana held the component up in Nina's direction, then promptly heaved it over the railing toward the pent-up waters of the Colorado River.

As Nina, wide-eyed, watched it sail over and out of reach, Dana grabbed Ashley's wrist and pulled her to safety behind her.

"Mom, shoot!"

A dull echo ricocheted across the expanse. Nina noticed that Dana and Ashley remained unharmed and whipped her head back toward the top of the canyon where the jeep was parked.

"What the hell?!"

Before she could take even a step, shouts of "Homeland Security!" came from everywhere at once as undercover officers pulled their sidearms from their scattered positions along the walkway. Joshua and his team fell into an array of shooting stances and revealed their badges on lanyards, belt loops, and vests. The remaining men on the walkway revealed their firearms in reply: folding-stock rifles, snub-nosed machines guns, and semiautomatic handguns pointed at the government agents, every firearm matched to another in the standoff.

"You stupid bitch!" Nina snarled.

All at once, they were surrounded by snapping and popping as the lawful agents and their adversaries returned fire, tearing open the tension that built on the bridge. Dana reached back and grabbed the carabiner peeking out the side of her backpack and clamped it on to the railing. She glared at her sister. "Ash, grab onto my chest, and whatever you do, *don't let go.*"

Dana lifted one leg over the rail, Ashley clinging to the front of her, spying from the corner of her eye Nina emerging from her cover. Nina lunged toward her, a metallic claw closing on the tails of Dana's jacket. A burst of silvery splinters erupted from Nina's forearm, liberating the coat from her grasp. Nina, armless, howled as the two sisters rolled over the rail toward the concrete embankment.

"Nice shot, Mom!" Dana shouted as the rope rapidly uncoiled out of her bag and the horizon line rocketed out of her periphery. Her back slammed into the wall of the dam, provoking a shrieking scream from Ashley. Dana spun herself around with a fumbling kick. Her knee cracked into the concrete, protected by the pad under her pantleg.

Just breathe, Dana. You can do this.

"Come on, girls, catch some concrete!" She kicked her left skate, then her right, trying to make solid contact with the wall as the cable continued to spool out of her backpack. The wheels of the skates spun madly in search of traction.

"Come on, Laverne! Come on, Shirley!"

The skates bounced off the wall and sparked sporadically. She reached around Ashley and attempted to grab the rope with her right hand. The pain as it ripped through her palm was blinding. Dana's ears closed as the white noise rose, her breaths getting shallower with every passing second. Her field of vision narrowed as gold flecks filled her remaining view. The panic shuttered her senses one by one as she fought for control. Then, her mom's voice buzzed in her ear.

"Hang on, Star, you're almost there."

Her heart slowed its pounding in her chest. A rush of warm blood filled the sinews of her legs. Dana gritted her teeth and pushed through her legs into the wall.

"Laverne!"

Contact.

"Shirley!"

Contact.

Adrenaline sprinted through her veins. Her thighs and calves tensed as the wheels rolled against the concrete, the river below racing toward them on their descent. The wheels on each skate whirred and roared in unison, unleashing a hailstorm of fire that danced down the face of the dam. Dana screamed in pain, her vocal cords rumbling and raging, her shriek turning into a long howl that then erupted into a primal roar.

"Come on, girls!"

Slack!

She felt the rope relax against her weight for a moment. She roared again, her gravelly scream twisting into a raucous laugh.

"Come on, girls!"

Ashley pressed her cheek against Dana's face as their descent slowed. There was still the sound of gunfire from above, but it abated as they approached the roof of the white expansive structure at the base of the massive wall.

"The eaglets have landed!" Dana yelled into her earpiece.

The sisters collapsed onto the panels. Dana rolled onto her side and clutched her knees. The roar of the river filled her ears as she gazed up at the orange-and-purple streaks in the evening sky above.

"Mom, what's happening up there?"

"Dana, it looks like the feds have everyone in custody. A couple of people down from each side." Dana noted the pause in her mother's speech. "A few of those were my shots."

"Mom. Good guy in a red windbreaker—that's Joshua. What's his status?"

Dana listened to the static reply over her headset. The silence lingered.

"Mom?"

"Dana." Her mom's voice broke as she said it. "When you went over the rail, one of Rhodes's men fired at you and Ashley. The man in the red windbreaker dove in front. He saved you both . . . but he took a lot of rounds. Too many rounds."

Ashley stared at Dana with a quizzical look. "Sis, what's wrong?"

She squeezed her eyes shut. "We just lost a good friend."

Dana reached her uninjured hand out and pulled her sister in as she broke into heavy sobbing, the weight of everything collapsing on her at once. She hadn't asked for anyone to give their life for her, but Joshua had done that. All Rhodes did was take people away *from* their loved ones. She hated him more than ever.

She buried her forehead in her sister's hair and held her tighter.

Chapter 50

The Pavilion (A Long Way Back) – Coheed and Cambria

The mob of nylon-jacketed agents, an alphabet soup of acronyms emblazoned on their backs, rushed from car to car. ATF, FBI, DHS, and USBR dominated the constant scat of consonants and vowels spiraling around Dana. Lining up in front of a dozen emergency vehicles was a convoy of gurneys, some carrying intubated or moaning men, others only black zippered bags that mirrored the evening's shadow enveloping them. Ashley sat on the concrete, legs crossed and wearing only socks—her skates having been taken during her abduction—and clutched the silver blanket gently placed around her shoulders by an emergency technician. Dana looked down at her bandaged hand and then over at her sister.

"Ash?"

"Dana?"

"I think we're gonna be okay."

A trio of men in tactical gear approached, led by a mature woman with neat short gray hair wearing a black pantsuit. She crouched next to Ashley and put a hand on her shoulder sympathetically.

Dana squinted as their eyes met.

"Dana, we met, sort of . . . once." She rose and extended her hand. "Carmen Jameson."

Dana awkwardly put out her uninjured left hand in return, but the director waved it away apologetically.

"Joshua was my favorite son, so to speak. He thought highly of you. He was so fond of your tenacity and resourcefulness. You were responsible for his promotion, you know. He said once that he wished . . . he wished more people like you existed. 'She's one of the good guys' were his exact words." She cleared her throat and looked away at the dam.

Dana bit her lip as she fought an outburst of tears.

"Joshua . . . did Nick send him here?"

"Yes. He made sure to ignore your request to *not* tell Joshua about your plans tonight. I think he regretted not doing the same thing last night at the airport. Joshua and his partner left Nick at a safe house en route, then came right here. You'll be reunited with Nick later." Director Jameson took a deep breath and continued. "As for Joshua, his family is going to be more than taken care of. I want you to know that. And so will your mother."

"My mother is—"

"I know all about your mother. Someone with clearance equal to mine— which, I might add, is very high—filled me in. That was some excellent shooting she did from up there." She surveyed the sisters' faces for a reaction. "Walk with me, ladies."

Director Jameson led the sisters away from the unwinding chaos of the federal and state agents to the parking lot at the base of the dam facility.

"Dana. Ashley. I know that there are still malevolent forces out there. Joshua and his partner relayed to me that someone associated with One Hundred Roads was intercepting their communications, staying a step ahead each time they moved. It's cliché, but we were playing chess without being able to see all the pieces on the board."

"Rhodes is still out there," Dana said. "He has Ashley's skates. There's a lot of tech jammed into them."

"And I suspect he also has some of your parents' projects, or at least parts of them or plans for them."

"This must be the part where you try to recruit us." Dana laughed dryly.

"Just you." She looked at Dana's sister and smiled. "Ashley, I'm afraid you're too young to be on any official payroll. But Dana, I'm offering *you* the chance to join my Technology Information Archives Recovery Agency."

"TIARA. Cute."

"I thought so." Director Jameson extracted a folded paper from her inside coat pocket. "You *and* your mother will work under Daniel Sun, Joshua's partner. You can trust him like I trust you." She extended the paper. "He's one of the good guys."

Dana wearily took the paper and scanned the words, letting the obtuse government verbiage sink into her still-muddy brain. Her eyes darted from Director Jameson to the paper and back.

"This mentions a civilian assistant." She nodded her head at Ashley.

"We could make that work *if* it's not a paid position and for behind-the-scenes work only."

Ashley's face broadened into a smile.

"Oh, right, right. Got it. This is a lot to process. Does my mom know?"

"She's still being checked out, but we'll share the news together. There's also a spot for Nick Andrews."

"Please don't offer this to Nick." Dana looked her directly in the eye. "Please. It's a condition of me agreeing."

"Then get me another name." Carmen glanced back at a small train of vans and trucks rolling out of the parking lot. Two SUVs remained at the far end of the lot. "You'll need someone you can trust, absolutely and without question. Someone who can keep secrets and handle themselves, if you catch my drift."

"I'll need to think on that." Dana handed the paper back to Carmen. "When you say my mom's going to be taken care of, what exactly does that mean?"

"We will expunge her record of any illegal activities. Anything that can't be tidied up without complication will be under Simone Jefferson, deceased. Or Ruby Jones, or Diane Ferguson, or Madelaine Thomas." Dana's features screwed up into a confused expression. "I'm guessing she didn't tell you her other aliases?"

"Not one."

"I know Ruby Jones," Ashley chimed in. "That was in Alaska."

"Going forward, she will need to be Jessica Walker."

Dana nodded. "Director Jameson, I don't understand. It's like you knew this was all gonna go down like this, like you were prepared for all of it. "

"The moment I got wind that a federal inmate with deep pockets in prison for running high-level black ops was sprung from a train by his bionic daughter, I knew what had to happen." She raised an eyebrow and turned up the corners of her mouth. "I don't get scared. I get prepared."

"How did you know I'd come out on top?"

"Because you don't *have* an X factor—you *are* the X factor."

Dana took her backpack off and carefully pulled out Laverne and Shirley one at a time with her uninjured hand. The wheels on both showed signs of major wear. Single strands of coiled wire stuck out from Laverne, and Shirley's shin guard was cracked. The scrapes from colliding with the dam wall dug deep into the paint and exposed the raw alloy.

"Nonnegotiable if you want me to agree: I need resources to get Laverne and Shirley fixed, and a new matching pair for my assistant here. I give you the material list; you give us the materials. No questions. You never see the blueprints. *None* of my mother's blueprints."

"Done. So, you're in?"

"You're damn right I'm in." Dana enthusiastically extended her hand, forgetting about her injury. "We join your team, we get Rhodes, we live happily ever after."

"I'll set up the meeting with Agent Sun, then. You think of who you want to have Nick's place. I also have one more person in mind for TIARA, but he's not available at the moment. But trust me, he'll be the perfect fit."

Dana looked out over the western ridge of the canyon, where the sky glowed in a lavender haze muted by desert dust floating through the breeze. She wished Joshua was standing with her right now, congratulating her on her new assignment and warning her to be more cautious next time, even though he knew she wouldn't be. She pulled her wallet out of her jacket and delicately removed the folded photo-stock paper from the seam. She looked at the happy family: father, mother, and child. Her heart ached for them.

One family torn apart, another reunited.

"Dana, what's next?"

"I don't know, Ash. But it ends with Rhodes in a body bag." She put the photo back in her wallet. "That, I promise."

The melee on the dam had unfolded in rapid stages, every person a potential threat to be analyzed rapidly before taking a shot or moving to a viable target. Simone replayed every moment of the evening in her head.

Brian rolling down the truck window and resting his rifle on the sideview mirror. Dana's command to fire. The slow exhale as she squeezed the trigger of her Barrett. The kickback smacking into her shoulder like a sledgehammer, partially knocking the wind out of her as she watched her shot hit its mark. Brian slumping over the side of the door. Next, she had frantically trained her scope on her next target, a one-armed bionic woman she had first met so long ago as an innocent child, before she became her sinister father's lab experiment. The bullet shredded Nina's other arm.

Then she focused on a long-haired man with a snub-nosed machine gun, the one who had aimed at her girls but hit Joshua instead. Then she targeted another, and another, and another.

She revisited every hammer blow to her shoulder from every shot as she fired the massive .50 caliber bullet. Every shot was a decision, a consequence.

Four, she had counted, plus Brian and Nina. She didn't know how many had died by her direct action, how many would live to see justice. She did what she had had to do today to keep her girls safe tomorrow, as she had done over and over for years to stay alive. This time felt different, desperate.

The last thing she remembered was seeing Dana and Ashley being helped off the roof of the building complex at the base of the dam. Then she started to cough, her chest burning as she tried to fill her lungs with air. The pain of her injuries from the past forty-eight hours conspired against her. Each inhale was met with a violent coughing exhale. The coppery taste that rolled over her tongue blanketed her with a quiet unyielding fear.

A spot of blood landed on the sand below.

She coughed again and watched the red spittle stain grow.

She closed her eyes and laid down on her back.

Simone was awoken from her blackout by two Homeland Security officers standing over her. One trained his gun on her as the other slowly removed her rifle from her limp hands. His kind smile in the evening light told her she was not in danger.

"I'm going to take this, just so we're all safe. Are you Simone?"

He extended a hand. She sat up on her elbows and sucked her teeth.

"Yes, but I go by Jessica Walker now."

"I'm Agent Daniel Sun. Are you hurt?" He knelt next to her.

"I took a few mule kicks from the Barrett," she said, trying to stand but wincing.

"Easy, Miss Walker. I've got you. Your girls are safe. You should be proud."

"I am," Simone said. She noticed the other agent inspecting her rifle. "It's clear, buddy. I emptied it out."

"We have to take a statement and have you checked out, but we'll get you back to them as soon as possible."

"Alright," she responded. Simone brushed her boot over the blood spot on the dirt to bury it. "Don't get me wrong, I can't wait to see my girls . . . but would you mind if we just walk a little slow? I want to take in the view."

Chapter 51

Stolen – Dashboard Confessional

The flight board at Roswell flickered with changing letters and numbers as planes landed and taxied to their gates. Dana rechecked the gate and confirmed for the fifth time in as many minutes that she was waiting for the right flight.

She smoothed the pleats in the skirt of her blue sundress with her still-bandaged hand.

"You're going to make it worse if you keep that up," Simone chided, her eyes rolling behind her oversized square sunglasses. A white satin scarf covered her hair and was knotted under her chin. She retied the waist belt on her thin black overcoat.

"Mom, you look like an actress from a French arthouse movie," Dana said as she peered beyond the TSA staff to the arriving mob of passengers. *Where is he?*

"Dana, this is a hornet's nest of surveillance. Airport security is the number one way most criminals get caught." She pushed the glasses up the bridge of her nose. "Can't be too careful."

"Director Jameson says you don't have worry about that now, *Jessica*."

"Yes, but there's always a chance someone is looking for Maddy or Diane."

"Or Ruby Jones, bounty hunter?" Dana smirked. Her mother did not return the expression.

"Especially Ruby," she snickered. "You're welcome for the dress, dear. I haven't worn that in ages. It fits you better than me for sure." Simone tugged at the straps on Dana's shoulders. "You're on laundry duty when we get home. I'm assuming that Ashley finally woke up and got the grocery list I taped to her phone."

"Did she say anything last night?" Dana dragged the toe of her white canvas slip-on along the seams between the tiles.

"She said she supports your decision."

Dana nodded and swallowed hard.

An extended family of children, parents, and grandparents lumbered into the waiting area. A trickle of passengers followed behind, couples and businesspersons and some military personnel. Dana kept her eyes fixed on the opening. At last, she saw his blond hair, his reliable uniform of jeans and a flannel shirt, the backpack hoisted over his shoulder. A smile bloomed on his lips as he gazed beyond the crowd.

"He's here!" Dana puffed her cheeks, and her hands felt drenched in sweat. "Mom, I don't know how to do this."

"Dana, I'll be right here. Right here." She squeezed her daughter's hand and left her to meet Nick alone.

A flash of warmth ran down the sides of her neck. Her pulse raced as they walked toward each other. Nick slid his backpack off his shoulders as he stopped in front of her. He grinned as she wiped a tear that suddenly sprang from her eye.

"Hi," he whispered.

Dana took a breath and wrapped her arms around his neck. Nick slid his hands around her waist and stared into her eyes.

"Nick, I–I just," she stammered, "I just . . ."

She pressed her lips against his, firm but shaking. She let herself breathe his air into her lungs, her fingers tracing delicate lines on his shoulders.

He pulled back, smiling to himself. "Dana, I—"

"Please, Nick," she whispered, "wait. Let me go first." She looked down, no longer able to meet his gaze.

"Dana, what is it? What's going on?"

"Nick, just shut up, please. Let me do this."

"Do what?" He gently dropped his arms from her waist and stepped back.

"We can't . . ." Her voice broke just like her heart. "Listen, it's my fault Joshua died. And I can't put you in danger like that. I can't lose you."

Every feeling rushed through her veins and pressed against her sternum in a beating rage. She had told her mother and Ashley that she needed to do this, but the moment in action was more terrifying and painful than she could have ever imagined. Nick had given her so much and asked for nothing in return, and now she was hurting him.

Dana turned to walk toward the exit.

"I don't understand," Nick said following behind her. "It's not your fault Joshua died. I want to do this. I want to be by your side through this!" His voice cracked. "I *would* die for you, Dana. I thought we were a team. Best friends. Something . . . more."

"I *can't*. You're too important to me, to your father, and I want you to be happy. But I will *not* be responsible for putting you in danger ever again. Ever." Her eyes darted back and forth as he looked over her shoulder. "Nick, I feel . . . everything for you. *Everything*. I do. But that's why I have to do this. I'd rather rip the bandage off now instead of seeing you end up like Joshua." Her lip trembled.

"I don't accept this, Dana. I'm not even sure I understand. Shouldn't I have a say in this?" His mouth hung open as he drew shallow breaths, panting with frustration.

She fumbled in the pocket of her dress and placed the key to his pickup in his hand.

"The truck is parked right outside. My mom is taking me back to her house."

He stared at the key in his palm, then looked up at Dana.

"Dana, I love—"

"Don't say it," she whimpered. "Maybe sometime later."

She hated this. There were no easy choices for her anymore. She would never be carefree again.

He walked past her, his head down, and through glass double doors to the parking lot. She lost sight of him in the swarm of cars and pedestrians.

"But just know . . . I do, too," she whispered to herself.

Dana felt her mother's hand on her shoulder.

"I don't agree, but I support your decision."

"Oh, Mom." Dana buried her face in her mom's chest.

"Dana," Simone soothed, stroking the long black curls shuddering against her, "you did what you thought would keep him safe. I know what that's like. I did it for you and Ashley." She kissed Dana on the top of her head. "The right thing isn't the easy thing. If it's meant to be, you'll find each other again. We did, didn't we? And I'm here for you for now." Simone coughed lightly. "I'm here for now."

Dana loosened her grip and placed her hand over her mother's collarbone.

"I need to do something before we go."

She turned back to look at the concourse. Above, through the glass atrium, she noted the sky was almost the same color blue as her dress. She felt her hair move gently as the automatic doors behind her opened and closed. She heard the whine of a single twin-engine plane as it passed high above. She inhaled a trace of cinnamon wafting from the nearby coffee stand. The tile below her feet was white with thin jagged gray veins of silvery stone. She slid her foot over the lines and traced them with her toe.

"Dana, is everything okay?" Simone asked.

"I'm good now. I just wanted to remember everything." She held up an imaginary camera in her hands and pushed the shutter button. "I just needed a photograph to hold on to."

Chapter 52

Drops of Jupiter – Train

We have a few new faces in group tonight."

Tara opened her arms to the circle of occupied chairs. Dana sat on the opposite side of the circle, arms crossed, leg twitching up and down nervously until the week-old bruises and brush burns from the dam irritated her enough to stop. She leaned over to Lilly, seated on her right.

"I think it's easiest to get it over with and go as early as you can."

Tara pointed her open hand at Dana. "Dana, did you want to start?"

"Sure." She bolted upright and placed her bandaged hand on her knee.

The group's turnover as people got better—or worse—and no longer decided to come had become a disappointing element for Dana. However, new faces also allowed her to refine her continuously changing narrative, which Tara obliged despite the inconsistencies.

"My name is Dana, and I guess where I need to start off is, I'm feeling a little alone right now." She caught Lilly smiling encouragingly out of the corner of her eye. "I lost a friend this week, someone I hadn't seen in a while. And I found out my father—he's deceased, to all you newcomers—was a bit of a bastard. I wasn't his ideal child, and that upset him. Also, I had to . . ." She paused and scanned the faces riveted to her opening salvo. "I had to terminate a new relationship because I didn't want them to get hurt."

Tara placed her thumb under her chin and nodded. "Dana, these are very difficult things on their own, and compounded, it's more than many people can bear. I hope you understand what wonderful insight it takes to be able to separate these challenges and confront them. Why exactly did you come tonight?"

Dana smiled at Lilly. "I came tonight because I am responsible for people. And I need to get better so I can help *them* get better." She rolled her eyes at the light patter of applause from the group.

Lilly timidly raised her hand. Tara again pointed an open hand to grant her permission to begin.

"I'd like to go next. My name is Lilly. I was assaulted, and I can't *not* see his face. I feel like everyone is a threat now. I had to quit my job. I'm behind on my rent, but I'm getting some help with that . . ." She started to cry in silent puffs and single tears.

"Lilly, welcome. This group is about anxiety and depression, but often it's about getting that control we all want when the wheels come off the wagon. Thank you for sharing."

Dana winked at Lilly and nodded. "Keep going, Lil."

"Dana," Tara cautioned, "remember we only speak when we're comfortable. If Lilly doesn't want to talk anymore, she can—"

"He's dead," Lilly interrupted. "I found out today that the man who assaulted me died. And I'm angry I didn't get to kill him. I'm angry I didn't get to see him get punished. I'm angry at Dana."

Tara recoiled. The group fell silent except for the dropping of an empty coffee cup from a flustered young man sitting next to Tara.

"Lil, I'm sorry—"

"Dana." Lilly spoke slowly and stared at the floor. "I'm angry that Dana was the only person I felt I could confide in. The only person who saw me in a crowd. The only person who screwed up with me but actually tried to fix things." She smiled through her tears. "I'm mad she's going away."

Dana pulled Lilly into her shoulder. "Lilly, I will always be your friend. And this group isn't going to fix you. You're going to be what you are now. You're a broken roadrunner or something." She laughed as she waved to Tara. "Help me out here, boss."

"Dana, you're doing okay on your own. I think we'll all be sad, but also happy to see you moving forward. Lilly, and the rest of our new members, let me tell you about the roadrunner."

Dana held Lilly's hand as Tara's exposition floated through the room. The next two hours alternated between tears and laughter, silence and screams, pain and healing as the group members each dissected their own stories with the help of each other. Lilly spent the last hour in a broad smile as she listened to every tale of triumph. Dana held her hand despite the sting of the bandage until they adjourned.

Dana hugged Lilly goodbye before walking to her mother's compact car under the familiar ugly yellow light of the community center parking lot. She let the warmth of Lilly's words settle into the cracks in her heart she had made by pushing Nick away. Lilly would find someone special, someone who loved her not despite her tragedy, but because of the person who emerged from it. It reminded her for a moment of Angela, and the secrets and moments they had shared not long ago but in a world far away.

She clicked the keychain remote. The compact's headlights flashed, revealing a black SUV idling one spot over with the driver's window rolled down. Dana threaded her keyring around her left middle finger to create a self-defense claw and marched head-on at the truck.

"I don't have time or patience for this," she yelled. "Come at me, bro!"

The driver turned on the interior light and Director Jameson gave a short wave. Dana jogged over but stopped short when the door opened.

"Dana, how are things?" Director Jameson extended a paper bag and shook it. "Muffin? I got an extra one."

"Things are fine, *Carmen*." She snatched the bag and took a whiff.

"Are you ready for tomorrow?"

Dana put her hands on her hips and lowered her head. "I don't like what you're proposing. But I get it."

"I mean, are *you* ready?"

"I don't have a choice, really. I have to be ready."

"Don't get dark on me. I need an optimist to lead this glee club."

"Glee club? Should have went with beauty pageant because, you know, TIARA?" Dana laughed at her own joke.

"There's my Little Miss Sunshine. Go home, get some sleep. And set your alarm."

Chapter 53

The Rising – Bruce Springsteen

Open your eyes, Olsen."

The steady stream of beeps was interspersed with the shallow whooshing of the oxygen pump next to the bed. Olsen's eyes fluttered open and immediately closed at blinding white of the lights above. He could feel a tube in his nose and a web of sensors on his chest. His cheeks felt stiff and his lips were cracked, but he forced some words to come out.

"Who are you? And where am I?"

A woman in a black pantsuit with short gray hair sat in a chair next to the life-giving machines at his bedside. Athletic in build even at an advanced age, she reminded him of his mother, though he had not seen her in years. Her hands lay folded over a file on her lap.

"My name is Carmen Jameson. I'm director of the GAO. You're in a US government hospital facility in a secure room, signed in as a John Doe. You were found in a field the morning after a messy incident at a local airport. According to the surgeon, you had been shot and were left for dead."

Olsen adjusted his eyes and struggled to sit up. "How did I survive?"

"You were shot point-blank in the chest, but lucky you, the Kevlar phone case in your pocket stopped the bullet. I must say, you are indeed one lucky man."

"I wouldn't say lucky," a familiar voice echoed from across the room. "But you are a stubborn son of a gun."

Dana crossed quietly and stood at the foot of his bed.

"You." Olsen sunk back into the sheets. He attempted to smile, though his swollen face wouldn't allow it. "You got my message."

"Your message," started Dana, "is the only reason you're here and not in federal lockup." She looked him over slowly. "I'm not going to deny it: I'm happy to say you look like shit."

"Did you stop him? Rhodes?"

"We didn't," replied Director Jameson. "We stopped the operation, retrieved stolen components, and prevented both possible arson and a massacre at the reservation. We scooped up just about everyone involved, but Rhodes ghosted us."

"I tried," Olsen replied quietly.

"You did," Dana answered. "I guess I should thank you at some point, but you'll have to pardon me if I'm not buying you a teddy bear and a get-well-soon card."

Olsen sighed. "But Rhodes got away. You have no idea what he's capable of now. He's lost it. He's angry and wants to tear this country apart." He gave a short laugh. "Funny—he feels betrayed for being a ripe bastard and he decides to burn the world. I was betrayed, by a friend, and all I feel is . . . regret. Everything I did on behalf of Rhodes was wrong."

Director Jameson held up her hand to pause his speech. "I'm very glad to hear you've come to that realization on your own. That's the only way to move forward. Dana and I and some others want to help you do that."

He noticed then a teenage girl and a woman, who both shared similar features to Dana, stood in the doorway. The older woman, wearing a fatigue shirt with the sleeves rolled up, stepped up to his bedside.

"I'm Jessica Walker, but you may know me as Simone Jefferson, who designed the Atomic Juggernaut. That is my daughter and Dana's sister, Ashley. Your 'friends' kidnapped her after they shot you." She steeled her gaze. "If you mean what you say and you want to make amends, this is the time. What, exactly, is Rhodes up to?"

Olsen surveyed the group. Director Jameson, calm and collected, starkly contrasted with the impatience visibly stewing inside Dana. Ashley looked on from the edge of the room, curious and inquisitive without an air of malice or threat. He strained to read Simone, who had juxtaposed a maternal reprimand with a demand for knowledge. He coughed a dry, shallow breath. Simone handed him a glass of water with a straw. He sipped and nodded his gratitude.

"Silver." He sipped again. "He's going to find Silver."

"What's *silver*?" Ashley asked.

"Not what, but who." He examined the ceiling, the walls, and the counter across the room. "No one knows I'm here? The room is clean?"

"No one, and yes," said Director Jameson.

"Silver is a person. Silver and Rhodes are . . . in the same business. They both want to rewrite history. Rhodes wants to smash things with a hammer and get paid to do it. But Silver . . ." He paused to fine-tune his thoughts. "Silver is someone who can make a president disappear. Silver can overthrow a dictator with the flick of a pen. Silver can erase a family tree with a phone call. Silver is accountable to no one." He stared into Dana's eyes. "Not even God. Silver thinks he is the divine right, that he is God, but in actuality Silver is the devil."

He watched Ashley's eyes widen. She stepped closer to the bed, but she stopped as he pointed at her with a shaking finger. "You're just a kid."

"That is correct."

"Why are you here? Why are you *all* here?"

Director Jameson clasped her hands in front of her chest and spoke assuredly. "We're here because we've got no time to waste. You've got the inside track on Rhodes. You're our only and best lead. I'm taking a leap of faith here—you called Dana before you were shot because you saw that he needed to be stopped. I think you're going to agree to join us. We need you to help us apprehend Rhodes, and apparently Silver as well."

"Did you forget how broken I am?" He attempted to wiggle his toes under the blanket. "Dana, you broke my back. I can barely fire a gun, and I can't walk without my canes."

Dana swallowed. "I was really hoping you wouldn't bring that up," she chirped. "I broke your back. I'm not exactly sorry about that, but you're right. You can't even fight a three-legged puppy in your current condition. But you *know* things. And we need to think like you and learn what you know to have a chance of catching Rhodes."

The fire in her eyes dimmed, her brow relaxed. He could see that she was no longer his enemy, but not quite his friend.

"This certainly is the odd welcome wagon here," he muttered.

"Desperate times," said Simone, "desperate measures."

"Help me sit up."

Simone slid her arm behind his shoulders as Director Jameson adjusted his pillow. As he rose to his upright position, Olsen's chest and shoulders, still muscular and sinewy, flexed under the bandages and wires. On his chest, buried in a litany of scars, a tiny black-and-white flag of the United States presented itself. He tapped the tattoo with his hand.

"I'll tell you everything I know. But I need something in return. I need my records expunged from a few international databases. And I need citizenship." He stared at Director Jameson. "I've done some terrible things, misguided by promises from Rhodes. I thought I was doing things for the betterment of this country and was going to make a king's ransom in return. I know better now." He paused for a moment, in thought. "Only when I was left for dead did I see the light. I was dancing in a snake pit and ignoring the venom coursing through me."

Ashley cleared her throat. "'You are a den of vipers and thieves. I intend to rout you out, and by the eternal God, I will rout you out.'" She rapped her knuckles on the bed rail for effect. "Andrew Jackson? Anyone?" she said to baffled looks around the room.

"She's one of our many resident geniuses," Dana scoffed. "She's showing off."

"Dana, I am not the man you broke in half." He closed his eyes and rested his chin on his chest. "I will help you. With everything I have left in my body, I will stop Rhodes. With all of you."

A gentle knock at the door interrupted them. A man with short black hair wearing a polo shirt and khakis walked in, carrying himself like the litany of federal agents Olsen had met over the years.

"Sorry we're late. Traffic from the airport was a mess." He held his hand up in greeting but kept a stoic look on his face. "I'm Dan Sun. I'm your handler."

The door swung fully open, revealing a second silhouette backlit by the fluorescent lights in the hallway. Olsen's jaw dropped, and his eyes flashed wide. "You?"

Behind Dan, a tall blond woman entered the room. Her thick-heeled black boots propelled her to six feet in height. Her black jeans traced long muscular lines up to her blue Asbury Park tank top. Her arms, chiseled and tanned, flexed as she crossed them over her chest. Her long golden locks caressed the angular cheeks of her perfectly symmetrical face and rolled over her shoulders. She smirked as she made eye contact with Olsen. Her fierce blue eyes narrowed.

Dana looked at Olsen, enjoying his discomfort. "You remember this lady, right?"

"I almost beat the crap out of you once, Aussie." The woman laughed. "But you had to cheat and bring a knife to a fistfight."

"Are you still about a size ten in a roller skate, Angela?" Dana asked.

"I still am."

Epilogue

Malibu – Miley Cyrus

Simone dropped the bucket of tools onto the dirty linoleum floor. Small piles of desert dust decorated the corners of the main room of the open floor plan. She counted the bullet holes in the walls, scraping her boot against a smear of dried blood. The refrigerator lay on its side with the door open, and the faint smell of remaining rotted foodstuffs wafted across the kitchen. Dana entered the open front doors, holding a box of trash bags, and shook her head.

"Yeah, they tore this place apart."

Simone nodded as she finished her inspection of the rancher. It had been years since she had been here, the home Samuel had made half safe house, half project lab. "At least my painting is still here." Simone pointed a gloved hand at the mantel and smiled. "Your father didn't know I had such an artistic streak until I started working on landscapes. He was a brilliant man, but he tried to create a hybrid of paint thinner and ammonia to clean my brushes."

"I don't get it."

"They were water-based paints."

She handed Dana a pair of gloves, which she donned carefully over a fresh patch of gauze taped to her left forearm.

"I thought your hand was all healed. Is that new, sweetie?"

Dana peeled back the dressing. A slimy coat of clear ointment shined in the midday sunlight that crept through the tattered drapes. She turned her wrist toward Simone and revealed a two-inch tattoo of a red pickup truck.

"Just something I needed to have."

Simone nodded. She was moved by Dana's ability to make hard decisions. She had made enough of those over the years and wished none of it for Dana or Ashley going forward, but at the same time she recognized the challenges of the mission ahead for the family.

"You do you." She checked a text message from Ashley. "Your sister says she finished her application for the linguistics fellowship. I'm proud of her."

"I'm proud of *you*, Mom."

The decision to sign off on Ashley's application was a struggle, but Simone felt it was better to guide her out of nest rather than push her out— or worse, stand by and watch her run away.

"I'm proud of you, too, Star." She suppressed the swelling urge to cry. "You gave me back my family. So, let's get on with this."

She kicked an iron pot away from the basement threshold with her boot, flipped the switch at the top of the stairs, and peered down the staircase.

"Lights still work. Thank you, solar panels."

They walked cautiously, step by step, into the cellar, a mother leading her child.

"Keep an eye out for any critters. They love it down here," Dana warned.

In front of them, the table that housed the power plant display lay in pieces on the floor, robbed of most of its components. The computers had all been stripped or stolen, leaving only a vineyard of cables and severed zip ties on one side of the room. Dana walked over and picked at the plastic pieces from the ruined diorama.

"Mom, they took everything. It's like we held a yard sale for One Hundred Roads." She shook her head sadly. "I guess we didn't need to bring the empty horse trailer." She jumped as a spider waltzed across the floor in front of her.

"I wouldn't say that." Simone placed a hand on the wall next to the stairs and ran her fingers across the drywall. She continued to slowly feel across the wall, carefully stepping one foot in front of the other, toe to heel, counting her paces.

"Sure, I mean, we can salvage some of the furniture, and I have some clothes to grab from the bedroom. I can run the pots and pans in the dishwasher a few times when we get home."

After a few moments of silence, Simone laid both of her palms against a spot in the drywall. "Dana, you may want to step back a few feet."

Her mother grabbed a hammer from the tool bench and smacked the wall to make a small hole. She measured one hand-width to the right and hammered again. Two more holes, each about a foot below the others, plotted a rectangle. She slipped a utility knife from her pocket and carved out a portal in the sheetrock to reveal a gray metal box nailed to the stud.

"Mom, what is that?"

Simone glanced over her shoulder and smiled. "It's why we brought the horse trailer."

She pried the lid off the mounted box and uncovered a pair of buttons, red and green. She pushed the green button forcefully. A whirring and rattling erupted from the middle of the room. Simone broke into a wide, almost sinister smile. "I told you to stand back."

A cloud of dust erupted up from the tile seam in the middle of the floor. Slowly, the tiles separated into two doors, each ten foot by five foot, that swung away from each other to reveal an opening in the floor.

"There's my baby."

Simone gleefully stared at the brown tarp covering a mound in the middle of the recess. She grabbed one corner and pulled it slowly toward her. Dana joined in, tugging the rest of the tarp to the side until the contents were exposed.

"Mom . . . Mom? Mom. What is that?"

"Something that TIARA could use."

The carbon fiber components glistened in the light. The central body was a tapered barrel housing with a segmented waist connected to two streamlined legs. The arms were thicker than those of a human, covered with more carbon fiber sections at the elbows and shoulders. A shiny black dome rested where the head would be. The word PEG adorned the chest, hand-painted in capital letters. Even on its back, its seven-foot height was formidable.

"This is Peg, or rather, a protective emergency guardian," Simone announced with pride. "This is what the juggernaut was intended to become. Independently powered by near-zero energy batteries, impenetrable against radiation, debris, EMPs, and the occasional anti-tank ordinance. Internal temperature control shield so you could walk through a volcano's boiling spray. Rescue and retrieval at its finest."

Dana removed her glove and placed it on Peg's chest.

"Is it a robot?"

"Not really," Simone replied. "It's more like a suit. We'll have to take the limbs off to haul it up the stairs, and it's going to need a lot of work to finish it." She hopped down into the cavity and lifted one of the legs, inspecting the ankle housing.

"And when it's finished?"

Simone spat on Peg's head unit and rubbed away a layer of grime. "We save the world, sweetie."

Dana Jefferson and TIARA will return in

PHOTOGRAPH: NEW WHEELED ORDER

Simone Jefferson's story

will be told, someday, in

MADELAINE AND THE MANE

Acknowledgements

My Wife:
As always, my favorite person in the world. Thank you for your fandom and for everything. When this is all done, I'm going to retire to the couch.

Amy Reeve:
I could not have completed this journey without your help and support. Thank you for pointing me in the right direction throughout this series, and for constantly questioning Dana. She appreciates you as much as I do.

Cleo Miele:
Thank you for your investment of your skills into the world I've built. Thank you for knocking the lights out in the ballpark and the magical dust you sprinkled into the final draft.

John Allemand:
Your encouragement and enthusiasm have been an inspiration, It has been a wonderful journey learning the value of perseverance through your encouragement and guidance. Thank you for talking to me many moons ago at a flea market in Flemington. I'll see you on the road.

Darren Auck:
When my motor slows down, I'm just reminded of any of our conversation and your enthusiasm for the arts and creators. There were many times where your words helped me burn the midnight oil and keep on writing out of love for what I create. Thank you for SPACE MADNESS!

Mom:
Thank you for being my biggest fan.

About The Author

Michael Blatherwick was born and raised in New Jersey. He is a graduate of Villanova University and worked in the world of finance for over twenty years. He currently works at a nonprofit organization.

Photograph and the Atomic Juggernaut is his first fiction novel after several years in the trenches as a technical and business writer. This is his second full length novel. He currently resides in Bordentown, New Jersey, with his wife, their dog, a menagerie of cats, domestic and feral.

Website: michaelblatherwick.com
Twitter: @blatherwords
Instagram: @jackowick